Buffy held the young man's face tenderly in her hands.

She felt the roughness of his afternoon stubble, the slightly rubbery quality of his cheeks. She couldn't imagine how things had become so intense so quickly, and found herself wishing for a moment that there was a way to turn back the clock, to restore things to the way they had been. But she knew there wasn't.

She put the face back down on the street where she had found it, and silently vowed to destroy whatever creature had torn it from some unsuspecting victim. Sunnydale crawled with vermin, supernatural beings that seemed to be here only to kill.

Buffy was fed up with them.

Buffy the Vampire Slayer™

Buffy the Vampire Slayer
  (movie tie-in)
The Harvest
Halloween Rain
Coyote Moon
Night of the Living Rerun
Blooded
Visitors
Unnatural Selection
The Power of Persuasion
Deep Water
Here Be Monsters
Ghoul Trouble
Doomsday Deck
The Angel Chronicles, Vol. 1
The Angel Chronicles, Vol. 2
The Angel Chronicles, Vol. 3
The Xander Years, Vol. 1
The Xander Years, Vol. 2
The Willow Files, Vol. 1
The Willow Files, Vol. 2
How I Survived My Summer Vacation,
  Vol. 1
The Faith Trials, Vol. 1

Angel™

City of
Not Forgotten
Redemption
Close to the Ground
Shakedown
Hollywood Noir
Avatar
Soul Trade

Available from ARCHWAY Paperbacks and POCKET PULSE

Buffy the Vampire Slayer ™

Available from POCKET BOOKS

Buffy the Vampire Slayer™
ANGEL™

UNSEEN

DOOR TO ALTERNITY

NANCY HOLDER AND JEFF MARIOTTE

POCKET BOOKS

New York   London   Toronto   Sydney   Singapore

Historical Note: This trilogy takes place between the fourth and fifth seasons of *Buffy*, and between the first and second seasons of *Angel*.

This book is a work of fiction. Names, characters, places and incidents are products of the authors' imagination or are used fictitiously. Any resemblance to actual events or locales or persons, living or dead, is entirely coincidental.

An *Original* Publication of POCKET BOOKS

POCKET BOOKS, a division of Simon & Schuster, Inc.
1230 Avenue of the Americas, New York, NY 10020

ISBN: 0-7434-1894-8

First Pocket Books printing July 2001

10 9 8 7 6 5 4 3 2

POCKET and colophon are registered trademarks of Simon & Schuster, Inc.

Cover art by Anna Dorfman

Printed in the U.S.A.

To Lisa Clancy, for believing this could be done, despite the odds, and making it happen. And for our families, who make it all worthwhile.

Acknowledgments

The authors gratefully acknowledge some talented people without whom . . . well, you know: Joss Whedon, David Greenwalt, Sarah Michelle Gellar, David Boreanaz, Debbie Olshan, Caroline Kallas, Lisa Clancy, Micol Ostrow, Liz Shiflett, and the rest of the crew who keep Buffy and Angel coming our way every week. Thanks also to agent Howard Morhaim and his assistants, Florence Felix and Lindsay Sagnette.

DOOR TO ALTERNITY

Prologue

Los Angeles

FRIDAY NIGHTS WERE ALWAYS BUSY AT COWTOWN BURGER Ranch, and this one was no exception. Tall, thin, and eager to get the hell out of fast food as soon as he could scrape some bucks together, Michael Buckley had been on shift since nine, and he would stay until six in the morning. He worked through the late dinner crowd, and then the rush at two, when the bars closed down and the hard-core drinkers came in for some greasy food to supplement their liquid diets. At nineteen, Michael was one of the few people on staff who could work the graveyard shift—eighteen and older only.

Lucky him; he got an extra ten cents an hour for being such a loser that at nineteen, he wore a paper sheriff's hat to work.

He'd always hated that term, though. Graveyard. Definitely something sinister about it; like what, they buried the dead hamburgers then?

Why couldn't it be the moonlight shift?

On this night, this great old graveyard shift, Michael

worked with Julianne Mercer and Eric Vicente. Eric was okay, a nice enough guy even though he hated to actually work if he could avoid it, and the dude had definitely lied about being allergic to onions in order to get out of ever having to slice them. So when it was onion-slicing time, Michael and Julianne had to take turns. Tears streaming down his face, Michael offered up a few choice words about his co-worker—not for having thought of the allergy dodge, but for having thought of it *first*.

Graveyard with Julianne was cool, though. She was a year older than he was, and she went to USC. Her long hair was brown and sleek, and he had to resist the urge to comb his fingers through the ponytail that cascaded through the opening at the back of her Cowtown ball cap. She had really cute freckles that dusted her nose and cheeks, barely showing against her sun-browned flesh.

And she inhabited a truly awesome body; even a cotton-poly Cowtown polo shirt and an apron (which featured Rusty the Wrangler, the cartoon cowpoke who was Cowtown's public symbol and spokes-cowboy) could not disguise her curves. Michael lusted for her constantly, even while slicing onions.

At Michael's suggestion, she usually worked the counter when they were on duty together—he figured customers would rather be greeted by her than him—and he burned more than the Cowtown-approved number of burgers, ignoring the grill as he watched her move about the restaurant, wiping down tables or scooping onion rings into a paper cup.

Tonight was business as usual. Eric jockeyed the drink dispensers, making shakes, and keeping French fries and onion rings happening. Michael flew the grill, flipping Ranchburgers and Meat Lover's Double Ranchburgers with effortless precision, taking time out to dunk the occasional Fishwich into a deep-fat fryer. When things were cooking—pun intended—there was a kind of dancelike perfection to their work.

Once the bar rush ended, Eric would leave, and it would be just he and Julianne until six. Michael was counting the minutes. The last time they'd covered the shift together, it had been dead and they'd had a long and surprisingly intimate talk about love, romance, and life after death. He hoped to pick up where they'd left off.

Oh, do I hope.

"I said, two Ranchburgers!" Julianne shouted at him.

Michael realized he'd been staring into space.

"Thank you," he replied, giving the company-mandated answer to any food order from the counterperson.

She looked hard at him, as if to make sure he had really come back down to earth. A stray strand of her long hair slipped from her hat and rested lightly across her high cheekbone. Her hazel eyes blinked a couple of times. He smiled, and she returned it, then showed him her back as she faced her customer.

Which, hey, there are worse views.

Michael pulled two more frozen Ranchburger patties, separated by slips of waxed paper, from the freezer compartment next to the grill and slapped them down on the hot surface. They spat and sputtered. He tossed the paper squares into the trash and pressed the patties down with his long spatula. Flipping three more Ranchburgers and one Meat Lover's Double Ranchburger for the last time, he drew some buns from another cabinet, split them open, and lay them down on the grill's dry edge to brown. As he did, Julianne stepped away from the counter for a moment, passing him and glancing at him from the corner of her eyes as she did so.

Oh, yeah, I am definitely getting somewhere.

He pictured the two of them leaving in the morning, hand in hand, getting into her car (he rode a bike to work) and heading back to her apartment. There he'd put on some Sting music—she had a kind of throwback hippie, tree-hugger spirit that he was positive meant that she had Sting on CD, and maybe even on vinyl, and showing himself to be a connoisseur would certainly get him—

"Hey! How can a guy get some service around here?" There was a guy in a black tee shirt and jeans at the counter, and a few other people behind him. No one was smiling.

Michael looked up. Julianne was gone, and a line had formed while Michael had been watching his burgers and dreaming of sweet sticky love.

"Julianne!" he shouted. "Eric!"

A moment later, Eric emerged from the men's room, drying his hands on a long sheet of brown paper towel. Probably where Julianne was too, he figured, only in the women's version. But it wasn't like her to leave the counter without saying something.

Of course, the way I've been tonight, maybe I just didn't hear her.

"You seen Julianne?" he asked Eric.

"Not for a few minutes," Eric said. He slipped back behind the counter.

"Can I get a Ranchburger and some fries?" the guy at the counter asked testily. He had short, cropped hair and double earrings in one ear. His tee shirt read No Fear No Fun, and Michael felt a tingle of envy for whatever lifestyle the guy had; him on the other side of the counter with earrings and a 'tude, Michael on this side flippin' burgers like a high school student.

The front door opened and a group came in, six people, laughing together. Obviously, the bar rush had begun.

"Ranch and fries," Michael repeated. "You didn't, uh, see a girl here when you came in, did you?"

"Brown-haired chick? She was standing right there," the guy said. "Then she looked like she was going in the back for a second, and she never showed up again."

"In the back," Michael repeated. Yeah, she'd passed by, but she hadn't come back. Back there was just a sink area, the walk-in freezer, the manager's office, the lockers where employees stored their personal things, and the back door. She wouldn't have left the building, and the manager's office was locked.

"Got raw onions?" tee shirt asked.

Freakin' tons of them, Michael thought. "Sure thing." He caught Eric's eye. "Work the counter."

Eric nodded. "Got it covered, dude."

Michael went back, passing the grill and turning the corner. A big stainless steel sink, where employees washed their utensils and cut the damn onions, filled a small room. No Julianne there. He yanked open the door to the walk-in. Shelves of burger patties and fish, buns of various sizes, huge containers of French fries and breaded onion rings and ready-made milkshake mix. No Julianne.

"Three Meat Lovers!" he heard Eric shouting.

"Thank you!" he replied, closing the walk-in.

He returned to the grill. The burgers he'd left there still sizzled, but now they had become small, black disks about the size of silver dollars. Cowtown cow chips, good for raising the cholesterol and not much else.

There went six more burgers, including one double. Daily inventory reports would show that, and as grill man it would be his job to explain where the waste had gone.

Sighing, he scraped the tiny burger nuggets off the grill and flipped them into the trash.

Unseen

Eric stuck his head back around the edge of the grill. "Couple people up here wanna know where their food is."

Michael indicated the trash with his spatula. "They sort of charred when I was looking for Julianne. I'll get new ones going."

Eric looked a little put out. "Cook 'em fast, dude. The mob is unruly."

"Where do you think she went?" Michael persisted.

"Maybe she booked." He shrugged as if he didn't care. "You know, just hung it up."

"She wouldn't do that."

"Whatever, man." Eric gestured with his head to the grill. "Keep that meat coming. Remember our company motto: 'A hungry drunk is a mean drunk.' "

"Where's my food, man?" tee shirt whined. "I'm, like, starving to death."

"I think there's a fire," a sleazy chick said to tee shirt, nuzzling his neck. She looked like Wendy O. Williams from The Plasmatics, white hair, black eyes, the works. "It smells like smoke."

"Dorks," tee shirt sneered.

Eric turned to the deep-fat fryer and dunked two baskets of French fries, snapping his head toward the counter as he did so. "Hey, man, chill," he snapped. "We're a little busy here."

"Attitude, Eric," Michael reminded him.

"Bite me." Eric rattled the handles of the baskets, his shoulders hunched and his jaw jutting forward. "I hate guys like that," he muttered.

Michael slapped some patties down on the grill, pressing them flat with the broad blade of the spatula so they'd cook faster. As he pulled more out and slipped the paper off and threw it away and flipped them onto the hot grill, he watched Eric working sullenly but frantically, filling

6

drinks and packing fries, ringing up sales, passing out extra ketchup and salt.

Sweat dripped off Michael's brow and splashed the grill, sputtering and evaporating. The front door just kept opening and closing, and the line grew longer and longer. People may have been joking and laughing when they came in, but after waiting around for a while, the jocularity faded. There was a restaurant full of angry customers out there.

"I'm gonna see if her car's still back there," Eric said, passing the grill again.

Michael didn't want to be left alone. He had a sudden, vivid image of getting shot or something.

"You need to stay with the register," he argued.

Eric snorted. "Dude, I can't ring 'em up any faster than you can cook 'em, can I?" He shook his head at Michael and headed for the back door. Michael watched him go.

But before Eric reached the door, his form began to shimmer. He seemed to be walking into a glow, a patch of yellowish light hovering there in the back of the kitchen where there shouldn't be one.

"Eric!" Michael shouted.

But there was no one there to hear him.

Eric's shape seemed to blink once, and then he was gone. Vanished.

For one instant, maybe two, Michael strained to make sense of it. Trick, joke, hallucination. He gaped, open-mouthed, his mind rushing through a handful of scenarios, none of which worked.

He didn't know he was moving until he reached the door. There was no hole in the floor, no trick curtain, no magician's mirror. The glow that he had seen was gone, if it was ever there at all.

"Hey, I think your kitchen's on fire!" shouted the chick with tee shirt.

"Shut up!" he yelled. "Just shut up, because something happened!"

There was grumbling, the door opening, closing as the angry customers started leaving. Michael couldn't really see them. He was blind with panic. His heart was pounding so hard he had to grab his chest with both hands to keep it from bursting through his chest.

"Freakin' psycho," tee shirt flung at him.

Fran will bust me, he thought, thinking of the manager. *I'm gone.*

"You guys?" he shrieked, whirling in a circle. "You guys?"

After a while, he slid to the floor in a sobbing puddle, and finally, somebody called the cops and they took him away.

The Friday night graveyard roundup at Cowtown Burger Ranch was over, at least until some fresh meat came along.

And if there was one thing Los Angeles had plenty of, it was fresh meat.

Chapter 1

Los Angeles

POLICE OFFICERS AT EITHER END OF THE SHORT ALLEY held guns aimed at Buffy, Riley, and Angel. Headlights and floodlights from their cars washed the alley with stark white light. Riley was the first to put his hands in the air, and he turned to the nearest pair of cops with a friendly smile on his face.

"It's cool, officers," he said. "No one's here to give you any trouble."

Speak for yourself, Angel thought. Having recognized the voice of Bo Peterson, crooked cop, he was perfectly happy to make some trouble if he had to. A quick glance revealed that the other cops were Luis Castaneda, standing near Bo, and Doug Manley and Richard Fischer at the other end of the alley. Peterson's comrades in corruption. If Angel had been alone, he'd already have been on them, or past them and on his way home. But Buffy couldn't survive a hail of bullets—she was Slayer-tough, but not immortal. So he tried a different tactic.

"On the ground, now!" one of the cops called. "Bellies down, arms out!"

"Just do what they say," Riley instructed. His Initiative experience had, Angel supposed, given him an affinity for law enforcement. It was not something Angel shared. Not only did he not want to take a chance that any of them would end up in jail, he didn't trust Peterson for a second. The guy and his buddies had killed one person that Angel knew about, framing an innocent man for their crime— and Peterson was aware that Angel knew it, which made him dangerous. Chances were good that if they were put into a police car now, their only destination would be someplace quiet where they could get bullets pumped into their heads. *Which again, not that big a deal for me, but bad news for Buffy and Riley.*

He turned toward Peterson, who was already walking toward them, in front of the lights, his weapon clutched in both hands, motioning to the ground with it.

"You heard him!" Peterson shouted. "Get down!"

Angel gave him a wide smile, as if recognizing an old friend. "Bo!" he called. He spread his arms wide and started toward the big cop. "What's shakin', pal?"

Peterson paused, caught off guard by Angel's approach. To cement the deal, Angel let his vamp face flash for a fraction of a second—so briefly that anyone who saw it would think it a trick of the light.

Anyone except Bo Peterson, who was already terrified of it.

Bo froze. Angel moved superhumanly fast, but casually, to cover the ground between them in an instant. When he reached Peterson, he caught the man's beefy arm in a steel grip, paralyzing it from the forearm down. He moved the arm carefully, making sure Peterson's gun no longer pointed toward anyone.

"It's been too long, man," Angel said loudly. With his body, he blocked his grip on the cop's arm from the sight of the others. Peterson started to say something, but Angel just increased the pressure of his grip and the man's face reddened. He blew out a sharp breath.

"Tell your friends to put their weapons away," Angel snarled under his breath. "Unless you want me to snap your arm off. You know I can do it. You know I will, too."

Peterson's face broke into a sweaty sheen as he struggled against Angel's grip. He was a strong man, a lifter, probably not used to being easily overpowered. "Are you nuts?" he asked.

"What do you think?" Angel replied. He spoke softly, so only Peterson could hear. "Have you told the guys about our conversation yet? You want *me* to? Let 'em know you've turned over already?"

Peterson shook his head, almost imperceptibly.

"This guy's okay," he called to the other cops. "It's cool. Holster your weapons."

The other three cops just looked at each other. "Bo?" Castaneda said. "What's going on?"

"Those two are friends of mine," Angel said softly, to Peterson. "They come with me."

"I don't know if I can do that," Peterson muttered with a whimper.

"You can. You will."

"But—"

"This isn't a negotiation," Angel said.

Peterson's eyes filled with tears as Angel kept up the pressure on his arm. The slightest additional force and the big man's forearm would shatter. As it was, he'd be wearing long sleeves for a while to cover the bruises.

"Okay, okay," he said finally.

"And you might want to talk to those guys about con-
fessing," Angel added.

"They'll never do that," Peterson told him. "They'd kill
me if I even suggested that I would."

"We all take chances in life."

"Not that kind."

Angel kept the pressure on. "Nothing happened here.
We were chasing the guy who broke that store window.
We'd have had him if you hadn't shown up and blocked the
alley. If you need to file a report, that's what you can say."

Peterson looked at his fellow officers. "These other
two, they're friends of my friend here. He says this is all a
misunderstanding. They can skate."

"You sure about that?" Manley asked him. He scowled
at Angel, who smiled pleasantly back. Angel knew guys
like these had all kinds of side deals going, made friends
with a motley variety of the semi-legit and the occasional
real innocent. You never knew if somebody's "friend"
was his drug connection or his kid's soccer coach.

"That's the way it's going to be," Peterson confirmed.

"You okay there, Bo?" Castaneda chimed in.

"Fine. Just do it." Peterson's arm was just about to go
and his voice was getting shaky.

"Okay, you two," Castaneda called to Buffy and
Riley. He motioned them toward him with one hand.
"You can go."

Buffy and Riley came toward the police cars, out of the
glare of the spotlights. They stopped in front of Angel,
Riley giving him a "what the hell was that?" look. Angel
ignored it and released Peterson's arm.

"Let's go," Angel said.

"So, how illegal was that?" Buffy asked cheerily.
"What you did back there. You know, the interfering with

the police part, combined maybe with the assaulting an officer part."

They sat on truly hideous orange Naugahyde booth benches in a twenty-four-hour coffee shop about a mile from the Boyle Heights location where they'd lost Sleepy Ramos. Dozens of cigarette burns, from the days that cigarettes had been legal in southern California restaurants, scarred the edges of the wood veneer table.

"Moderately, I guess," Angel replied. "What were you doing there?"

"Looking for a gang meeting that Salma's brother Nicky was supposed to be attending." Buffy answered. Riley quietly sipped his coffee, letting the other two carry the conversation. Which wasn't really Angel's strong point, so pretty much letting Buffy carry it, which was fine with her. "Which, once the police cars and everything showed up, you have to figure was most likely rescheduled for some other time and place." She paused to take a breath. "What about you?"

"Sleepy Ramos, the guy we were chasing, was supposed to fill me in on some details of collusion between gang members and corrupt police officers. The four cops we ran into, by the way."

Riley let out a whistle and put his cup down on the table. "So chances are, if we hadn't been there when we were, Ramos would still be sitting there in his car."

"That's the way I figure it," Angel said. "Only he'd have a bullet in his skull and he wouldn't be waking up this time."

"We saved his life," Buffy said. "But . . ."

"But then he disappeared through that . . . that whatever that was," Angel continued for her. "What was that? Why'd you stop me from going in?"

"I have no idea," Buffy said, remembering the shim-

mery golden circle Ramos had disappeared into. "It just
felt like going through it was a spectacularly bad impulse.
I mean, there's so much going on, here in L.A. and in
Sunnydale. Anything freakish like that should, I think, be
investigated, not just charged into."

"You're probably right," Angel admitted. "Thanks."

Buffy had already given Angel the short version of her
last few days, but this seemed like the time to bring him
up to speed in more detail. She and Riley had gone to
Boyle Heights looking for Nicky de la Natividad. The
brother of Willow's friend Salma had been missing for a
week now, and seemed to be mixed up in an oil field explosion that had taken out a Sunnydale oil patch belong-
ing to a billionaire named Del DeSola. Since Nicky's
disappearance now seemed to be linked to various types
of woo-woo stuff (she imagined Giles's grimace if he
heard her calling it that), finding him suddenly seemed all
the more urgent.

Sleepy Ramos would, they'd been told—after some
not so gentle persuasion of the type both Buffy and Riley
could be good at when they needed to be—be able to
point out precisely where the gang meeting was taking
place. But then, before they got a chance to talk to him,
Angel had materialized out of nowhere in that billowy-
coat way he had and Sleepy had done his fastest forty-
yard dash into nowhere.

As she sat in the coffee shop and watched him drinking
a cup of actual coffee, no blood added, Buffy realized
she'd been half-hoping that the phone call they'd shared
would be the extent of their contact, that she wouldn't run
into him while they were here in Los Angeles.

And two-thirds hoping she would.

It didn't add up, but not much about her feelings for
Angel added up anyway. They'd been in love, once.

Deeply, passionately. That love had survived even her killing him.

Ultimately, though, it hadn't survived him surviving. A moment of true happiness would turn him evil again, and true happiness seemed a strange thing for a couple of young lovers to have to avoid. *Or, one young and one very old lover,* she mentally corrected. It definitely put a damper on the relationship. Angel had moved to L.A. and taken up fighting crime, trying to atone for the wrongs he'd committed in his evil-vampire days, and Buffy had remained in Sunnydale, where eventually she had hooked up with Riley.

Who was, if not entirely human—military test-chip removed, drugs out of his system, but who knew?—at least more so than Angel.

She caught Angel looking at Riley over the rim of his coffee mug. "I don't like him," Angel had once said of Riley. From the appraising look he gave her new boyfriend, she figured that sentiment hadn't changed over the last few months.

"I'm not too worried about those cops," Angel said when she got to the end of her story. "They're crooked anyway. I just can't prove it yet."

"Nothing worse than dirty cops," Riley offered.

"Except maybe treacherous government agents," Buffy suggested. Riley's wrinkled brow showed that he didn't see the humor in her reference to the Initiative. "Or not," she amended quickly.

Riley smiled patiently at her. He was fidgeting with a sugar packet. *Ill at ease.* He didn't like Angel any better than Angel liked him. *What is it with boyfriends, anyway? Girls can sometimes be friends with their boyfriends' exes, but guys can never quite put those feelings in a compartment and leave them there.*

"What have they done?" Riley asked. "Those officers, I mean."

"Murdered a drug dealer, for one thing."

"There are worse things," Riley replied.

"And framed an innocent man for the murder. The dealer may have been involved with the Russian Mafiya. And I think the cops might be, too. So the innocent man was in a lot of trouble, and now it looks like I am."

But Angel didn't look troubled about being in trouble. Buffy had always liked that about him; he saved his passion for the real battles, didn't sweat things he knew he could handle.

Riley's the same way, she reminded herself. *In fact, he's even cooler, cuz it's a lot easier for him to die.*

"I've heard about those Russian Mafiya guys," Riley said, putting down the packet and taking a sip of his own coffee. "You really don't want them mad at you. They're ruthless."

"Most bloodthirsty criminal organization in the country, is what I hear," Angel offered.

"And you made enemies of them?" Buffy asked. She flashed her ex a look. "You never did do things the easy way, did you?"

Angel shook his head. "Where's the fun in that?" he replied, gracing her with a quick grin.

She remembered that smile. *Rare as a double rainbow and twice as precious.*

She almost glanced over at Riley, but she had the distinct feeling she would look guilty. *No need,* she reminded herself. *I'm on board with him. Angel is of the past.*

"But it sounds like I'm not the only one with a gang problem," Angel continued. "If this Nicky is mixed up with one."

"It's looking that way," Buffy responded. "And then,

just to make things more complicated, today his sister Salma, Willow's bud, vanished from her house. Poof, just like that." She snapped her fingers, something at which, despite her coordination in all other areas, she'd never been particularly adept.

"That's strange," Angel said thoughtfully, scratching his chin in a remarkably human way.

"It sure is. I mean, we were all there, and—"

"I know," Angel interrupted. "Poof. I mean, it's strange because I'm working on a similar case. Well, Cordelia and Wesley are, mostly, but I told them I'd look into it."

"A disappearance?" Buffy queried. She looked at Riley, who raised a brow.

"A teenage girl vanished from right in front of her friends," Angel said.

"Multiple poofings?" Buffy asked. "Mysterious."

"So it seems," Angel said. "One poof could be a problem, but multiple poofings is more of a situation."

"If there are two . . ." Buffy began.

". . . there may be more," Angel finished.

Riley sighed. *No grins there.*

"We'll need to find out," Angel insisted. "I'll have Cordelia check into it, see if there have been other disappearances reported recently. Especially of teenagers."

"This is Los Angeles," Riley pointed out. "How many teenagers run away here every day?"

"This *is* Los Angeles," Angel echoed. "This is where kids run away to. The girl who vanished was a runaway."

"And Salma would never do that," Buffy said. "What's she got to run from?"

Riley folded his hands together, bringing his two extended index fingers to his chin. Buffy considered him extremely handsome under any circumstances, but this thoughtful thing he did sometimes was especially yummy. His dark blond hair was still in casual disarray from the fight, and his blue eyes flashed with intelligence.

"Having money isn't always a sign that there are no problems," he said, looking at Buffy. "Maybe she's running *from* the money. Didn't you say she wanted to go to college in Sunnydale specifically to be away from the family and the wealth and all that?"

"That's what Will said," Buffy agreed. "But she just doesn't seem like the type to take off. She loves her family. She wouldn't have put all this effort into finding her brother if she just intended to vanish. I think it's more complicated than that."

"I have to go with Buffy on this one," Angel put in. "The multiple disappearances thing is a problem. We need to investigate further. We should assume that Salma is a victim of the same thing that took Cordelia's friend Kayley."

"Wow, Cordelia's got friends and can't keep 'em," Buffy drawled. Angel shot her a stern look. She knew he'd been spending a lot more time with Cordy lately than she had. She thought it prudent to move on. "So, what's our next step?"

"We go into the headquarters of the Echo Park Band and we force them to give up Nicky," Riley said. "Nicky'll know what happened to his sister."

"That's an assumption," Angel pointed out.

"Yeah, but a good one," Buffy chimed in. "We told you it was woo-woo. Nicky's grandmother is a *bruja,* and she majored in woo down in Mexico."

"Still, it may not be a valid assumption," Angel insisted. "I think we should get together with Cordelia and Wesley, and whoever else came up from Sunnydale. Willow's here, you said?"

Buffy nodded. "Will's here. At the de la Natividads' house."

"We should put all our heads together and come up with a plan," Angel suggested. "Otherwise we're just running in circles, maybe duplicating efforts."

"You're right," Buffy said. She glanced at Riley, who didn't look thrilled about being overruled. "Well, he is."

"Yeah, he is," Riley admitted, moving his shoulders. The moving the shoulders, also especially yummy.

And I am not comparing him with Angel, she reminded herself. *I am not trying to focus on Riley because having them both around is wigging me.*

"Where to?" Riley asked Angel.

"Your office, Angel?" Buffy asked.

"My office . . . uhh . . . kind of blew up," Angel said. "We're using Cordelia's apartment as kind of a tentative headquarters."

"Cordelia's. How charming," Buffy said with fake sincerity, sliding from the booth. "Let's go."

Riley left a five on the table for the coffees, and they headed for their cars.

"It's been on the radio all night," Wesley was saying. "All-out gang warfare, they're calling it."

"Between which gangs?" Angel asked. He sat on Cordelia's couch. They were all crowded into her living room—Buffy, Riley, Willow, Cordelia, Wesley, and himself. He had felt a touch of smugness for Cordelia's sake when Buffy and Willow had so obviously gawked at her beautiful apartment.

Dennis was also around, presumably, though if he hovered, he kept a low profile. It was after three in the morning, and several of the participants had been startled out of deep sleep, but everyone had come willingly. After a few minutes of moderately awkward good-to-see-you chitchat they had settled in and Wesley had begun his report.

"Several gangs, apparently," Wesley continued, seated between Willow and Cordelia. The little redhead had been pleased to see him again, her natural friendliness bubbling over at running across someone she hadn't spent time with lately, and Wesley had clearly been flattered. "Primarily Mexican-American gangs battling Russian gangs, it seems. There have been five deaths during the night."

"I was afraid of this," Angel said.

"Yes, well, there was every indication that things were heating up. The release of Rojelio Flores from prison was taken as an affront by the Russian gangs, they say, as they still hold him responsible for the death of their man Nokivov."

"But he didn't do it," Cordelia inserted. She was leaning forward with her elbows on her knees, listening carefully to everything everyone was saying. "That's not fair."

"Fairness has very little to do with gang mentality," Riley offered. "They think they're all about fairness, but their version of it is pretty twisted."

"What's the Mexican gangs' beef with the Russians?" Angel asked, pondering. He was trying to pay attention, but part of his mind was wandering, thinking about the strangeness of the whole situation. Buffy, sitting so close by, didn't even remember the last full day they'd spent together—while he'd never forget it. Feeling her, touching her, being with her . . . Now she was with Riley, who sat on the floor in front of her chair, his head resting against her knees, in a definite possessive-boyfriend way.

There was no denying that it hurt.

"As far as I can tell, it's primarily economic," Wesley replied with authority. The ex-Watcher had blossomed since moving here; Buffy and Willow had barely taken him seriously back in Sunnydale, but here they listened carefully to every word he said. "These gangs have run large portions of Los Angeles for years, even for generations in some cases. Other gangs have come along, such as the Crips and the Bloods, but the Mexican-Americans have always managed to hold onto their neighborhoods, their 'turf,' as it were."

The others nodded. That was the L.A. everyone knew and did not love.

"But now the Russians have moved in with considerable amounts of money and muscle, and they don't have any respect for the old rules or the neighborhood boundaries. The Mexicans take offense at this, and they're striking back," Wesley concluded.

"But so far, no innocents caught in the crossfire?" Angel queried.

"So far, no." Wesley moved his shoulders as he regarded Angel. "Subject to change at any moment, I'm certain."

Willow raised her right hand as if she were back in school. "Umm, this is all sad and everything, but what does it have to do with finding Nicky and Salma?"

"We don't know yet, Willow," Angel told her, glad to have something to contribute. "But Nicky is involved with one of the Mexican gangs. So there might be a connection there. At the same time, teenagers are disappearing all over town—Cordelia said she found two more reported cases online, and there might be more that either haven't been reported to the police yet, or that they're not releasing. There may not be any association between the gang war and the disappearances, but the links are there so we need to check it out."

Willow nodded. Then she brightened. "Maybe there's some kind of spell I could do to enlighten us."

"If there is, Will," Buffy said, "then you should do it as soon as you can. A little enlightening would do us all a lot of good."

"A little *sleep* would do us all a lot of good," Cordelia added. "And can I just remind you all that you're in my apartment, which makes sleep pretty much of a lost cause for me?"

"We'll be out of your hair soon, Cordy," Angel assured her, as Willow nodded eagerly, covering a yawn. "We just thought it was important to get everybody on the same page as fast as possible."

"Because of the poof factor," Buffy added helpfully.

"I'm not even sure we're on the same book," Riley said. "I'm still not convinced that these cases are related at all. Except for Nicky's tie to the Echo Park gang—"

"The Echo Park Band?" Wesley asked, perking up. "That's one of the gangs involved in the war. Apparently they have already made some sort of overtures to the Russians, in hopes of ending this conflict before more lives are lost."

"So that's a pretty strong connection right there," Angel said. The rest of the group looked more convinced. "You guys go back to Salma's family's house. See if you can find out any more about what might have happened to Salma. Willow, do your spell. I'll be looking into the gang thing from the streets, while Wesley and Cordelia try to find out what they can about any historical disappearances of kids or teenagers." He wanted everyone to get some rest, but part of him couldn't help wanting Riley to get out of there—and Buffy too, if they were just going to hold hands and play with each other's hair all night.

"Kind of a Pied Piper thing, maybe?" Willow asked.

"Maybe," Angel agreed.

"Sounds good," Buffy said. "We'll talk again in the

morning—later in the morning, the part where the sun is up—and see what we've come up with. In the meantime, let's hope no one gets hurt."

"I'm sleeping first," Cordelia announced. "I can't even keep my eyes open, much less sit at a computer keyboard and type, type, type, while Wesley leans over my shoulder and breathes all over me."

As if on cue, the front door opened.

"Dennis, be polite," she admonished.

"I do not breathe all over you," Wesley said, as everyone stood and began to drift tiredly to the door.

"You do," she shot back. "And by the way, the cinnamon-scented Altoids are definitely the way to go."

"Good night," Buffy said.

Riley put his hand on her shoulder, and they left.

Angel stood at the doorway, and watched her go.

Nicky turned to Che, who pulled his midnight black Porsche Boxter into a parking space on the street. "You sure about this, man?" he asked the leader of the Echo Park Band.

"How many times you got to ask me that? The man wants to talk. We talk. We don't get satisfaction or respect, we walk. Simple as that."

Nicky opened the passenger door of the little car, unfolding himself onto the sidewalk. Che had stopped in front of a café, closed at this hour and sealed tight with a metal grille. The café comprised the ground floor of an expensive downtown office building, though, and on the nineteenth floor, lights burned despite the hour.

"Just seems like if the guy really wants to have a serious talk, he'd meet us in the daytime or something."

Che rolled his eyes and moved his shoulders. He stuffed his keys into the front pocket of his tight black leather pants. "You know what these Russian dudes are like, dog. He's just jackin' us around a little, make us come to him, make us operate on his schedule. We let him think he's pullin' the strings until we make our demands, then he'll find out we're serious people. Anyway, dude's kid got killed, *macho*, he probably ain't sleeping too good these days."

Next to the coffee shop, double glass doors led into the building's lobby. They passed through unlocked doors, and a sleepy-looking guard appraised them from behind a deep counter as they entered.

"Help you?" he asked.

"We're here to see Teodor Nokivov," Che told him. "We're expected."

The guard nodded. "Nineteen," he said. "Elevator's right there."

Nicky and Che crossed to it, their shoes resounding off the marble floor in the quiet of the predawn morning. As they approached, one of the cars opened up for them. They stepped into the elevator, and the 19 button glowed.

"Guard's operating the elevator from the desk," Che said as the door slid shut. "Other buttons probably wouldn't work even if we wanted 'em to."

"Let's find out," Nicky suggested. He pressed the button marked 17. Nothing happened.

Che fixed Nicky with a dark stare. "You're strapped, right?"

Nicky touched the right outside pocket of his windbreaker to answer in the affirmative. He had a 9mm semi-auto in there, and three clips on the other side.

"That's cool," Che said. "You don't ever want to meet these guys without some protection." The elevator rose and rushed them past the seventeenth floor, stopping on the nineteenth.

The elevator door gapped open. Three big men in dark suits waited outside it, hands held behind their backs.

One of them met Che's gaze, then Nicky's. "My name is Karol Stokovich," he told them in thickly accented English. He had long dark hair, slicked down and pulled back into a ponytail. To Nicky, he looked like a parody of a Colombian gangster from the eighties, someone he'd seen on *Miami Vice* back in the day. But the flat expression in his eyes showed no trace of humor. "Mr. Nokivov asked me to meet you."

"That's why we're here," Che said. "To pay our respects and see what we can do to make a peace."

"You'll have to talk to Mr. Nokivov about that," Stokovich said. "These gentlemen are going to search you. Do you have anything you'd like to warn them about before they do?"

"I got a piece which I don't give up for nobody," Che replied. "It's in a belt holster at my back. That's all I'm carrying."

Nicky tapped at his pocket again. "A nine," he said. "I keep it."

"What if I told you that you can't get in to see Mr. Nokivov with your weapons?"

"Then, *adios*," Che responded. "No talk, no peace. I don't think that's what Mr. Nokivov wants. But we ain't handing over our straps to nobody."

"That's what he thought you would say. You keep those weapons. These men will make sure you don't have any others that we don't know about. Fair?"

Nicky watched for Che's response. Che nodded, removed his Sig Sauer automatic from its holster and held it in the air, with both hands raised. One of the Russians moved in to pat him down. Nicky followed Che's example, raising his own gun high. The other Russian thug frisked him.

After a moment, both Russians stopped, nodded to Stokovich.

"Replace your weapons," Stokovich instructed Che and Nicky. "We'll be in the room with you. If you reach for the guns, you're dead."

"Cool," Che said, sounding casual about the whole thing. Nicky was impressed by the way he kept his head at times like these. He aspired to the same kind of composure. His Night of the Long Knives had certainly helped—even though the invincibility of the one-night spell had worn off now, he felt a confidence that he had never possessed before, a certainty of purpose and of his own abilities. He would always remember the way he'd felt, strolling through the oil field fire he had ignited, feeling the heat rush around him, smelling the hair singe off his body, and knowing that he could feel no pain from it, that it couldn't kill him no matter what.

Stokovich led the way out of the hall and into a lushly furnished office suite. The blue carpet was thick and welcoming, the wooden fixtures gleamed with polish. Nicky mentally compared this place to the barrio houses the Echo Park Band, and his own Latin Cobras, used for their headquarters, and decided that the Russians were doing something right. This looked like his own father's corporate offices, not like a headquarters for a bunch of gangsters. He was used to wealth and comfortable in such surroundings, but he doubted that Che shared his background.

They kept following Stokovich through the office suite. He paused before double doors of a rich dark wood. Then, with a glance back at Che and Nicky, he pushed the doors open and stepped back to let the guests enter first.

They went into a plush conference room. A vast table,

the size of some of the entire rooms Nicky's fellow Cobras slept in, dominated the room. Leather chairs were arrayed around it, the buttery softness of them apparent even from the doorway. At the far end of the table sat the man that Nicky knew was Teodor Nokivov, head of L.A.'s Russian Mafiya. A legal pad and an assortment of manila file folders littered the tabletop in front of him.

As they entered, Nokivov set down the Mont Blanc pen with which he'd been writing something on the legal pad, and rose. "Welcome," he said with a broad smile. A powerful-looking man, his chest was deep and his shoulders wide, straining his expensive suit. His kept his thick, steel-gray hair neatly trimmed and combed back from a ruddy, heavy-jowled face. His prominent, bulbous nose reminded Nicky of nothing so much as a new potato. "Be it ever so humble," he said, spreading his hands as if to indicate the conference room surrounding them.

Behind him, Nicky was aware that the other three Russians had entered the room and closed the doors. But he focused on Nokivov, who came around the table, hand extended in friendship. Che took the hand and gave it a quick, nervous squeeze, then released. The Russian continued on to Nicky. Nicky offered his hand, and Nokivov took it in a firm grip, touching Nicky's forearm with his other hand as he shook.

"Nice place," Nicky said casually.

"Thank you. The beauty of America," Nokivov said. "Back home, when I lived there, only the most influential party members had offices like this."

"Were you an influential party member?" Nicky asked him.

"Me?" Nokivov shook with silent laughter. "No, not me. Not then. And after, of course, the Soviet Union fell apart. Under the rulers we've had since then, Mr. Gorbachev and Mr. Yeltsin, and now Putin, all the rules are changed. Who knows where I would be if I were back there? Prison? Siberia? Head of the KGB?"

Che didn't seem to know what to make of Nokivov's monologue, so he just launched into the speech he'd already prepared. Nicky had heard it twice in the Boxter on the way over, although it had been spoken more forcefully then.

"Mr. Nokivov, we're here to express our sorrow for the death of your son, and our sadness that members of your organization, and ours, are now dying in the streets. We want to work out a way that we can both operate and share the wealth that Los Angeles has to offer."

Nokivov chuckled once, but without any humor in his laugh. "Sharing the wealth is a concept close to my heart," he said. "I am, after all, a Communist. One who has taken an interest in many aspects of capitalism, but a Communist nonetheless." The smile vanished from his face. "However," he continued, sounding suddenly angry, "you are not here to negotiate a deal. I am a Communist, but I am also a father, and my son has been taken from me. I have reason to believe that he was killed by a Mexican—maybe the one who was arrested and then, inexplicably, set free, or maybe another one. But his murder is a crime that must be avenged, and if the killer doesn't come forward it will be avenged with the spilling of as much Mexican blood as possible."

"I don't care for the sound of that," Che said. He sounded all attitude, and Nicky felt a thrill of fear. "We have apologized, and—"

Now Nokivov threw in some attitude, holding up a hand to silence Che and saying, "If there is anything you'd like to tell me—"

"We don't got nothing more to say," Che said angrily.

"Very well," Nokivov said.

Behind them, Nicky heard the unmistakable sound of weapons being cocked.

"Nicky, go!" Che shouted. He had heard it, too. He dove to the right side of the room, rolling underneath the thick conference table as he did. Slugs tore into the heavy wood and the room was suddenly aroar with the thunderous boom of weapons fire. Nicky hurled himself the other way, tearing the 9mm from his jacket as he did. A burst of pain flared from his arm as he hit the ground. Without even aiming, he rolled himself into a ball and fired his gun toward the door.

Acrid smoke filled the air, and Nicky knew he would die here in this close quarters gunfight. He couldn't see or hear anymore, smoke stinging his eyes and his ears ringing from the echoing gunfire. But, blinking away the smoke, he thought he saw Che on his feet, motioning wildly toward the doorway. Che had his Sig Sauer in his fist and he fired it several times at a mound of bodies on the floor.

"Run, man!" he thought Che was saying. Then Che threw the double doors open and disappeared through them. Nicky followed. At the last moment, he hazarded a glance behind him and saw Nokivov raising a shotgun from beneath the conference table. Stokovich, on the floor, shoved the corpses of his two thugs off himself and scrabbled for his own dropped weapon. Before the man could locate it, Nicky darted through the big doorway.

His left arm burned. A bullet had torn through his upper arm and blood soaked his jacket. He couldn't stop to worry about it, though, and he couldn't take any time to deal with it. Che was already out of sight up ahead.

For a moment, Nicky feared he wouldn't remember the way out of the office suite. But rounding a corner, he saw the main doors just ahead, and he knew the elevator waited on the other side of those doors. If there had been anyone outside, then Che would be dealing with them now, and he'd hear the signs of a fight. So he banged the door open with his left shoulder—his nine was still clutched in that fist. Che stood on the other side, breathing hard, panic in his eyes.

"We got to go, man," Che implored. "I was just about to give up on you. We got to hurry."

"You push the elevator button?" Nicky asked.

"Stairs, fool," Che said. "Last thing you want to do is get on that elevator. Dude downstairs controls it, right?"

Nicky had forgotten. Without Che, he'd have been one stupid dead *cholo*.

Che led the way to a staircase with a green EXIT sign over it and they ran downstairs, leaping from the fourth or fifth step each time. Every hard landing sent a new jolt of pain up Nicky's arm and shoulder and he thought once that he would faint. But above them, they heard the stairwell door open, and he forced himself onward. A couple of random shots were fired from above, bullets pinging around on the cement stairs, but the shooters fired blindly. In another moment, the ground floor door loomed before them.

Che paused for only a second. "We don't know what's out there, *mano*," he said.

Nicky glanced up. "*Orale,* we know what's up there."

Che grinned. He looked manic, but sincere—like there was some part of him, maybe a big part, that genuinely enjoyed this. "*Vaya con dios,* baby," he said. "Let's boogie."

He and Nicky, weapons in hand, burst through the door into the lobby like Butch and Sundance at the end of the movie, Nicky half expecting to be cut down by rifle fire from a hundred Bolivian soldiers. But no one waited for them—even the front desk guard was gone from his post. They dashed through the empty lobby and to the waiting Porsche. A moment later they were laying rubber through the streets of Los Angeles, screaming and whooping like maniacs.

No, Nicky thought. *Like survivors.*

Teodor Nokivov was furious.

Filthy Mexicans. I should have realized they could not be trusted.

He made the necessary phone calls, barking orders into his cell like a drill sergeant at boot camp. He was already comfortably ensconced in the back of a black Lincoln Continental with dark, tinted windows, being driven across town. Within ten minutes of the gunplay—before sirens even wailed their way toward the office building—Teodor's crew swept the offices, emptying every desk and filing cabinet and wastebasket, wiping down every doorknob, removing any evidence of who had been using the space. The bodies of the two men shot by Che were on their way to a final resting place in the Pacific Ocean. The KGB had prided itself on the effectiveness of its cleaner crews, and Teodor Nokivov had instituted that same pride in the Los Angeles Mafiya.

The brisk efficiency of his people pleased him. He was angry, though, at Che, who had so easily escaped his trap. He was angry at Stokovich's men, who had let two punk gangsters escape them—if the men hadn't died, he would have killed them himself, or made Stokovich do it for him. He still hadn't decided what to do about Stokovich, but he realized the indecision would work for him—as long as Stokovich knew he was mulling it over, he'd be on his best behavior. And the next thing Nokivov ordered him to do would be done, without fail.

But he really had wanted Che dead before another sun rose, and now that wouldn't happen. The Mexican gangs, he believed, had run the city for too long. Now they were in his way, interfering with business, their petty turf wars and battles over pride and honor getting in the way of his agenda.

And Teodor Nokivov's agenda was an ambitious one indeed. He desired nothing less than the restoration of the Soviet Union, with himself, if not at its head, then as the power behind whoever sat there. If the Soviet Union itself proved too hard to bring back, there was one fallback position for which he would settle—Mother Russia herself, once again under Communist rule.

He knew how to do it. All it took was money.

And money, the United States had in abundance. It was a matter of directing it to the proper ends.

Forty minutes later, the Lincoln pulled up to a modest suburban ranch house in Hawthorne, near the corner of Mount Vernon and Fairway. No one would ever suspect that the key to returning Russia to Communist grandeur lay inside that purely American construct—the epitome of postwar capitalist society. But it did. Teodor chuckled softly to himself as he walked the flagstone steps from the driveway to the front door.

As he approached the door, it swung open, from within. Mrs. Vishnikoff stood there, blond head bowed slightly, eyes cast away from him. He swept inside without breaking stride. As she closed the door behind him, he took the foyer in with a single turn of his head, and spoke the two words that would change the course of human history.

"It's time."

Chapter 2

Los Angeles is a very lonely place at night. It's not like New York, the city that never sleeps. In New York, you can do anything at three o'clock in the morning, including shopping for antiques or going to graduate school. In Los Angeles people go to bed early—successful people anyway, by Los Angeles standards—working actors and directors, who have to get up early to start shooting; their busy managers and aggressive stockbrokers, whose lives revolve around the opening and closing of offices and markets all over the globe.

When it's six A.M. in Los Angeles, it's already nine A.M. in the Big Apple, and almost time for tea in London. You want the big bucks, you gotta hustle.

Nights in Los Angeles don't smell of perfume, champagne, or money; the most common odor is a combination of ozone and freshly watered grass. Lawn sprinklers skitter on just before dawn. Before first light, alarm clocks chime and house lights blink on. Computerized coffee makers grind the Jamaica Blue Mountain and drip the first batch of the day, usually the first of many in this high-stimulation environment.

Willow wondered what the de la Natividad house was like this early in the morning. She couldn't wait to get back, get into bed, get some sleep.

The meeting finally concluded, Willow stumbled sleepily from Cordelia's apartment, slightly behind Buffy and Riley. The world of Los Angeles was just beginning to rise. It was surreal, as Willow's life often was: scratch the picture the world saw, and scarlet demon eyes glowed from the shadows. Arched palm tree trunks became the spiny curves of dragon backs; trash cans were squat trolls, eager for something—or someone—to gobble up.

And we're not just talkin' fairy tales, Willow thought.

Buffy and Riley were both sleepy-quiet as they led the way to the black SUV Riley had borrowed from one of his old Initiative buddies. It was parked at the curb and there was a fluorescent flyer underneath the windshield wiper advertising a gig by an L.A. band called Velvet Chain. Willow took it and glanced at it while Riley unlocked the car doors. Old habit, maybe, but her life with Oz had left her with an interest in the music scene.

They wearily began to climb in. Riley had mentioned to Willow that his own car was still back in Iowa, and she wondered if it bothered Buffy that he hadn't brought all his stuff out to Sunnydale. To Willow, it meant that he still considered Iowa to be his home. He was still hedging his bets about staying permanently in southern California. Maybe she was reading too much into it, or not; at any rate, she herself had been devastated when Oz had sent a note to Devon asking him to send on the rest of his stuff. That had pretty much signaled the end of their life as a couple—whether Oz had realized it at the time or not.

Riley started the car and pulled out into the not-yet-traffic, although there were a fair number of cars. Willow was not a big fan of busy highways; Sunnydale was still, in many ways, a small town, and gridlock wasn't one of their problems. Too many things that ate cars, maybe, but not too many things that drove them.

"Cordelia seemed like a nice gal," Riley said conversationally. "Not as snobby as you guys made her out to be."

"She seems a lot mellower now," Willow agreed.

Riley glanced from the wheel at Buffy. She only said, "Sure."

She's distracted. Is she feeling nostalgic? Willow wondered. *For this? Maybe it's being around Angel. Weirdness. Riley seems stressed too—I'll have to tell him not to be worried. He's the one.*

In the predawn lavender gray, the homeless were shuffling from the streets toward alleys and doorways. They wore raggedy layers and their faces were cast with a patina of gray, age, and poverty. The sidewalks were cracked and the buildings spray-painted with graffiti. Metal grates protected all the storefronts.

It's like Los Angeles is a big prison, Willow thought, *and we're on the inside, looking out.*

"Sorry for all the driving," Buffy told Riley. "You must be really beat."

"I'm good." He flashed her a smile. "Not a heck of a lot of traffic. I thought L.A. was always jammed."

"The freeways will be heating up pretty soon," Buffy said. "All the movie stars going off to work in their limos. These guys . . ." She gestured out the window at the street people. "They're not going anywhere."

Willow leaned back and closed her eyes. She wished Tara had come. *Or, not. I'd prefer her to be out of dan-*

ger. Which, Sunnydale, you have to figure danger, sure, but—

"Willow!" Buffy screamed.

At the exact moment that the windows on either side of Willow shattered.

With a *piiing,* something whizzed past her nose. She knew gunfire when she heard it, only usually, not this close. She freaked for one full heartbeat, then flung herself to the floor of the SUV, covering her head with her hands.

Screams and shouts erupted outside; the vehicle swerved as Riley cranked the wheel and slammed to a stop. His door opened and he shouted, "Willow, stay down!"

"What—?"

"Stay down, Willow!" Buffy yelled, also opening her door.

Willow said "Okay" in a tiny voice as a bullet tore through the door; she felt the hair on the back of her head lift as it missed the hollow at the base of her skull by a fraction of an inch. Chills shot up and down her spine; she trembled violently, realizing she had barely missed being hit. Struggling to concentrate, she murmured a quick protection spell for herself, the ex-Commando, and the Slayer, and thought once more of Tara.

There were more shouts; also, grunts, screams, and guns. Willow could hear her pulse in her ears. Her breathing was rapid and shallow. She whispered more words, in Latin, tears welling. She was frightened out of her wits.

"You'd think I'd get used to it," she muttered. "Life in danger, gunfire. Not so much gunfire back home."

Riley and Buffy slammed their doors and barreled around the car to a row of overflowing trash cans. Riley spared a glance at the car, where Willow remained on the floor, and scoured the street in the flat, gray dawn. Buffy had seen the shooter first, but Riley had also caught a glimpse of him beneath a streetlight as he ran; he'd been a blond guy in a leather jacket carrying a Kalashnikov. Bastard had run up to the car, blasted directly into the door, and disappeared on this side of the street. There were lots of nooks and crannies to hide in, and Riley was very aware that he and Buffy presented excellent targets.

"Did you see where he went?" Riley murmured to the Slayer, as he crouched beside her. They both squatted on their haunches, poised for action. She shook her head.

Riley ducked his head around the trash can, which reeked of something rotten. It was too dark to see what it was, but it couldn't be anything good.

"Gotta be a gang thing," he said. "Who'd want to shoot an innocent SUV? Or some innocent-looking people inside it?"

"Hey." Buffy nudged him. "Look."

Riley swiveled his head in the same direction Buffy was jabbing her thumb. Blue neon from a sign that said, PAY-CHEX CASHED MONEY ORDERS illuminated the silhouette of a guy wearing a knitted cap. He was creeping down their side of the street, completely unaware of the two of them. He was wearing baggy cargo pants and a plaid shirt. In his arms he held an Uzi, and he cradled it like a veteran soldier.

The creeper swore in Spanish. His eyes were riveted on the other side of the street. He was not a veteran street soldier, that was for sure. He was making so many mistakes that Riley figured he wouldn't make it to the ripe old age of, say, nineteen.

Sure enough, the sound of the blond guy's Kalashnikov ripped the *sshussh* of passing cars, their drivers unaware of what was going down, and the Spanish-speaking creeper screamed and crumpled onto his back.

He wasn't dead. Groaning weakly, he tried to find his

Uzi, his right arm anxiously sweeping the pavement. Blood ballooned from beneath him, and the weapon lay about a foot beyond his reach.

From across the street, Blond Guy yelled something in Russian. Riley smiled grimly. Buffy took in his expression and asked, "What did he say?"

"That all Mexicans are something that can't be said during prime time," Riley replied. When she waited for more, he shook his head.

She grimaced, blue eyes half-closed and that mouth he loved hinting that she was touched by his sense of decorum. "Sometimes you just go all Iowa farm boy on me. I'm no delicate maiden, you know."

"Oh, I know." They shared a mini-moment, glancing at one another through the darkness, and then they both were all business again. Actually, being shot at was not conducive to building romantic memories that last a lifetime.

He said, "I knew I should have gotten my gun out of the glove compartment when we left Cordelia's place."

"Not loving gun-toting," Buffy said. "However, dying also sucks." She gestured toward the direction of the Russian-speaking person with the potty mouth. "You think he's alone?"

"Could be. We haven't heard any additional gunfire." He tensed. "Except—"

"Yeah," she said.

There was someone behind them, coming up stealthily and slowly. Riley shifted his gaze toward Buffy. She counted off her fingertips on her thigh, *one, two, three,* and they both dove away from the trash cans, Riley to the right and Buffy to the left.

Clockwork.

Bullets ripped into the cans, slamming them into the street. The force gutted them open as they rolled, strewing coffee grounds, wet newspapers, and pieces of melon rind everywhere. Riley and Buffy both tucked and rolled; and as the shooter ran forward, Riley sprang from the completion of his forward roll and threw himself at the guy. Both of them went down; Riley knocked the gun away and Buffy grabbed it up.

Then she executed an awesome 360-degree turn followed by a kick, snagging the chin of a second guy. A chest-high side kick to the left, and she downed a third one.

Fire opened across the street again, only this time it came from more than one weapon. The body of Buffy's second attacker quickly became a corpse as she barreled out of harm's way, not taking him with her. The first guy started shouting and scrabbling out of the line of fire; it would have been funny if it didn't look like he might die within the next oh, ten seconds or so.

Directly above Riley's head, a second-story window shattered as fresh gunfire erupted; a wooden door to his right slammed outward and half a dozen guys swarmed out, shooting as they started gathering up their wounded and possibly dead. Riley was not in any special mood to help out, but he didn't relish being shot, either, so he grabbed attacker number two under the arms, hoisted him up, and handed him over to a couple of his buddies.

While they were dealing with that, Riley caught up with Buffy, who rushed toward the car. Willow must have been watching, because the front door on the driver's side opened.

As the single working headlight diffused the darkness, Buffy flew inside and crawled past the wheel to the passenger side. Riley dove in after her and slammed the door.

The engine roared to life and the car went from zero to slamming into the pale blond guy, who had run in front of the car in preparation for shooting everyone inside it. He went down and Riley skyrocketed into reverse, hung a sort of a trapezoid, and caught the ragged edge of one of the trash cans as he raced down the street.

"Willow? Doing a protection spell?" Riley said, as the car fishtailed down the streets. The right front tire was flat, and the resultant rocking as they rode the rim was extremely bad.

"Hecate, hear my plea," Willow intoned. "Divine goddess, make straight our path and guard our way. We beseech thee, keep us in safety and bind us to thee."

The front left tire blew. Riley reacted quickly, giving the car its head, not making any move to hit the brakes. The car struggled to keep going; and bare metal scraped the asphalt as it ground to a stop.

"What's up with Hecate?" Buffy asked sourly.

"Buffy, look," Riley said.

On their right, more guys with weapons charged toward the car. On their left . . . more guys with weapons charged toward the car.

Riley gunned the engine, floored it, and . . . the car lurched about two inches forward. Then something caught, and it burst forward with impressive speed.

Riley glanced into the rearview mirror at Willow, whose eyes were shut in concentration, but who wore a little smile. He took time out to smile, too, then returned his attention to their regularly scheduled crisis. The car was badly damaged, holes everywhere, smoke pouring out from beneath the hood. It was a miracle that no one had been hurt.

No one I know, anyway, Riley thought, remembering the guy who was lying back there in a pool of his own blood. He felt a moment of disgust: all the gunfire, and the injuries, and no police sirens were blaring to the rescue. Soldier's life—good and evil, right and wrong, with no shades of gray—but Riley was not naïve. Some of these gangsters had started life hoping for fair treatment and justice, and had turned to lives of crime not because they were poor but because they had had enough of being harassed just because they had brown skin and spoke Spanish. They were tired of getting plopped into special ed classes simply because their first language was not English. Many of them were American citizens, but cops stopped them, searched them, questioned them, as though they were in their own country illegally.

Still, Riley thought, *you don't let someone kill you just because you felt sorry for them. And you don't let them get away with murder.*

They went under a bridge, and it was spider-dark there; Riley was not loving it. Neither was Buffy, who sat up straight and kept her eyes glued to the windshield. And neither was Willow, whose chanting got a bit shaky and who, at one point, opened her eyes to take in her surroundings.

Riley had prepared for situations like this for most of his adult life; he'd been pulled from Special Ops to join the Initiative. Then Maggie Walsh had souped him up, transformed him into a supersoldier.

He almost knew the brick was plummeting from the bridge before he saw it; it hit the windshield with the force of a grenade, spraying the three of them with fragments of thick glass. He finally lost control of the car and it wheeled to the right, hard, metal squealing as Buffy's side of the car impacted a huge stone column.

Shards pierced his forehead and cheeks, but he was damn lucky: nothing hit his eyes. Willow screamed; the dome light was on; her face in the rearview mirror was traced with a dozen puncture wounds. Beside Riley, Buffy was worse off; her entire face was bleeding profusely.

Still, as the car gave up and died, Buffy unbuckled her seat belt and tried to open her door. Wedged as it was by the concrete column, Buffy switched to Plan B and plunged through the webby debris of the windshield. She got her footing on the hood, then leaped off the front end and raced toward a pedestrian stairwell.

Inside, Riley reached for the glove compartment, going for his gun, but it was jammed shut by the crash. Giving up, he threw open his door, and raced up beside her. The rush of adrenaline eased the burning pain of his face, and he made good backup as Buffy located a dark-haired guy in the shadows and threw him up against the side of the stairs.

"Hey," she snarled. She clenched the front of his shirt in her fist and threw him backward again. "Who are you people, going after anybody who drives into your precious territory?"

"Hey, man," the hood protested. "We were here first."

"No, the Indians were here first," Buffy said, "as my friend in the car will be happy to explain to you." She threw back her fist, ready to punch him out. "Excuse me, the Native Americans."

Gunfire blatted above their heads. The guy shouted something in Spanish; Riley spoke a smattering of various languages but he couldn't make out the words in all the percussion. Bullets hailed all around them; he forced himself into that cool, quick alert space he had learned to find in Special Ops and almost calmly headed for the stairs. He ascended, taking them two at a time.

Buffy picked up their new friend and shouted, "Hey! You wanna take your own guy out?"

There was more Spanish, the gist of which Riley got this time, and it was not something one would read in a college textbook. Grimly, Riley sprinted across the bridge, the sun just beginning to peer over the horizon.

A guy in a black sweatshirt and jeans was crouching on the other side of the bridge, zeroing in on a target below.

Riley dove, landing on top of him; the two rolled to the right, into the stairwell, and tumbled down the concrete stairs. Riley felt each bruise; *no Slayer superpowers for me.* Using the momentum of his fall, he managed to end up on top of the guy at the bottom of the stairs. He slugged him a good one, knocking him out.

Riley retraced their path and found the jerk's semiautomatic. Assuming a shooting position, he scanned the area for more shooters. There was no more gunfire. The air was filled instead with the grunts and groans of someone being rabbit-punched; it did not sound like Buffy.

Sure enough, she was pummeling the other bad guy in the stomach, who had given up trying to talk to her.

"Honey," Riley said. "We're good."

She gave the guy one more punch and said, "If we have scars, you are dead."

Blood streamed from the guy's nose. "Hey, hey," he protested, as she backed off. Her face was covered with blood.

Bad guy number one dropped to his knees. "Hey, man." His whine was little-boy pathetic.

"Think you're a big man as long as you can throw a brick at someone?" Riley said dangerously. "As long as you've got a gun in your hands?"

Buffy said, "I'm checking on Willow," and dashed to the car.

The guy fell forward onto his palms. He was groaning. He looked up at Riley and said, "But this is our turf, man," as if that justified his actions.

Riley shook his head in disgust and walked away.

Sunnydale

It was still dark out, and the magick shop was far from officially open. But the current proprietor knew bad vibes when he felt them, and he had eagerly let Giles, Tara, and Anya into the store to purchase warding supplies. He was a tall, heavyset man with balding strawberry blond hair and so many folds of skin around his eyes he vaguely resembled a pig. He himself had already taken care of the shop and his home, setting protective wards in place, but admitted that that had tested the limits of his own magick abilities.

"I got a plate in my head," he explained, tapping his skull. "From the war. Screws me up, spell-wise."

"I'm so frightfully sorry," Giles told him, as he and Tara gathered up plain brown paper shopping bags and moved toward the door.

"It's hell going through metal detectors," the man continued. "Airports." He shrugged. "Whatcha gonna do?"

"You might try replacing your brain with one of a freshly murdered psychopath," Anya suggested helpfully. Then, seeing the expressions of horror on the faces of Tara and Giles, she said, "That was a movie, right? Not a documentary." She shrugged and flashed the other man a little moue of apology. "I occasionally confuse the two."

"Let's go, shall we?" Giles suggested. He nodded at the man. "Thanks for opening up the shop."

"No problem." The man waved a beefy hand at them. "Glad to see we got some concerned citizens ready and willing to take action. It's hell out there." He sighed. "I keep thinking I should move, but, hey, I own a house, ya know?"

"Try not to get killed," Anya said in reply. "So many of

the people who have owned this store have died horribly."

The man frowned at her. Giles said, "Please, girls, come along."

The bell on the door tinkled merrily as the trio left the shop. The air outside was cool and crisp.

Half a block away, something bobbled from an alleyway and blocked their path. The thing resembled a dimensional portal, about half an inch thick, hanging in the air as it glowed and pulsated. Heat emanated from it, so intense that Tara could feel it standing a good five feet away from it.

Clutching the shopping bag of warding supplies, she stared at the shimmering crimson form and said, "What is it?"

Anya's eyes gleamed. "Wow. I'd forgotten about these. It's a . . ." She paused. "I don't really know what they're called. I just know what they are."

"And that would be?" Giles queried, as the shape drifted toward them. He took a step to the left, off the curb. "Let's keep moving, shall we?"

"It's the residue of a spell of some kind. In this case, I'd say something cast in anger." Anya observed it with keen interest, a wistful smile on her face. "You should have seen the residue that came off Nostradamus after he had sex."

"Come off," Giles repeated, as he continued to skirt the object. "A-are you saying that this is some sort of artifact? That someone—or something—shed this, as it were?"

"Sort of. It's like sweat. Or something." Anya cocked her head, regarding the shimmering. "Maybe an afterglow."

Following Giles's lead, Tara cautiously minced sideways. She held the bag more tightly and said, "You had sex with Nostradamus?"

Anya sighed. "He wasn't as good as Xander, of course. No one is as good as Xander." As she came abreast of Tara, she peered into her sack. "There's not much of anything in these bags that can help us with this."

Suddenly the shape rushed over to Giles, who dodged it; the glowing circle wafted past him, then bobbled toward him once more.

"So our best defense is . . . ?" he prodded.

"Running," Anya said calmly. "Otherwise, it may scald us to death."

"Running now?" Tara suggested.

"Yes. Now is good," Giles replied.

They ran, clattering down the street, only to be confronted on the other end of the block by a flash of something green and lizardy; it ran past so quickly that Tara didn't have time to really see it. But it wigged her mightily; she took the lead toward Giles's place, listening as Anya said, "Now that was a Vordulac. I've never seen one in this dimension before."

"Dangerous?" Giles asked as he jogged up to Anya.

"Only if it's hungry." Anya juggled a small, beaded purse and her shopping bags, looped her currently blond, curly hair around her ears. "Then, watch out."

"Is that one hungry?" Giles asked, glancing over his shoulder.

"Hard to say. If it devours one of us in a single gulp, I'd say yes." Her voice rang with calm authority. She knit her brows and said to Tara, "What? You're looking at me very strangely."

"I-I was just thinking what a great t-tour guide you'd make," Tara fibbed as she worked to keep up with Giles. He was much taller than she, and his legs were longer.

"Tour guide." Anya considered. "That might be an interesting occupation. But what would I be a tour guide of?"

"Hell, maybe?" Tara blurted.

Anya's face fell. "Their union's really tight. It's hard to get in."

The green lizardy thing flashed past them again, coming from the other direction.

"Running faster?" Giles suggested.

"Running faster," Anya agreed.

"I thought you were going to sleep," Wesley said. He was stretched out on her living room sofa, his feet up on the armrest, a cushion under his head.

"Aah!" Cordelia shrieked, startled. "I thought you were going to leave." She had passed through on her way to the kitchen for a cup of tea, dressed in sweats and looking decidedly unglamorous. "You are still paying rent on a place, right? Not living here? Because I have to inform my landlord if anyone moves in with me."

The lights flashed once.

"Anyone but you, Dennis," she amended.

"Of course I still have my own place," Wesley said. "But that meeting . . . I thought it would be easier if I just stayed here, so that when we woke up we could get to work on that research."

"My one joy in life," she said, sinking into a chair. "Researching demons."

"Not this time," he reminded her. "Researching disappearances in Los Angeles."

"Right," she said. "In case there's a history dating back to primeval times, or something like that." She yawned.

"Have you slept at all?" he asked.

"I've been in bed. Does that count? Look at my hair."

She ran her fingers through it, tugging at knots. "I guess more tossing than sleeping. What about you?"

"I've been trying to puzzle this all out," he said seriously. "The gangs, the vanishing kids—there's got to be a link somewhere. I just haven't found what it is."

"Why does there have to be one?" she asked. "Why can't it just be a coincidence? The world is full of them. When Angel and I both came to L.A., and we ran into each other at Margo's party? That was a coincidence, right?"

"Well, yes, I suppose," Wesley admitted. "But I can't shake the feeling that—"

"Now, when you came here and found us," Cordelia continued, ignoring him, "that was anything but a coincidence. You tracked us down like some kind of . . . tracker thing, and—"

"I beg your pardon, but that was indeed a coincidence. The demon I was actually tracking came to you for help. I merely followed its course, and that led me to run into Angel."

"Okay, see? Coincidences abound! They're more common than . . . whatever their opposite is."

"Point taken, Cordy," Wesley said. It was his turn to yawn. "Perhaps we should try to get some rest before we get started on that research."

Cordelia nodded. "I'm with you on that one," she said. "If anybody needs me, tell them to wait." She padded back into her bedroom and shut the door.

Left behind while the ladies went on their shopping expedition, Xander was dozing on the couch. Spike had carried his currently best-beloved vampire chick Cheryce into the bathroom, and they were curled around each other in the tub with a blanket over them both to ward off the sun when it finally rose. That was so much better than watching him sigh over what in human terms could be called a real messy corpse. Xander got that she was going to heal, and he got that vampires were immortal, but the whole thing just creeped him out.

If a monster did that to one of us, he thought, and let the thought just lie there.

The phone rang at the same time that the door burst open, a sort of a surprise in stereo, and Xander leaped straight off the couch as Giles, first in, said, "Xander, for heaven's sake, get the phone."

"Hey, gee, hi to you, too," Xander replied, smoothing back his hair. When Anya threw him a look, he said, "What? I'm guarding Spike."

Giles grabbed the phone as Tara hurried through the door and shut it behind her.

He said, "Hello?" and Tara said to Anya, "Can it go through walls or doors?"

"Nostradamus could penetrate anything," Anya said, with the same smile on her face she got after Xander did the bed-thing she liked best. "But then, he was . . . Nostradamus."

Xander's head swiveled, trying to multitask all the goings-on; then a blurry voice from the bathroom bellowed, "Hey! Can't a vampire get any sleep around here?"

"Buffy, hello." Giles held up a hand for quiet. "Interesting." Xander took a couple of steps closer, trying to hear Buffy. "Disappearing," Giles said carefully. He listened again, then interrupted. "Well, things have been a bit busy around here, Buffy. More than busy, I should say."

"But it's not from sex," Anya added to Tara, "so it's probably safe to assume it can't, you know, burrow through and get us." She raised her voice and half-shouted, "The residue is not from sex."

Giles shot Anya a look and carried the phone into the kitchen, where he might, he hoped, be able to find some privacy.

"What's going on there?" Buffy asked.

"Oh, it's Anya, for heaven's sake," he replied. "You know how she is."

"No, I mean, you said it's busy down there," Buffy said. "What's happening?"

"Oh, that. I wouldn't want to, you know, worry you. Except that, it's just a bit worrying." He pushed up his glasses.

"How so? Details, Giles?"

"Sorry." He leaned against the counter, moved the phone to his other ear. In the living room, Anya and Tara were still carrying on. "Umm, monsters, I guess, would be the best way to put it."

"There were monsters before I left."

"Indeed. They've got worse, Buffy. More numerous, and I think, more vicious, as well. It's . . . it's bad, Buffy." He swallowed once. "It scares me."

"I'm coming home," she said.

"But . . . you're busy there, right?"

"Yes, but, hello, Hellmouth? If things get bad in Sunnydale, the rest of the world isn't far behind. I think Angel can cope with L.A. in my absence."

"I really don't mean to alarm you."

"I know, Giles," she said, her voice soothing. "But if I need to be alarmed, then I need to be. That's what I'm here for, right? And as my Watcher, you're the guy who's supposed to point me at the major badness and pull my trigger."

"I suppose."

"So it's settled. I'm coming home."

"Very well, then," Giles said. "I'll see you soon."

"Hold on." Buffy listened to someone else for a moment. "Is Tara there?"

"Yes, she's-she's in the other room."

"Willow wants her."

"All right, hang on," he said. "And Buffy, be careful." He carried the phone to Tara. "Tara, Willow would like to speak to you," he said.

Tara's face brightened as she took the phone and murmured softly, "Hi." Her cheeks grew rosy; her lips curved into a sweet smile.

Giles turned away from the intimate moment, not wanting to disturb, moved from the living room and headed for the bathroom. His voice trailed off as he said, "Spike, how's your girl . . . friend?"

From the tub, Spike sat up and pulled off the blanket. He growled, "Not bloody good. She's all bloody. See?"

Indeed she was. It was a truly horrific sight.

If the same monster got hold of one of us, he thought. *Perhaps it's for the best that Buffy is coming home.*

He liked to think of himself as capable. He had been a Watcher, after all. But since being fired from the Council—particularly, and a bit oddly, since losing his librarian's job at the high school that no longer existed—he knew he'd been at sixes and sevens. Not really in charge of anything, not really responsible for anything. Trying to keep useful. And all the while, Buffy matured and honed her abilities, leaving him that much farther behind.

He turned and went back into the living room.

"People," he said, almost as if calling together a class. "Everyone, we have a problem that must be dealt with."

"It wasn't me," Xander said. "I put the seat down every time. I've been trained."

"No, umm, thank you for sharing, Xander, but that's not it."

"What is it, Mr. Giles?" Tara asked.

"Well, of course, all sorts of things are wrong. But there's still a deadly shadow monster at large in Sunnydale," he announced. "Or at least, until we have proof that it's gone, we have to believe there is."

"You'd better believe there is," Spike said. "And it's stronger than Cheryce, which is going some."

"Indeed," Giles said. "That seems to be fairly substantive proof that we still have this problem. And we're not, may I say, doing anything about it sitting around here."

"So you want us to go out and fight this thing that was tough enough to beat the crap out of Spike's sweetie?" Xander asked.

"I think we should do exactly that," Giles said. "Buffy just called and said that she's coming back to Sunnydale, because there are so many monsters showing up here."

"So you think you failed her," Anya pointed out with her typical guileless honesty.

"Failed?" Giles repeated. "I don't know that I'd say that, but . . . well, perhaps. Perhaps there was something we should have done differently. All I really can say is that she trusted us to do the job here, and now she's coming back. What does that tell us."

"We suck?" Xander offered.

"Not to put too fine a point on it," Giles said.

"So what's the plan, Mr. G.?" Xander asked. "Go out and kill it?"

"I rather think we should put a little more preparation into it than that, Xander," Giles suggested. "But in broad strokes, yes. Something like that."

Xander raised his finger. "Just say the word, Giles. We'll be here. Have Scooby snacks, will kill."

"Thank you, Xander," Giles said, "for your loyal support."

As Doña Pilar and Willow finished applying a creamy healing unguent to Buffy, Riley, and Willow's own face, Buffy sniffed the air and said, "Does this stuff come in vanilla?"

Doña Pilar smiled gently as she screwed the cap back on a beautiful alabaster jar encrusted with turquoise and silver. "It's good for wrinkles. too. I gave Salma some to take to school with her. You should wear it every day, like sunscreen."

"Check," Buffy said. "Magickal Bain du Soleil."

Buffy touched some of the cuts on her face. She had a lot of them, but the stinging sensation was already going away. Slayers healed faster than other people, and Riley and Willow were the proof of that, each with several stitched-up cuts on their cheeks and foreheads. Riley was heavily bruised, too, and he was walking with a stiff-legged gait.

But there was no time to worry about a few minor injuries. They needed to go back to Sunnydale, and he was obviously extremely tired.

"We'll take a nap first," Buffy said.

Riley shook his head. "I'm good to go."

"Nap. *I'm* tired." Buffy felt a little like she was covering for him, doing the girl-thing to assuage the male ego, and that saddened her a little. Willow was watching them, and she had the feeling her best buddy had her number.

And speaking of numbers . . .

"I'd better call Angel, give him the update," Buffy said. "Sunnydale's in the middle of a monsterama and I am, after all, the superhero in charge there."

She crossed to the phone, picked it up, and paused.

"What's up?" Riley asked.

She frowned for a moment, then fished in the pocket of her pants for her handwritten list of Angel and Cordelia's phone numbers. Scanning down, she located ANGEL and started punching in the numbers as she said to Riley, "Couldn't remember the number."

Riley's face didn't change. Neither did hers.

The connection was made; on the other end a phone rang.

Los Angeles

"Dammit," Angel swore as his cell phone trilled, breaking the silence.

The two young gangbangers behind Angel took off.

He took off after them.

The boys zoomed around a corner, ducking into an alley; they knew the area and they led Angel on a wild ride down the alley and into another one, where they dodged a maze of trash cans and a clutter of wooden crates filled with wilted bok choy and celery roots. Angel leaped over the crates, keeping pace, and he had a momentary image of himself as a character in a video game. Around the trash can, ducking low for the fallen rain gutter, then pouring on the grease as the boys skidded back onto the street, narrowly missing being hit by a stretch limo with black tinted windows.

The littler one got away, but Angel tackled the taller one and brought him down. As the kid rolled over, Angel was shocked to realize he was even younger than Angel had at first thought; he couldn't be any older than thirteen, fourteen tops.

"Hey, man," the kid protested. "What're you doin', man?"

"You were gonna jump me," Angel informed him.

"And you were gonna let me?" the kid asked warily. "You a cop?"

Angel paused and held out his hand. The kid took it, still unsure, and allowed Angel to help him to his feet.

"The streets aren't safe." Angel let go of him and let the kid reclaim what was left of his dignity. "People are disappearing."

"Man, I disappeared a long time ago." The kid gave him a crooked smile. "Streets are safest place I know."

His accomplice peered out from behind a parked car. Angel ticked his glance to the younger one.

"That my little brother," the kid said. "We got it together, man. We're doing all right."

"Jumping strangers and stealing their wallets?" Angel asked, gazing levelly at him. The kid must have seen something there, seen one one-millionth of the terrors Angel had witnessed—*had caused*—and took a step away from the vampire.

"Go home," Angel said tiredly.

The kid looked like a kid for a moment. A tired, hungry, frightened kid.

"Man," the kid whispered, "we *are* home."

He turned away, gesturing for his little brother to join him. The smaller boy darted up to him and checked Angel out over his shoulder. The two walked on down the street like two wraiths. Then the little boy shouted at Angel, "This our place! This our turf!"

His brother slapped him upside the head and Angel moved back into the shadows. He tugged the phone from his pocket, hit *69 to call back whoever had just called him. Buffy's voice answered.

"Did you call me?" he asked.

Unseen

"Depends," she said. She sounded like she was stifling a yawn. "Did you hang up on me?"

"I was following someone," he said. "You sort of blew my cover."

"Sorry, Angel."

"You couldn't have known. So, what's up?"

"Monsters," she said. "In Sunnydale."

"Tell me something new."

"No, I mean more than the usual. Above and beyond, according to Giles. Serious invasion."

"So," he said cautiously, "what you're saying is . . .?"

"I have to go back."

He felt a strange numbness, and recognized it for deeply suppressed disappointment. *I was hoping . . .*

No, I wasn't.

I wasn't.

"Now?" he asked.

"They're not going to sit around waiting for me to come back, Angel. They're killing people. And I'm worried—what if it's a Hellmouth thing? Like somebody got it open again and all the bad is spewing?"

"Does Giles think it is?"

"Well, no," she replied. "It hasn't seemed to be. But if that becomes the problem, I need to be there pre-problem."

"Okay," Angel sighed. "I know."

"You can handle stuff here, right?"

He chuckled. "Hey, it's my town."

"That's what I hear." There was an edge to her voice, and he knew she still resented that comment. He hated having to say it.

"You go, then," he said. "We'll be okay here."

"All right. I'll, uh, keep in touch when we get there."

"We," she had said. Riley would be going back with her, then.

"Good," he said. "Talk to you soon, then."

"Okay. Bye, Angel." She clicked off. He put the phone back into his pocket. Time to get home.

Day would break soon.

He had to miss the sunrise.

Chapter 3

AFTER BUFFY AND RILEY GOT UP FROM THEIR NAPS AND left the de la Natividad home, Willow drank a cup of strong coffee laced with Mexican chocolate and ate a yummy pastry. Sugar and caffeine helped make up for some, but not all, of the lack of sleep. Her brain was fuzzy and she had sandpaper eyelids, plus, okay, residual jitteriness from enduring Buffy's driving.

Oh, yeah, and monsters.

Doña Pilar found her standing beside the kitchen sink, trying to wash her dishes, although an insistent maid really, really wanted to do it for her. The family matriarch spoke gently to the other woman in Spanish, who smiled shyly and shrugged, then said to Willow, *"Con permiso."* She handed her the kitchen sponge and left the kitchen.

Doña Pilar poured herself some coffee in a large cup and leaned against the counter, watching Willow as she sipped. She was wearing a black silk dress and black low-heeled shoes, her hair in a chignon. An ornate golden crucifix dangled from a chain around her neck.

She said to Willow, "I've been to Mass."

Willow took that in; as she put her cup in the dish drainer, she asked politely, "Do you know I'm Jewish?"

The *bruja* eyed Willow across the rim of her cup. "Of course."

"Does it, um, concern you? Maybe about how our magick works together, or—"

The older woman looked pleasantly amused and rather touched by Willow's confession. "*Mi'ja*, I honor all the souls on this plane—or on others—who align themselves with the power of good."

Flushing, Willow rinsed off her plate, put it into the drainer, and squeezed out the sponge. "There've been a couple of times I've been pretty tempted to do something kinda black-arty."

"As have I," Doña Pilar said bluntly. "And not just tempted. But I've always paid in the end for taking a shortcut." She wagged a finger at Willow. "Don't forget; it all comes back—"

"Three times multiplied," Willow finished, nodding. "Or seven, depending on which Wicca tradition you follow. I know."

Doña Pilar inclined her head. "Let us simply say, 'multiplied,' and leave it at that. Now, I think we should perform a new spell. Buffy and her *novio* told me about some of the things you saw around my granddaughter, back in Sunnydale. The strange creatures. I think you and I should investigate further."

"Oh. Well, it might get kind of violent out there," Willow said. "With the investigating. There's only so much a warding spell can do . . . I think." She made a little face. "Not to imply that your magick is as weak as mine." As she kept processing, she brightened as the realization dawned. "But you mean investigate magickally. With a spell."

"*Sí.* You're a very intelligent girl. If only Salma had been thinking straight . . . she should have come to me as soon as she began to worry about her brother."

"She probably didn't want to worry you," Willow ventured. She dried her hands on the dish towel and straightened her orange mandala-symbol tee shirt. "I'm up for a spell, if you are, Doña Pilar."

"*Bueno.*" The woman crooked a finger at Willow as she led the way out of the kitchen. "And as for Salma, her fear was for Nicky, not for me. She didn't want to get him in trouble. That has been the whole problem with my grandson. No one wanted to take a stand. Be firm with him."

She looked at Willow over her shoulder. "If you had a little puppy you loved very much, and you lived on a busy street, would you let her run loose without a leash?"

"Of course not," Willow replied.

"Nicky never had a leash. His parents believed that they needed to prove that they loved him by not imposing limits. So he has never learned that there *are* limits. For him, all restrictions are unseen."

Willow took that in, following Doña Pilar back into her spell-casting room. On the floor was a circle of glass jars containing what appeared to be clear water. In the center of the circle lay a single brown hen's egg.

The older witch handed the younger one a sack the size of her fist. It was burlap, sewn shut, with small, flat silver charms sewn around the neck. Willow examined them. One was a heart, another an eye; a third, a small bird. It smelled vaguely of anise.

"There are powerful spices herbs inside that *saco.* You probably smell cinnamon, but there are many others. I will explain it all to you later. For now, we should do the work, eh?"

Taking up a second sack, which had been lying on her worktable, Doña Pilar walked to the center of the circle, beside the egg. She passed her sack over the egg three times, chanting. She said to Willow, "Join me in the circle, and close your eyes. Imagine yourself as either the wing or the claw."

"I'll be the wing," Willow ventured, not liking so much the notion of claws. *Talons, ripping, and we're back to the monsters and the violence.* "Unless you want to be the w——"

A blinding flash surrounded Willow, accompanied by a rushing sound and a *whum-whum-whum* like a huge electric generator. Vertigo hit her like a blow to the stomach, and flashes of glare alternated with washes of gray as she tumbled and waved her arms, trying to catch her balance. *I'm falling.*

She blinked and waved her arms harder. Her rate of descent slowed, and she saw that she had been plummeting down the side of an office building constructed of concrete and glass. In one of the panes, she caught her reflection: Willow had been transformed into a medium-size bird with shiny black feathers.

I'm a crow!

Giddily, she had a moment where she pictured Xander saying, "And after the bird, you'll become a fish, and then you'll pull the sword out of the stone, right?"

The traffic below her was awesome. Cars, trucks, and limos vied for tiny patches of space in multiple lanes of traffic. The sidewalks, were crowded with jostling pedestrians and panhandlers. Car horns blared; music pounded; a jet flew overhead. The air was thick with exhaust fumes and the smells of coffee and deep-fryer grease.

"Pay attention, *mi'jita*," Doña Pilar admonished. Willow ticked her glance left and right until she realized the witch was speaking to her in her head. "Have you not traveled in other guises before?"

"Not really," Willow admitted. "But I have been dimension-hopping. Oh, and I have this friend named Amy who turned herself into a rat and hasn't been able to change herself back. We haven't been able to, either. So I'm thinking when I get back that we could work on that."

"Pay attention," the woman said again. "Flap your wings. Try to find an updraft."

Willow felt a little silly as she flapped harder. "I'm doing the chicken dance," she muttered.

Warm air pushed her upward, and she straightened out. Glancing at herself in the mirrored panes of glass of what she guessed was a different building, she watched the reflected bird fly, *and quite nicely too.*

Experimentally, she angled downward, nearly losing it when the ground rushed up toward her. The brilliant, blue sky wheeled overhead. She was incredibly dizzy. *I'm not sure birds even have inner ears, but my sense of balance is off the charts.*

"Good?" Doña Pilar asked her. "Can you control your flight?"

"I'm doing okay," she reported to Mission Control. "Not great, but I'm maneuvering."

"Then I'm going to perform the second part of the spell."

"The *second* part?"

Suddenly, it was very dark. Colors and shapes evaporated; Willow was very cold, and heartbeats pulsed through her. Some were fast, some slow; a few were irregular. All of them were distracting.

"Doña—"

"Ssh, Willow. I'm listening," the witch reported. "It is my hope to locate Nicky's heartbeat."

"Wow," Willow breathed, then fell silent.

She kept flying through the blackness, which encompassed everything, until she was literally flying blind. She wondered if it was possible in this state to hit a building, a tree, or a power line. *Or I could ram into another bird, or get sucked into a jet, or fly upside down and crash into the ground, and I am not loving this at all.*

The blackness shifted and moved, and she was aware of shapes trying to grab her. Darting and soaring, she managed to avoid them, but as they reached for her, they tore the sky into thick lines of an even darker blackness. Red gushed from the rips, dripping down the shadowed blackness like blood from terrible wounds.

Willow dodged the scarlet waterfalls. "Um, I'm not sure this is going right."

"Willow, stay calm. Still your thoughts," said Doña Pilar. "Strange creatures are entering our dimension in some way. I don't know yet how. But I will protect you."

Willow took a deep breath, held it in, and exhaled slowly. She tried to remind herself that Doña Pilar was a powerful witch, and she knew what she was doing. Her demeanor and her spells carried with them an air of authority Willow had yet to assume. *She's not the kind of person to send someone out on a suicide mission.*

Um, I think.

"It should become better," Doña Pilar said.

The dark lightened to a semitransparency, and the heartbeats, though still audible, became quieter. Cool air slid around Willow's body; then she was swooping gracefully downward, to an unnaturally silent street. Everything was filtered through a strange, muted light, giving people and other objects a strange off-gray aspect, the colors odd and slightly off, as if everything had been hand-tinted.

She kept flying. And then, at the far end of the street, she saw a lone figure. It was that of a man, and more importantly, unlike everything else, he cast no shadow.

"Nicky," Doña Pilar said. Her voice raised to a shout that echoed through Willow's head. It was a command, a wail of anguish and a roar of anger all at the same time. It made Willow's head ache so badly she was afraid it might split open.

"Nicky!"

This time Willow groaned, although it came out more as a strangled caw. Then she was zooming straight for the figure, diving directly at him, but she couldn't control her speed. She cawed wildly. Her head was about to burst.

Just before impact, the figure turned around and shouted, *"Abuelita!"*

Immediately, Willow found herself back in Doña Pilar's spell-casting room. The elderly lady grabbed Willow's shoulders and eased her down onto a three-legged stool. Tears streamed down Doña Pilar's face.

"He's still alive," she said to Willow, crossing herself.

Willow's head no longer ached, but she was extremely drained. She was so worn out that even her fingernails were tired. She asked, "What part of Los Angeles was that? 'Cause now we can go in and get him."

The woman shook her head. "I couldn't tell. Could you?"

"Not an Angeleno here," Willow reminded her. "I didn't see any street signs, either. Or buildings I recognized from movies. This being L.A. and all." She raised a brow. "Finder's spell?"

"Perhaps it will work this time." Doña Pilar looked uncertain. "If it doesn't, maybe we can figure out the location if we write down everything we saw. Get some clues."

"Or I could go back." Willow stifled a yawn and tried to look like she wasn't about to keel over.

"You need to rest. You're exhausted." The woman looked mildly regretful. "And I'm too old to take the wing myself."

Willow placed her hand in Doña Pilar's and gave it a squeeze. "We'll find them both, Salma and Nicky," she promised the worried grandmother. "And they'll be okay."

Doña Pilar patted the back of Willow's hand and smiled weakly, a smile that didn't reach her eyes. "Of course, Willow. Thank you for your faith." She bent over and kissed Willow's forehead. "Go to your room and take a nap, little one."

Willow felt badly leaving the woman alone, but she could barely move. She nodded and rose, her thoughts drifting as she made her way back to her room.

I flew. It was so cool. I can't wait to tell Tara about it.

She entered her room and pulled back the bedclothes, kicking off her scuffies before she crawled into bed.

She was asleep before she pulled up the covers.

Back in her apartment, Cordelia was having a half-serious tussle with Phantom Dennis over possession of the TV. She was trying to watch a video Wesley had turned up, a history of crime, especially famous kidnappings, in Los Angeles, but Dennis was one of those people who just couldn't stop watching the news. Each time Cordelia aimed the remote and clicked back to Robert Stack's monotonous drone, Dennis would switch over to KTLA or CNN.

"Phantom Dennis," Cordelia groused, wearying of the game.

Then Kayley Moser's picture showed on the screen; Cordelia sat forward and said, "Dennis, wait."

The sound went up, and Cordelia leaned forward, listening. The gist was that more disappearances were occurring, and Kayley's parents had offered a reward of $100,000 for information on her whereabouts.

"That's a whole lotta sling-back pumps," Cordelia breathed. She was very worried for Kayley, and also mystified yet again by the strangeness of growing up: Kayley had been convinced that her parents didn't care a thing about her, yet here they were, offering a fortune for help in finding her.

If only she had been around to see this effort—or if it had been made while she was here to appreciate it. But it looked like it might be too late now. Wherever Kayley had vanished to, it seemed unlikely that she got L.A. channels.

About then, Angel dragged into the living room from outside, looking, well, like he'd been dragged in, and murmured, "Hi, Cordelia."

"Coffee's on the stove, blood is in the fridge," she said, still watching the broadcast. "And you need to hit the streets."

Angel watched along with her. "Already my plan," he said.

He padded into the kitchen and opened the refrigerator. "There's no coffee in here," he muttered. "Then, oh. Right. Coffee pot. Kitchen counter."

She grinned to herself.

Angel was *so* not a morning person.

Kate Lockley read through the abbreviated report filed by Bo Peterson at the end of his shift that morning. She had put in a request to have copies of any paperwork generated by, or involving, Peterson, Manley, Fischer or Castaneda, routed immediately to her desk.

There was precious little detail in the report—an unknown subject who broke a shop window with a garbage can lid, and then escaped on foot. He had to file a report of some kind, she figured, since the store's alarm had gone off and two units had responded. But she couldn't remember, in all her years of police work, a report that used so many words to say so little.

It also disturbed her that it had been these two particular units that had been close to the scene, after what Angel had told her about them. The thought of four dirty cops, possibly involved in a homicide, sickened her. *Sure, we have a tough job, and there are a lot of temptations along the way, but how come so many of us think we're above the law we've sworn to protect?*

Do men like them think no one sees what they're doing? That they're invisible?

To make it worse, she found herself oddly annoyed that it was Angel who had brought these four losers to her. But it didn't do any good to shoot the messenger, as much as she sometimes thought she might enjoy that. She wondered how his investigation was coming along.

Guess I'll have to pay him a visit, she decided. She glanced up at the morning sun. *After he gets some sleep.* She was exhausted, but not sleeping well these days. There were periods where her father's death—and the events leading up to it—bothered her more than usual. It was almost cyclical, but she couldn't point to any particular cause for it. But during those times, woe betide the bad guy—*or vampire*—who crossed her.

Angel liked to play fast and loose with things like procedure and rules. She used to think he wasn't big on sharing unless he had to, in order to get his man . . . or demon . . . or other loathsome, creepy thing from hell. Lately, however, she was beginning to realize that Angel gave her things he didn't need to, because he wanted her to catch her criminals, too. That should make her trust him.

I don't.

But I trust him more than four dirty cops.

She stood, yawning, and stretched beside her desk. *I'll give him a few hours,* she thought.

"Hey, Detective, rough night?" asked a young officer, passing through the squad room with a rolling cart of evidence files. She was fresh out of the Academy, ready to do her bit for *Xena* and the American way. She wore no makeup and her hair was tucked under her cap.

Kate shook her head. The woman continued, "What about all the missing kids? Anything on that?"

Kate found herself grinning inside. This was one ambitious rookie, looking to put herself in the loop, trying to befriend her higher-ups. Kate liked that. She liked *her.*

"Nope." Kate shook her head. "Have you heard anything on the street?"

The cop shrugged. "People are scared. They're talking about the Rapture." She chuckled. "That's when all the good people go to heaven and leave all us sinful bastards behind." She snapped her fingers. "Just like that. Folks around you disappear, and you know you're screwed."

"The Rapture," Kate repeated. "That's what they're saying?"

"Yes, ma'am."

Kate sighed. "Maybe they're right. That would explain a few things."

"Yes, ma'am," the cop said again, uncertainly.

Kate looked at the woman's name. "Valdez," she read off her badge.

The cop nodded. "Yes, Detective Lockley."

"You're a good cop, Valdez," Kate said. "Stay that

way." She gave the woman a halfhearted salute, and walked toward her squad car in the late morning sun.

Sunnydale

Spike woke up extremely groggy, and alone.

Hang on, that's not right, he thought, as she shook himself awake.

Having prevailed upon his fellow Englishman and Willow's girl chum to put poor Cheryce back in order, they'd performed various magicks for the healing of vampires—*thank God ol' Rupe left the bloody Council; they'd excommunicate him for that, ha*—then insisted Spike take her elsewhere, in case she woke up hungry. He understood their concern and, frankly, agreed with it. His brilliant trailer park queen was a woman of impressive appetites. There was no telling what she'd do to the lot of them once she recovered.

Fun to watch, but the mess . . .

He'd considered taking her back to her trailer, but change of plan: he'd have a better chance of not getting kicked out again if he took her to his place. Xander drove him over, Spike doing the blanket-over-the-head trick, and together they got her into home sweet home.

Then he carefully laid her inside the sarcophagus he usually slept on, pushed back the lid, and took a snooze himself.

Worn out, still hung over, he let himself drift down to the deepest levels of slumber. He had a dream, which unfortunately starred Dru, who then turned into Harmony, and the blond hair and face changed a bit. Then he realized he was dreaming about—

"Huh?"

Spike woke up.

He frowned, unable to recall the image of his dream girl, reached for his pack of cigs, and realized that the lid he'd been asleep on had been moved. Rather than sitting atop the stone vault wherein his lady love should lie recuperating, the slab was lying on the floor.

"Cheryce?" he said, as he struck a match to the cigarette, lit it, and took a puff. He exhaled and got to his feet, kicking up a few dry leaves as he walked back to the sarcophagus and peered in.

It was empty.

"Huh."

He shuffled over to the door and cracked it open. The daylight was hideously bright; he shut the door before a single ray could burn him and leaned against it.

If his heart could have pounded with anxiety, it would have. Cheryce was missing, and there was no subterranean tunnel connecting this crypt to the rest of the graveyard. To leave the tomb, one would have to go outside, in broad daylight. It had been nearly dawn when he'd brought her here, and he certainly would have known if she'd gotten up and gone out before first light.

Someone had either taken her, or she'd disappeared, just like those kids Buffy's pals had been discussing on the phone with Cordelia.

Not a good thing. I've got the chip, she's gone, maybe dusted, maybe yanked out of my dimension. At any rate, I'm back to square one.

He slid down onto his arse to finish his cig as he considered what to do.

Best go looking for her, then. Once the sun goes down.

Or find some other way to get to them what knows how to get this bloody thing out of my head.

Los Angeles

His name used to be Tony Tataglia—Tony T, on the streets back in Philly—but now that he was almost in Hollywood, he was Anthony St. James. He loved that name, loved to say it. The first road sign he'd seen that said Los Angeles, he started using it.

"Hello," he said in a deep voice. "I'm Anthony St. James."

He had planted himself at the Cowtown Burger Ranch, but nobody was picking up hitchhikers today, looked like. He had politely gone from table to table, trying not to look pitiful, threatening, or hungry, asking if someone could give him a ride "into town." That could mean a whole lot of different places in the sprawl that was Los Angeles, Tony knew that; but he was getting progressively more anxious about finding a place to park his carcass that was closer to the action than a fast-food restaurant with a HELP WANTED sign in the window.

A trio of girls in beautiful dresses burbled in, laughing and chatting on cell phones. Rich girls. Party girls. Tony T's spirits rose. Chicks, he was good at.

He grinned at them, knowing they saw a good-lookin' guy in jeans and a GOT FEAR? tee shirt. Tony had kept himself scrupulously clean during his travels, washing down in public bathrooms, rinsing out his wardrobe, and generally not looking like a vagrant. That was the secret to getting rides—out of Philly and into fame. If he had learned anything from the other males in the Tataglia family, that was it.

The chicks grinned back—*Whoa, is that Gwyneth Paltrow? Nah! Couldn't be!*—and Tony sauntered over to them as they jumbled up to the register and ordered fries, only to be told that it was still hash-brown time. This caused them to make little chick-pouts at the guy behind the register, asking him, *please?* But the dude was not even smiling, not gonna crack, just stood there like he was guarding the entrance to the Pentagon.

"Hi." Tony sidled up.

"Can you get us fries?" the tall redhead asked. She was wearing a strapless dark purple wraparound thing that was technically a dress. Before Tony's sister Angela went out the door in something like that, she'd better have her suitcases packed.

"Not here," he said confidently, grinning at her. "Back in Philly, maybe."

"Philadelphia," the little blonde cooed. "We have a house there."

"Where?"

She shrugged. "I'm not sure. I've never been to it." Then she grinned wickedly at him. "Who wants to go to Philadelphia?"

The other two girls laughed.

"Not me," Tony said. "Let's get fries downtown."

The three appraised him—the third girl had dark skin and her dark brown hair was very curly and lush—turned and giggled like they were guest-starring on *Sex and the City* and the blonde said, "Okay."

They took him outside to someone's cute little PT Cruiser, popped him into the back with the redhead, and started the engine.

"Do you have a place to stay?" the dark-skinned girl asked invitingly.

Tony grinned at her. "Y'know, I was gonna use this fake name, Anthony St. James. But I'm really Tony Tataglia."

The girls laughed again. The blonde said, "Do you have any idea who my father is?"

"Nope."

Merrily they drove away, drove away, drove away.

When Tony disappeared—*poof!*—from the backseat, they screamed and freaked out and ran back into the Cowtown Burger Ranch. The guy at the register verified their story, which they told for weeks at all the parties they went to. *Tony Tataglia: Jesus, the vanishing hitch-hiker, or a ghost?*

The blonde's father decided to make an HBO movie about the incident.

So the boy from Philly did not disappear in vain.

Chapter 4

Los Angeles

"Willow," Cordelia said brightly. She clutched the front of a terrycloth bathrobe. Pressing an elbow against it to hold it together, she put her arms awkwardly around the titian-haired Wiccan, kissed the air inches from Willow's cheek. "How . . . unexpected!"

"Didn't Angel tell you I was coming back?" Willow asked her.

"He may have mentioned it, I guess," Cordelia affirmed. "But you know how vampires are about details."

No," Willow responded. "How are they?"

"Oh, okay, I forgot," Cordelia said. "The place is a mess, and there have been so many people in and out of here, including you, and . . ."

"Cordelia, I'm not here on assignment from *House Beautiful* or anything like that. I don't care what your apartment looks like."

"Of course *you* don't," Cordelia agreed, with a shade of her former, Sunnydale tone. "But . . . why are you back? I mean, not that I'm not just thrilled to see you and everything. Even though, now that the apartment is finally empty for a change, I was about to take a bath."

"I won't stay long," Willow promised. She looked around the apartment, which, now that it didn't look like a Scooby convention, she thought was a surprisingly spacious, airy place for L.A. She figured spacious, airy places in L.A. probably rented for a pretty penny. "Angel called Salma's house. He was worried about you, what with all the disappearances going on around the city, and I told him I'd come back over and cast an anti-disappearing spell here."

Cordelia shook her head gravely. "What you need is an anti-alien spell," she said.

"Anti-alien?"

"Sure," Cordelia confirmed. "I've given this a lot of thought. This has all the markings of alien abductions. Beaming kids up to their spaceships, for, you know, icky experiments and things, and, um . . . probes."

"Probes?" Willow echoed.

"You know." Cordelia wiggled her index finger. "Probes."

Willow made a face. The mental image, she didn't need. "Got it," she said. "Probes. What makes you think it's aliens?"

Cordelia lifted her shoulders in an exaggerated shrug. "Why not? Not everything can be woo-woo other dimensional, you know? I mean, who else would want to steal random teenagers from all over the Los Angeles area? The casting director for one of those lame high school dramas on some start-up network?"

"That's what we're trying to find out," Willow told her. She began to draw the items she'd need for her spell from a canvas bag she carried. "But so far, we're not really checking into the alien angle, as far as I know."

"All I'm saying is, I think we should also look to the skies," Cordelia intoned.

After Willow finished with her spell—which didn't seem to have anything at all to do with aliens, *unfortunately*—and left, Cordelia continued her bath. She'd become used to bathing with Dennis in the apartment, and had in fact come to appreciate being handed a towel or a hairbrush from time to time when she needed one. She didn't worry any more about whether or not he was a voyeuristic type—figuring that a ghost, after all, could see as much as he wanted at any time, and it probably all got a little old to him after a while.

But as she bathed, she thought about the disappearances Willow had reminded her of, which of course made her think of Kayley Moser. And thinking of Kayley, she thought about the other girls, the vampire wannabes she had met. They had been under the downtown branch of the Los Angeles Public Library, the last time she had seen them, fighting off the assault of a vampire named Kostov and his cronies. Well, she and Wesley and some people she had later learned were Gunn's crew had been fighting—the girls had invited Kostov over in the first place, to turn them, in a misguided romantic fantasy, into vampires.

Suddenly stricken with concern, she quickly dried herself off, took her hair down, grabbed a red sleeveless top and dark pants, and headed out the door. She was going to be alone, but she didn't think that would be a problem—she was only going out to reassure herself that the impossible hadn't happened, because it was, well, impossible. There were a few hours of daylight left, and Angel was resting up after a tough night. Wesley had gone out to track down a demon said to specialize in abducting and eating small children—a long shot, they knew, since it was teenagers, not little kids, who were disappearing. But even if it turned out not to be responsible, Wesley pointed out, if the stories were true, the thing would certainly deserve killing.

Twenty minutes later she pulled up to a curb around the corner from the big library building. She knew a way to get to the abandoned corridors that honeycombed the earth beneath the building through the library, but it was awkward and carried a risk of being caught. So Cordelia bypassed the library's old California-style entrance and went instead to an empty commercial storefront across the street. Looking both ways to be sure she wasn't observed, she slipped inside, wading through the detritus of people who used this place as a shelter from the elements, and located the section of wall that slid to one side to allow access into the tunnels. She took a deep breath, holding it against the stench of the first section inside, ducked her head, and went into the cutaway tunnel. A few minutes walk and one creaky staircase later she was in the hallways underneath the library building.

Cordelia's footfalls echoed off the old tiled floor of the ancient passageway. There didn't seem to be anyone around. She looked into the nooks and crannies Kayley had shown her, but they were empty. She began to worry more—had the girls found more vampires? Did Kostov somehow survive and come back? Cordelia fought down the sense of dread that rose in her throat. Had the other girls fallen victim to the same force, space aliens or whatever, that had spirited Kayley away? What if—

"Cordelia?" a hushed voice said from behind her. "Is that you?"

Startled, Cordelia almost let out a cry. She clapped a hand over her mouth and spun around. Amanda stood behind her. A girl, maybe sixteen, with an athletic build but

Goth-style choppy haircut, pale skin, and dark eye make-up and lipstick, stood behind her.

"Amanda?" Cordelia asked, although she recognized the girl. Amanda looked haunted; even through her smudged makeup Cordelia could see deep circles around her staring eyes, and her cheeks seemed to have caved in over the last few days. "How are you?" Cordelia demanded. She raised her hands to indicate the empty passageway. "Where is everyone?"

"Gone," Amanda replied.

"Disappeared? Like Kayley?"

Amanda shook her head slowly. She looked completely defeated. "No, not like that. Just, gone. One after another after another. First it was Pat, then Holly, then the others. They'd had enough, I guess. They went home, or . . . somewhere."

"What about you?" Cordelia asked.

Amanda shrugged, clearly dejected. "No place to go."

"There must be someplace," Cordelia said firmly. "Anything is better than being down here all by yourself, isn't it?"

Amanda looked around the dark corridor as if for the first time. "It's not so bad," she said. "No one comes down here. No one bothers you."

"What about going home? Your parents must be worried sick."

Amanda gazed down at her feet. "My parents don't worry about me. They have other things to worry about. The stock market, the box office, the maid." She looked up at Cordelia. "They never have worried about me. Probably don't even know I'm gone."

"I'm sure you're wrong," Cordelia said, thinking of the large reward for Kayley Moser. Surely Amanda's parents were just as worried as the Mosers were.

"Yeah, and you've known my family how long?" Amanda snapped, her voice rising. She looked very much like she wanted Cordelia to tell her that she actually did know her family, and that she, Amanda, was wrong about them.

"Well, obviously I don't know your personal particular family," Cordelia replied. "But I have known families, in general, and some families in particular, and generally speaking. they tend to be very concerned about the members of them, the families, I mean."

"You're very articulate," Amanda shot back. "And very wrong."

Cordelia stiffened. She needed to convince this girl . . . because that was the only thing keeping Amanda from fading away, if not physically, then mentally. The hurt was coming off her in waves.

She said, putting on her best convincing voice, "I am not wrong."

Amanda's eyes welled. "In this case, you are. And you are not articulate, either. That was sarcasm, in case you didn't notice."

"I am *so* articulate," Cordelia shot back. "I can talk more than most peop—well, never mind that. Just . . . listen, Amanda." She put a hand on Amanda's shoulder. "I don't want you to do this. You can't stay down here forever. It's not safe."

Amanda roughly pushed her hand away and took a step backward, toward the shadows. "That's what you told Kayley, too. She listened to you, and then you came in and screwed up any chance we had of becoming vampires. Then Kayley vanished, right? You think if she'd been a vampire, that would have happened?" Tears spilled down her cheeks; she narrowed her eyes and clenched her teeth, raising balled fists as if she might actually hit Cordelia.

"You think if we'd all been vampires the other girls would have left like that? We'd all still be together, if you hadn't come along. We weren't a real family but we were the closest any of us had ever come to having one that worked. And one person destroyed that." Amanda fixed her with a malicious glare, the haunted look in her eyes replaced now by one of pure hatred. *"You."*

Cordelia was—as difficult as it was to admit—speechless. As for Kayley's parents . . . *Let's be honest here. It was too little, too late.*

Amanda didn't wait for her to find her tongue. She turned on her heel and slipped back into the darkness from which she had come.

Cordelia stood there for a moment, trying to compose a reply in her head. Nothing came. Maybe she had made a mistake. She had meant well. She still believed no good could have come from letting the vampires take those girls. She was convinced that the girls who had been here, and had gone home, had made the right decision.

But we all know where the road of good intentions leads, she thought.

So she didn't try to find Amanda, didn't attempt to talk some sense into her, as much as she wanted to.

She left the warren under the library, never, she hoped, to return.

Sunnydale

Riley drove, and the two-hour trip from Los Angeles to Sunnydale was strangely silent. Every now and then, either Buffy or Riley would try to engage the other in conversation. Buffy could tell when Riley was making the attempt, and she wanted it to work as much as he did. But she was awash in her own thoughts, her mind full of

Angel, which always *always* happened when she went to L.A., and those thoughts wouldn't get out of her brain long enough for her to string three sentences together. On top of that, she was unhappy to leave L.A. behind with Salma and Nicky still missing, but she felt that the monster invasion of Sunnydale required her attention right now.

So they drove, radio off, each in his or her own private world.

Riley, she suspected, was probably anxious about what the next mile or two might reveal: monsters, monsters, or monsters. Her mind mulled over what lay behind them.

But the road to Sunnydale was clear. The sun set to the west as they drove along the coast, dipping into the Pacific and flaring out as it did. By the time they reached the Sunnydale city limits, it was full dark.

And Buffy knew something was majorly wrong.

She gripped Riley's thigh, feeling his tension even through his jeans.

He nodded, a movement she could barely make out in the dim light cast by the car's instrument panel.

"It's bad," he said.

"I know it is," Buffy agreed. "I just don't know what is."

They sat in the quiet car for a long moment, atop a rise that led from the freeway down toward Sunnydale itself. Most of the town, vast tracts of it, lay in pitch darkness. Patches of Stygian black blanketed the city where there should have been streetlights and houses lit against the night. The town looked like a war zone, braced against the Blitz.

In other areas, they could see fires blazing, as structures burned uncontrollably. The flashing lights of emergency vehicles, fire engines and police cars and ambulances strobed down largely empty streets.

"You said 'bad,' right?" Buffy asked, surveying her domain.

Riley nodded. "I did."

"You were right." She sighed. "And also, not good."

"I think that applies," Riley agreed. "Definitely not good."

"And bad."

"That too. Very bad."

"Think we should go down there?" Buffy asked.

"Like we have a choice," Riley said.

She glanced over at him, loving him, proud of him. Wondering if he was up to this, or if his fatigue was going to get him badly hurt, even killed.

"You're right. Choices are limited. Options are few."

"It's Sunnydale," he said simply. "Our homes are there. Our friends. Your mom."

"And I'm the Slayer."

"And you're the Slayer."

His smile was filled with the same pride, love, and concern that had welled inside her for him. *We sync up so well,* she told herself. *I'm so lucky I have him instead of being like Angel, all alone. . . .*

"So no matter what's going on down there, I need to go help deal with it," she continued.

He took her hand and wrapped it around his own, brought it to his lips, and kissed her knuckles. His lips were warm. All of Riley was warm.

"And I'm the Slayer's boyfriend. So when the Slayer kicks butt, I'm right there."

"You're no slouch in the butt-kicking department, Riley Finn," Buffy said. She leaned over, gave him a gentle kiss on the cheek. "What are we doing sitting up here?"

"Haven't the foggiest," Riley said. He put the car in gear and drove it down the hill, toward Sunnydale.

They were halfway through town—close up, it looked more like a bombing target than ever, with curls of smoke wafting up into the night air from a dozen different fires, broken windows, cars smashed against one another and then abandoned in the street—before they saw their first monster.

It walked the silent streets on legs that Buffy guessed had to be eight feet long. There were six legs, skinny, oddly proportioned ones that had joints where it didn't seem like there should be joints. Where the legs came together, it had a heavily muscled, almost human-looking torso. But the head that sat atop the torso was nothing like a human head. Human heads tended to be basically oval, or egg-shaped, but this one looked like it had been flattened to a furry disk. Six eyes on long stalks wobbled around its perimeter. A cruel mouth, row upon row of sharp fangs, hung open, a red gash in the black, glossy fur.

The thing traveled down Seacrest Street, just two blocks from Main. Seacrest was a residential street, mostly small apartment complexes with a few small single-family homes interspersed. The creature's head was level with the apartment windows on the second floor of the buildings.

Buffy spotted it from the car, and gave out a small sound of surprise.

"What?" Riley asked, braking the car.

"That," Buffy said. The thing was coming toward them. A human leg dangled from the teeth, like a bit of spinach stuck there.

"It has a leg."

"It has lots of them," Riley observed.

"I mean, in its mouth. I don't know whose leg that is, but it looks human. And maybe the thing is still hungry. I say we slay."

"Have you ever seen something like that?" Riley asked her. "Do you know what it is? How to kill it?"

"No clue, no idea," Buffy replied. "But I'm betting there's a way. A thing that ugly can't be too tough, can it?" She began to assess its weaknesses, plan some moves.

Riley looked puzzled. "How do you figure?"

"The ugliness alone ought to be enough of a defense mechanism for anything," Buffy said. "Besides, those legs look pretty flimsy. I ought to be able to bring it down to my level pretty easily."

Riley killed the engine, set the emergency brake. "I've got your back," he said.

She gave him another smile. "You just make sure that if you see its big brother coming, you let me know."

Buffy climbed from the car and faced the thing. It took a few more steps in her direction, then seemed to notice her there. The torso, humanlike, but covered with the same black fur as its head, reared back. The disk of the head revolved, as if the various eyes were checking her out, taking a reading of some kind.

The legs twitched.

I've got to take this out fast, Buffy thought. *Because looking at it for very long is going to make me lose my dinner. Not that the Denny's on the freeway was any kind of fine cuisine, but still, the whole bulimia thing doesn't work for me.*

The thing's mouth opened, revealing the long, spiky fangs. The leg caught in its teeth slipped free, dropped, and smacked wetly on the sidewalk.

Yeah, that helps, Buffy thought.

The creature seemed to make up its mind. Buffy couldn't tell if it thought she was prey, or a threat, but it hunched its weird torso forward and charged at her.

Buffy braced.

She didn't have any weapons to use against this thing—well, she had a stake, but this was no vampire.

On the other hand, it didn't seem to have much going for it—long, twiglike legs with freaky joints, and lots of teeth. No arms. Nothing that could grasp, except that mouth.

Still, it had taken that human leg from someone. So it wasn't harmless.

She waited.

It covered ground in no time, with long strides from those six skittering legs.

When it neared Buffy, it bent—the wrong way, leg joints working in unnatural fashion—and thrust its head at her, mouth wide, snapping teeth glistening with spittle. Buffy dodged, but it followed. There seemed to be no rhyme or reason to how the legs could move—they turned and twisted like cartoon legs, not bound by any laws of musculature. The head kept coming, tracing Buffy's movements.

She dove forward, hit the ground in a roll, came up right under the monster.

The head charged between its own legs. Buffy could feel its hot breath, taste the rank smell that issued from within.

She wouldn't be able to keep outmaneuvering the head forever, so she changed tactics, grabbed it in both hands and yanked.

It wasn't well balanced, with its torso thrust so far forward and its head between its own long legs.

When she pulled, it went down.

Buffy had to leap to keep from being tangled in a forest of long hairy limbs.

The monster hit the ground with a furry thud, its bizarre legs already twitching and scrabbling for leverage. Buffy spun and kicked one of them, enjoying the sensation as it snapped under her assault.

But then one of the other legs swept in, knocking

Buffy's feet out from under her. She hit the ground, and the monster's head appeared before hers, mouth gaping. She could see strings of flesh left behind from its last victim, hooked on barbed, razorlike teeth. It bit at her and she scooted sideways. A couple of the teeth grazed her hip, tearing through the fabric of her pants.

Another forty bucks down the drain, she thought. *Maybe armor isn't such a bad idea, after all.*

When the head came back for a second try, she was ready. She reached for it, placing both hands on top of it, and pushed herself up, almost doing a handstand on top of the foul, furred disk. Doing so slammed the head down into the sidewalk. She heard its teeth clash together, hard.

She shoved off again, up into the air, reversed herself and came down feet first. Again, the head smashed into the cement walkway. This time, the thing seemed to whimper in pain.

She stepped back to get her bearings. The head wobbled unsteadily now. A thick, yellowish fluid—blood, she guessed—oozed from between its teeth. The creature sent another of its nasty legs skidding toward her, but she caught it and snapped it easily. It was obviously weakening fast. She felt a moment's pity—it was just a living thing, trying to get by the only way it knew how. But she remembered the human leg, and the way it had attacked her. It was a predator. If she let it go, it would heal up somewhere and continue its assault on humanity.

Anyway, it was a beast from some other place. It didn't belong here. It couldn't stay.

Buffy moved in for the kill.

When she was done, she went to Riley, who had watched the whole thing from nearby.

"No big brothers," he reported.

"Something to be thankful for, at least."

"Pretty unpleasant, huh?"

She nodded. "Tell you what," she said. "Next time there's a spider, and I say, 'Riley, there's a spider, get rid of it?' "

"Yeah?"

"Just get rid of it. Don't tell me what you do to it. I don't want to know. I just don't want to have to step on one for as long as I live."

Riley took her in his arms, held her close to his chest.

"That's a deal," he said.

Salma de la Natividad rubbed her eyes and wanted to be gone.

When she took her hands away, though, she wasn't. She was still here. The bad part was, she didn't know for sure why she was here, or even how she had come to be here, and she definitely didn't know where "here" was. The whole thing was terribly distressing to her.

She had been walking on the grounds of her own family home, enjoying a soft summer breeze, when suddenly the very air before her had seemed to glow. Intrigued, she stepped forward, into the glowing area, and felt a welcoming warmth there. The feeling was like coming home after a long time away.

But as she passed into the shimmering golden spot, a reeling sensation of vertigo made her nauseous. One moment she had been firmly on Earth, feet on a flagstone walkway, smelling freshly mown grass and listening to the chirp of distant birds, and the next she was tumbling-turning-twirling through nothingness. She couldn't see or hear or smell anything, and her stomach flip-flopped as if she were trapped inside the fastest roller coaster ever built.

When she—was "landed" the word for it?—landed,

she found herself on a rocky, windswept plain that she knew existed nowhere on Earth. The sky was a deep sea-green color, and the rocks blue and rust. Strange plants, like succulents she'd seen in Baja, but gigantic, the size of redwood trees, loomed here and there. The landscape was so completely alien it made her feel sick to look at it, dizzy and ill.

Salma tried screaming and crying, calling for various people—her brother Nicky, her parents, her grandmother, Willow and Buffy—but none of that helped. After a while, she determined that it was not going away. She was truly here, in someplace so strange it was like the realm of dreams, or nightmares. At length, she picked a direction at random and started walking. Various possibilities occurred to her, the most obvious one was that she had gone insane, or was suffering a very intense and bizarre dream. But the nausea from the gut-churning journey seemed real enough. And nothing she tried to wake herself up or restore her normal surrounding seemed to work. So, tears in her eyes, she walked.

Chapter 5

Moscow, 1971

ALEXIS VISHNIKOFF WAS EATING BEEF FOR THE THIRD
night in a row. At his previous assignment, a small
physics lab in Minsk, meat seldom made the menu. But
here, in the capital, he ate like a czar, and he was so ex-
cited that he was bursting to tell someone, anyone, about
it; only he was surrounded by people who had eaten beef
for five, six, even seven nights in a row. *Maybe more.*

He never wanted to wake up from this marvelous dream.

He sat in a cafeteria with around fifty or sixty other
white-coated scientists who worked on the People's Project, many of them his boyhood idols. There was Yuri
Pushkin, seated in the corner with Gregor Dorodin and
Anna Krasova. Wen Ho Ling and Amalia Felix. He could
hardly contain himself.

Alexis understood that nourishment and rest were necessary for the cause, but it was very hard to make himself
eat or sleep in his new environment. The scientists were
treated well, in part, because so much was at stake: the

future of mankind, the ability of people to forge their own destinies. The right to dream.

Beyond the secure borders of the Soviet Union, the world was going insane. The Americans had invaded Southeast Asia. Students in Paris were rioting. People his own age wandered the streets in a daze, high on drugs, starving and filthy, caught up in a terrifying mass hallucination that degeneration was in some way a return to more idyllic times. They were passing terrible diseases to each other, completely unmindful of what they were doing. More frightening still, they insisted that theirs was the best way to live.

The relentless bombardment of capitalist propaganda had finally achieved its self-serving goal. The masses of Europe and America had become armies of materialistic creatures whose souls had been bought for refrigerators and dishwashers. All initiative and judgment had been erased. Now that they had been made slaves to the military-industrial complex, the capitalist overlords would begin to rebuild men and women as they wished humanity to be—seeking to assuage the terrible, aching emptiness of their hearts with endless amounts of shoddily-made, unnecessary consumer goods.

The only nation on Earth that had withstood the onslaught was the Union of Soviet Socialist Republics. While the world had criticized his country for protecting her people, the U.S.S.R. alone carried the torch of steadfastness to the ideals of mankind. Alexis's motherland stood between the complete destruction of civilization and a return—if possible—to sanity.

Everyone around him ate and chattered. Alexis was already accepted as a comrade, and he was gratified by his quick acceptance. He understood that the project was the thing on everyone's minds, not making new workers feel comfortable, and yet they had made an effort. Of course, it was simpler to work with people who were cordial with one another.

Around nine P.M., Vladimir Markov, the chief scientist, announced that it was time to go in for the latest test. Cigarettes were put out, the last of the tea drained from the glasses. Coffee cups clinked against saucers. Almost as if they were members of the Bolshoi Ballet, and not the People's Project, some of the finest scientists in the entire world pushed back their wooden chairs and stood; as soon as they filed out of the cafeteria to the observation theater, the large serving women toddled in and began loading their plates on carts.

The test area was quite small, approximately twenty meters by twenty. There was a black curtain, such as one might find in a theater, and a thick sheet of glass that ran from the floor to the ceiling separating the audience of chairs from the testing sector itself. The chairs were on graduated risers, so that successive rows of spectators could see over the heads of those in front.

Markov appeared, a man of great stature, not only professionally but physically. He looked like a Russian bear, burly and hairy, with unkempt dark brown hair and a perpetual five o'clock shadow. His earlobes and knuckles were hairy and his hands were huge.

"Comrades," he said jovially, into a microphone that transmitted his voice beyond the thick glass barrier, "tonight is a special night. We have good hopes of a successful test."

A middle-aged woman with short, dark hair sitting next to Alexis muttered, "I hope they don't use a piglet again. Since Markov's smiling, I assume they won't be trying the patience of our comrade janitors tonight. Or perhaps he's given them permission to forage through our dinner leftovers, the great man."

Alexis was stunned by his comrade's cynicism, but had no time to voice his outrage, as Markov went on. "I assume that those of you who are new to the project have read the handbooks you were given when you were assigned to this facility. Let me summarize in brief."

The woman shifted in her seat and rolled her eyes. "Last time, his 'brief' summation took an hour."

"The Reality Tracer," Markov continued, "is the last, best hope of mankind. With it, we can change the world. Literally." There was a ripple of polite applause; most of these scientists had certainly heard that before.

"Radio, television, movies." Markov gave his hand a wave. "Muzak. Pornography. Subliminal messages. The human mind is bombarded constantly with images seeking to reshape thoughts and expectations, and the assault is committed with the skill and finesse of a surgeon. At the same time, it is a brutal and savage attack upon the sanctity of one's inner thoughts. Of one's self-esteem. Of one's aspirations."

The audience murmured in agreement.

"Misunderstanding the nature of their oppression, the victims of this atrocity seek to numb themselves from the pain by any means possible—drugs, sex, violence, and isolating themselves from the collective of man. The result? We have worldwide depression, malaise, and a sense of purposelessness that transforms a skilled, productive worker into a shadow of himself, watching television and drinking beer."

"Sounds good to me," the woman said under her breath.

"Comrade, please hush," someone hissed behind them.

The woman made a face. "He's afraid he'll miss something," she snorted. "As if Markov will do anything but spout propaganda."

"Comrade," someone else admonished her.

Markov's eyes ticked toward the woman. She smoothed out her smirk and gave every appearance of listening attentively. Alexis was unnerved, hoping that he would not be singled out for having sat next to this rude individual. Even in the Workers' Paradise, there was such a thing as guilt by association.

The scientist returned to his summary. "Therefore, we begin with the notion that reality has been shaped by exterior forces and will continue to be shaped by exterior forces. But what if we can select the good, the true, and the useful from the possibilities of reality? The collective would be able to see life as it might have been, but for the intervention of those who profit by the misery of the masses.

"After a while, this reality would replace the terrible oppression which has been visited on our fellow human beings."

Alexis could not stifle the fervent "yes" that spilled from his mouth. The woman snickered and said, "You've got it bad."

"Please be quiet," Alexis snapped, shifting away from her.

"Oh, dear," said the woman. "Another live subject."

A petite young woman in a white lab coat was carrying something small and fluffy in a cage. From this distance, Alexis couldn't see what the creature was, but he could feel the tension rising around him.

"What we hope to do tonight is to open a passageway from our reality to a different one. To send this chick through the portal we have managed to open."

"Without turning it into scrambled eggs," the woman whispered. This time, nervous whispers joined her comment.

"Comrade Vishnikoff," Dr. Markov said, "would you care to assist me?"

"I'd be honored," Alexis replied, in a loud, bold voice. He rose, pointedly ignoring the woman as she said, "Don't let him push you through," and made his way down the row and out into the aisle. His footfalls rang on the metal stairs as he descended.

When he reached the bottom of the stairs, another woman in a lab coat gestured for him to follow her. They went out the door and into the hall, down a few meters, and then through another door. Alexis was behind the barrier now, in the little room.

Rather like assistants in a magic show, the woman who had carried in the chick in the cage set it down on a wooden table and left the room, only to reappear leading two men who were pushing a wheeled, wooden pallet. Placed on it was what looked very much like a shiny silver fire extinguisher. It was unremarkable in the extreme, not at all resembling the ornate object depicted in Alexis's Project handbook.

"The Reality Tracer," Markov announced proudly. He raised his bushy eyebrows as his colleagues applauded. "The prototype of the machine that will transform the world." His big, wide grin was ferocious. "What do you think, Vishnikoff?"

"It's a marvel," Alexis blurted. His cheeks flamed. "I'm proud to be here tonight."

Markov flashed a grin at the woman in the audience, who smiled back at him. At once, it dawned on Alexis: *She's KGB. She was testing me. Testing my loyalty.*

"Very good," Markov said, clearly pleased with him. He held out a hand to his assistant. "The subject, please."

She handed him the cage with the chick in it. Markov pulled up a wooden stool that had been pushed to the side of the table and set the cage on it. He moved the stool to a spot marked on the floor with an X of black duct tape.

Then he flicked on a series of switches along the side of the Reality Tracer. It emitted a low hum. The audience shifted forward, eagerly watching.

Light began to form at the top of the cylinder, shaping itself into a sphere that gave off static electricity and sparkles like fireworks. The light had a pastel green tone that deepened slightly as the seconds passed into a minute.

"Please, hold this as I show you. Keep it steady," Markov instructed Alexis. From a pocket in his lab coat, he pulled a small metal box. He opened the lid and picked up what looked to Alexis like an ordinary glass prism.

"This will bend the reality beam," Markov said, almost casually. "Hold it just so, yes? I will work the controls on the side of the Tracer itself."

As Markov had demonstrated, Alexis angled the prism above the sphere. It began to narrow, like a bubble of mercury when pressed down in the middle. It stretched and grew into more of a circle, nearly grazing Alexis's stomach as he pulled it in.

The circle wobbled unsteadily. Markov pushed buttons on the side of the Tracer.

"Remove the prism and stand aside," he told Alexis, who did so immediately. Markov backed away.

The circle shuddered but began to raise up on its side. The crowd murmured.

"I have set it to remain stable for ten seconds," he said.

The circle floated forward, drifting toward the cage. Alexis, like everyone else in the room, held his breath. And waited.

The circle touched the stool and the light fell on the cage. The chick peeped. A membrane formed over the circle and began to shimmer with an exquisite, strange glow.

Please, Alexis thought, not begging God—after all, he

was a Communist—but the collective knowledge and wisdom of his comrade scientists. *Please.*

For one second, one moment in the time in which Alexis lived, the chick disappeared.

Then strips of wire, blood, feathers, and guts exploded from the circle and were strewn across the floor.

The circle collapsed, and vanished.

There was silence. Acute disappointment.

Then someone cried, "For one second, it worked!"

There was thunderous applause. Alexis joined in.

I will devote my life to this, he thought. *I will do whatever I can, give whatever I can, to making this come true. No matter the price.*

Sunnydale

The doorbell of Del DeSola's mansion rang.

Which should never happen, he thought. He employed security guards, paid for state of the art equipment—cameras, motion detectors, alarms—precisely so that he would not be surprised like this. He was particularly nervous now, having had one of his oil fields attacked by some kind of terrorist gang.

He picked up the nearest phone, punched a code. His security personnel knew to answer this phone on the first ring.

By the fifth ring, he gave up and replaced the receiver.

The doorbell rang again—a long, insistent buzz. Followed by a knock. *More of a pound,* he corrected himself.

He went to his closet, removed a loaded shotgun, and crept downstairs. The ringing and pounding continued.

Next to his office was a small security station, with monitors from which one could view the entire property.

He checked the camera over the front door. A young lady stood there—attractive, in a cheap way, like a showgirl. Her clothing was torn, in some disarray, and she was bleeding from the mouth. Maybe there had been some kind of accident. He hurried to the door, still clutching the shotgun, just in case, and threw it open.

She looked at him, looked at the gun. "I come in?"

"Are you all right? Are you hurt?" he asked.

"I'll live," she said with a sharp laugh. "Now listen up—can I come in?"

"Yes, of course, come on in. We'll get you cleaned up, call a doctor."

She crossed the threshold, her gaze wandering around the sumptuous interior. "Nice place."

"I-I'm surprised my security guards didn't see—"

"Oh, I saw them," she said. "They're dead."

"Dead?" DeSola said, shocked. He remembered the gun in his hand, raising it now as if there were something to shoot. "What—?"

The young lady wiped her mouth with the back of her hand, smearing the blood there. Then she raised her hand again, and licked it. "Tasty, too, that big guy anyway."

Something was very wrong here. He aimed the gun at her. "Now, listen here—" he began.

"No, you listen," she said casually. She passed him, going into the formal living room, and dropped onto an antique chaise so hard he thought she'd break it. "Yes, I killed your guards. Big deal. If they're that bad, you need new ones anyway."

"Point taken," he said. "But I'm still going to call the police."

"Fine," she said. "Do that. But then I'll leave, and you won't get revenge for your oil field."

"I've already put that in motion," he said, thinking of the Russians who had been in touch with him. The meeting hadn't happened yet, but he knew that's what it would concern when it did.

"Sure," she said. "Only, I'd bet money that whatever you think you've got arranged won't do diddley."

"And why is that?" He sat down in a chair opposite her, the shotgun across his lap. He couldn't deny that the girl intrigued him even as she repulsed him.

"Because you're human," she explained. "And whoever you've lined up to get your revenge, chances are, he's human too. But whoever torched that field—he's not human. That's where your plan comes up short."

He found himself nodding along with her. "Not human? Then what is he? Or it?"

"I don't know that yet," the young lady said. "I'm smart, not psychic. But I know that I can find out."

"You are resourceful," he said, thinking of his guards.

"And a whole lot more," she agreed. "Look, just think it through. Could anyone have survived that fire? The explosions? They rocked my trailer, miles away."

"No, certainly not. No one at ground zero."

"But didn't the investigators determine that the way the charges were set, whoever touched them off had to be right on the spot? No remote detonation, right? No timers?"

"That's true. I can't say it's not a mystery."

"It's only a mystery," she went on, "because you're not looking at it from the right angle."

"And the right angle is, I should be looking for some kind of super-villain?"

"Super something," she said. "You should be looking for some kind of monster, a demon, something like that. I can find out which one it was, and I can get your revenge for you."

"And what's in it for you?" He looked at her with a combination of curiosity and amusement. "Surely you're not the kind of person who would do this from pure generosity of spirit."

She laughed again. "Got that right, Del," she said, crossing her legs high up on her thighs. "I can call you Del, right? Seeing as how we're in business together."

"Business?"

"Money, Del." She almost winked at him. "You got it. I want some. I want a lot of it. You give me what I want, I give you what you want. That's what turns the world."

"I suppose it does," DeSola said. The fire had cost him plenty. What was a little more, to get some satisfaction?

By the time she left his house, Cheryce had convinced the oil billionaire to pay her to do what she wanted to do anyway. She hadn't been kidding—she was smart. She had thought about the oil field explosions, and the type of being that was most likely to survive same, and she had thought about the shadow monster that had attacked her, nearly tearing her in two despite her best efforts, and she had decided that the two had to be connected somehow. So she'd track down the shadow monster, and she'd make it pay for what it had done to her.

But she was ready to move on. Sunnydale had become boring. To tell the truth, Sunnydale had been boring within about twenty minutes of getting here, as far as she was concerned. Spike had a good idea with Paris, except for the part where he'd be coming along. *Also boring,* she thought.

Better to have Del DeSola bankroll her trip to the City of Light. She could travel first class, get herself a chateau outside of town somewhere, live right. She was trailer trash and she knew it—but there was no law that said trailer trash couldn't move uptown.

As Spike awoke from his fever dream—*something to do with Buffy*—he could tell by how refreshed he was that night had fallen at last. He was free to search for Cheryce.

He threw open the door to the crypt and took one step over the threshold. Then something jumped out at him, all teeth and bad body odor, and tried to eat his face.

Spike was not one to cower. Never had been, never would be; he slammed his fists into the thing's midsection, sending it flying, and began to kick it as hard as he could. When a mate's shoes have steel plates in the toes, that can hurt.

"Damn bloody bastard," he spat, as the creature made no sound. It was a flesh-eating ghoul, nothing more, and Spike made short work of it.

But while he was distracted, a few of its mates shambled up behind Spike and began trying to rip off his arms.

"Here, leave off!" Spike shouted, pulling his arms together. That smacked two of their heads together. The ghoul on the right slathered at the other one, teeth clacking, trying to take a bite out of its cheek.

"What the devil are you doing here, anyway?" Spike demanded. He wheeled around and kicked a fourth ghoul in the head, knocking out all its teeth, and sent another flying with a good, sharp punch to the gizzard.

He smoothed back his hair and straightened his duster, when all at once, just like in that Michael Jackson video he liked so much, shapes moved toward him from beneath the tree. Their steps were awkward and disjointed; their gait distinctly uncontrolled.

As they moved into the moonlight, their eyes were blank and their mouths hung open.

"Zombies. Crikey, what the hell is going on?" he shouted. "I have a rescue to conduct, d'you mind? So I'll just be on my way."

They
Walked
Toward
Him.

"Oh." He was more annoyed than anything. What were zombies going to do to him?

A lot, it seemed, if there were enough of them. And there were a lot. A whole bleedin' army of the buggers. They stumbled and lurched on, intent upon surrounding him, perhaps to have a nibble, even though, God knew, a vampire would probably taste like dried leather to a flesh-eating ghoul. . . .

Soon, he was completely overrun with them. They were like really big lice; no matter how many he picked out, there were more to take their place. *Disgusting.*

Kicking, punching, much with the chop-socky and every other trick he'd learned. Heavy boots, heavier fists; Spike head-banged them and shoved them, one against a file of them, like dominoes. He tore out large sections of them, only to face their reinforcements.

Bad news: at long last, he was beginning to tire.

And that was when Xander, of all people, happened along and called from the entrance gate, "Damn, Spike! What'd you do, blow your subaudible zombie whistle?"

"Ha, ha, very funny," Spike answered, as he rammed his fist into the face of an oncoming zombie. Its face crumpled inward and the lower jaw popped off. Spike barely took note. "I'm sure Giles and Tara are to blame."

Spike puffed out an explosive breath. "All that bleedin' magick. Come on in here and help me."

"And why?" Xander asked, stuffing his hands into his pockets.

"Do we really need a retake about you being one of the good guys and all that rubbish?" Spike groused at him.

Xander shrugged but nevertheless joined the fray, putting the lie to the Scoobies' constant verbal threats that if Spike eventually proved to be too much trouble, none of them would harbor any reservations about staking him through the heart. Here he was, being a lot of trouble—as he usually was—and this fine young bloodbag was risking his life to save Spike's. It was enough to warm Spike's heart.

No, actually it wasn't.

So they fought together. Xander tripped them up, usually by, well, sticking out his leg; and Spike punched them in the face so hard that their faces left their heads. There was mold everywhere, and desiccated skin and flesh. Brittle bones cracked. Xander kept saying, "Ew, yuck," like a ninny, and Spike experienced the nearly uncontrollable urge to haul off and hit him. However, he was no stranger to the chip-induced pain that would create. As long as that damn chip was inside his head, harming humans was *verboten*.

As long as . . .

They kept fighting together. Fight, fight, fight. Xander said, "Spike, let's book. There's too many of them and I'm getting tired."

"You big nancy-boy," Spike jeered.

Xander shook his head. "I take time out of my valuable schedule to save your butt, and this is the thanks I get?"

At that moment, a zombie shambled over and ran directly into Spike's face. It crumbled into an icky mess that left ooze the consistency of blood pudding all over Spike's nose, cheeks, and chin.

"What are you doing here, anyway, Harris?" he asked.

"Like I said. I came to save you." Xander looked at him. "Well, okay, I didn't know you were in trouble. But I thought someone should, you know, check in on you."

"Since when have you given a fig about me?"

"Since you can fight monsters and we've got more monsters than we can handle," the boy said frankly.

"And I can't hurt you."

"That's pretty much right. Makes you an asset—that's what Riley calls you. Well, one of the things. You should hear what Buffy calls you." Xander flashed him a sneer. "Anyway, you're an asset that we can use. So, since you're an asset, I figured someone should come over and drag your worthless carcass back to Giles's for a strategy session."

"Strategy." *I am not flattered,* Spike reminded himself. "Sounds like another of Riley's words."

"They have a way of rubbing off on you," Xander said. "Whether you want them to or not."

"Doesn't sound like you like him," Spike observed.

"I like Riley just fine," Xander countered. "You're the one I don't like."

It occurred to Spike that he could tell the lad to sod off. There was very little percentage in him fighting the baddies while Cheryce was off somewhere, and him still chipped up. But Tara had all that magick and maybe they could do some kind of finder's spell for Cheryce, and he could threaten her with a good staking if she didn't tell him about the chip.

Ought to get her hot, at least.

"Right, then," Spike said through a grimace. "Let's book." He sighed. "Sure was a good time."

Superheroes A and B disappeared into the night.

Willy had fixed up the Alibi. Now it was Willy's Place. He had a deep fryer because some of the demons liked onion rings. The jukebox had a few new CD's in it, which Willy had picked up at the Runaway Project garage sale for a couple of bucks apiece.

But Willy himself had not classed up. Once a snitch, always a snitch. Willy cost less than an order of fries. He cost less than ketchup.

"Buffy," Willy said nervously from behind his varnished wood bar, as the Slayer and Riley sauntered through the front door. "What brings you to my place of business?"

"Business." Buffy was not smiling. Neither was Riley.

"Oh." Willy looked so much less than pleased. "Um, like, a drink?" He reached for a bottle of Old Reliable.

Riley grabbed Willy around the collar and hoisted him up to eye level. "Like, who killed Rosalie Estrada?"

"Huh?" Willy was goggle-eyed. "She's dead? Who is she?"

"On the news. On the radio. On the computer," Buffy intoned, unimpressed by his act. Much as she regretted anyone's death, the loss of Rosalie Estrada was mainly important to her as a stepping-stone—if she knew who had killed the girl whose body had turned up, she could leverage that against the killers for information about Nicky.

"We're guessing you've heard about it." Riley narrowed his eyes as he glared at Willy. "We're guessing you'll tell us about it. Now."

A few demons started observing the goings-on. Those who knew Buffy was the Slayer usually kept their distance. Those who didn't quickly found out from those who did. There was honor among demons, of a sort.

Occasionally.

For a price.

"I've heard about it," Willy admitted. He lowered his voice, his eyes big and wary and not at all obvious with the guilt thing. "You want to get me killed?"

"I've been good all year round, Willy," Buffy replied coldly. "Santa owes me. And he knows who's on my list."

Riley took charge, hovering over the man, who seemed to shrink from the heat of Riley's scowl. "Word on the street is you're in thick with the Latin Cobras." That wasn't true; neither Buffy nor her sweetie had heard one about that. But Willy was the dumbest snitch on the planet Earth.

"Let's go in my office," he said quickly. Smiling too brightly at his patrons, he said, "I'll be back in a flash. You won't even miss me."

"You got that right," one of the barflies slurred. A few others chuckled at the humor.

"Man." Willy led the way down the hall and into his tiny, messy office. "You're going to get me killed one of these days."

Buffy and Riley waited. Willy raised his hands and said, "All right, all right. I do a little go-between work for the Latin Cobras and their, um, mother gang."

"The Echo Park Band," Riley filled in.

Willy paled. "Jeez, you guys know everything. Why bother me, huh? I'm just trying to get along. Pay my taxes, live decent—"

Buffy pushed him against his putty-colored filing cabinet. "Who killed Rosalie?"

"I don't know," he said. "I swear."

She pulled him back from the cabinet, then pushed him back again. "Who, Willy?"

"Murder. It's not so nice," he whined. "I try to stay out of that kind of thing. I got a mom in Jersey Heights."

Buffy glared at him. "I'll beat it out of you if I have to, Willy, but I am not leaving here without the name of Rosalie Estrada's killer."

"Okay." He held his hands chest high. "Only, no more hitting, all right? I just spent a fortune replacing my front teeth." He gestured for her to draw closer. "It was two Cobras named Little King and Dom," he whispered. "If you ever tell anyone how you found out, I will personally go to your worst enemy and offer him my services."

Buffy just shook her head. "All you do, Willy, is make it easier," she snarled at him, showing him her fist. "Every single time, it's just that much easier."

"Hey, I cooperate with you, okay? You have no right to threaten me," he insisted, as Buffy and Riley walked out of the office. "No right at all!"

"And you have no right to exist. Strange world," Buffy flung over her shoulder.

They walked back from his office through the bar, Buffy catching the expressions of hatred on the facial areas of several of the demons. Nobody challenged her, however, which was par for the course in Willy's Place. These demons might hate her, but they also feared her. They preferred to conduct their battles against the Slayer on far less level playing grounds.

"Let's go find Little King and Dom," Buffy suggested, once they got outside. "Find out what we can about Nicky, then take them to the cops. Serve up some justice."

"Liking that idea," Riley replied.

Then he tapped Buffy's shoulder and gestured sky-ward.

A long-tailed creature was flying across the moon. It looked like a Chinese dragon. Or some poor little kid's worst nightmare.

"Also, we need to check on my mom," Buffy said.

"Liking that one, too," Riley said.

Together, they moved into the night.

Chapter 6

Sunnydale

Huddled in her white pajamas in the corner of her living room, Joyce Summers was not having a very good night. She was under siege, with no moat, no drawbridge, and no Slayer on a white charger in sight. Her house was surrounded by so many different kinds of monsters that someone in the underworld should get awards for best special effects makeup.

And that's the best joke I can make at the moment, because if Buffy doesn't come home soon, these things are going to break in and kill me.

Because some of the monsters were body-slamming the house, and others were rattling her doorknobs. Horned demons, winged creatures, monsters so different from anything she'd ever seen before she didn't even know how to describe them: things that were half-mist, half-liquid, creatures that were covered with talons or mouths filled with needle-thin fangs. Things that growled, and shrieked, and wailed.

And then, there were the things that were so eerily reminiscent of childhood nightmares: a witch in a pointy hat, cackling as she rode her broom; a scattering of trolls; and a beautiful young girl with pale skin and blue-black hair, wearing a dark gray velvet gown and a snood, surrounded by a tribe of dwarves.

Snow White, Joyce thought, unaccountably comforted by the sight as she looked through the window, still maintaining her distance. *Maybe because Snow White was a nice fairy-tale heroine, and not someone who might grind my bones to make her bread.*

Something was lobbed against the window, making the glass rattle. Joyce pushed herself farther into the corner, stifling a scream: it was the head of a demon, still fresh and bleeding, its green blood smearing down the window as it tumbled to the ground.

"It figures," Joyce muttered to herself. "I just washed those."

Then the outside lights revealed something that gave her hope, but sent her fear skyrocketing: her daughter, Buffy the Vampire Slayer, and her boyfriend, taking on the monsters.

They worked as a team, the two young people, Riley setting them up and Buffy knocking them down. Buffy was astonishing, doing backflips and high kicks and whirling in circles, to land at precisely the right spot to attack her enemy. Riley, though obviously weaker and lacking superpowers, was nevertheless impressive. He was tall, and very strong, and while careful, utterly fearless. Joyce noted how often he took his attention off his own fight to make sure Buffy was all right, and a faint smile crossed her face.

As she watched through the window, a demon with skin the color of blood and a wild, leering face appeared in front of her, hands pressed against the glass. Joyce let out a shrill cry. But Buffy saw it—her eyes locked, momentarily, with Joyce's. She grabbed the thing's shoulder and spun it around, meeting it as it turned with a sharp kick to the midsection.

The demon's flesh surrounded Buffy's foot and, Tar Baby-like, seemed to suck it in, refusing to let it go. Buffy yanked, but the foot was stuck. Buffy made the classic mistake of pushing off the thing with her hand, pressing it against the demon's chest, but that got drawn into the demon's gooey flesh as well. The demon, absorbing Buffy bit by bit, clawed at her with big hands, raking sharp fingernails across her cheek and drawing blood.

Joyce watched the whole thing in horror. Riley couldn't help—he was under a dogpile of demons as it was. And there was nothing she could do to help Buffy; she knew if she so much as set foot outside, they'd grab her and all she'd wind up doing would be serving as a distraction, not an assist, to her daughter.

Buffy strained, trying with all her might to tug her arm or leg free from the demon's grasp. Nothing seemed to work. But Joyce Summers hadn't raised a quitter. Buffy, apparently giving up, went limp, and then, with the demon caught off guard, just as suddenly threw herself backward onto the lawn. As she landed on her back and rolled, the demon flew over her. Buffy directed his landing so he hit headfirst. He slammed into the grass with a squooshing sound that Joyce could hear all the way inside, and his head seemed to spread over a patch of lawn.

This seemed to work. Buffy disentangled herself from him and stepped back. As she watched, the demon liquefied, running into the grass, some of him flowing over the sidewalk and spilling into the street, where Joyce had no doubt he'd eventually wind up in the sewer.

She made a mental note to have a gardener tear out the

grass in that spot and put in new sod, as soon as possible. Heaven only knew what might grow where the demon's head had splattered.

With that demon dispatched, Buffy raced for the door. Riley had climbed out from underneath his, and followed. Joyce had the door open in time for both of them to sail over the threshold and into the house.

"Thanks, Mom," Buffy said, panting. She held her midsection as she caught her breath.

"Thanks, Mrs. Summers." Riley looked at Buffy and nodded. "Let's get your mom to Giles's place."

"Mr. Giles?" Joyce asked, coloring. It was no secret— *not any longer*—that she and Buffy's former Watcher had had sex. *Under the influence of cursed chocolate bars,* she reminded herself. *Not that anyone gives us any slack because of that.*

"Everyone's there, Mom," Buffy said. "You'll be safe . . . safer."

"Okay." She hesitated. "Do either of you want anything to eat?"

"I'm good," Riley said politely. "Thank you."

"Let's go. Stay between us if you can, Mom. That way we can protect you better."

Joyce took a breath and nodded. Before she was ready, they were out of the house, Buffy in the lead, kicking and slamming horrible-looking creatures out of the way. A blue, gilled thing slithered on all fours toward them and Riley rammed his heel into one of its eyes; black liquid jetted into the air and sprayed Joyce's pajamas.

They made it all the way across the lawn and had reached the sidewalk, when an ice cream truck jangled up beside them, playing a tune Joyce could not identify. Xander was seated in the driver's seat; he gave a jaunty wave and said, "Hop in."

They did, and he took off, at, oh, about twenty miles an hour.

Buffy and Riley continued to fight, joined by Spike, who appeared from the interior, slurping on a 50–50 bar. He said, "Evenin', missus," to Joyce, then finished off his ice cream and joined the other young people pummeling the demons who tried to board the truck.

After a very, very, very, very long time, they reached Giles's condo. There were very few monsters around, and Buffy, Riley, and Spike killed enough of them to make a dash for the door.

As they ran up the stairs, Buffy said, "Come on, Mom," looked down at her, and added, "Why weren't you wearing a bathrobe?"

"I'm so sorry, dear," Joyce countered, padding along in her bare feet. "What could I have been thinking of? Perhaps my life?"

"You were the one who used to tell me to put on clean underwear, in case I was in an accident."

Giles opened his front door.

"I never did," Joyce protested. "Good evening, Mr. Giles."

"Good evening." He smiled as if they had never had sex on the hood of a car and moved courteously out of the way. His smile faded when he saw Spike. "What are you doing back?"

Xander plopped down next to Anya, on the sofa. "It must be cold outside," Anya observed. She smiled at Joyce's chest.

"Oh." Joyce was abashed. She looked to Buffy, who said, "Giles, where's your bathrobe?"

"Upstairs. In the loft," he said.

"I'll get it, honey." Joyce turned and started up the stairs.

Buffy turned to Giles and she and Riley began telling him about the situation both in L.A. and in Sunnydale. Which was: demons, demons, demons.

"What?" Anya said in response to something Xander had murmured to her. Only she spoke in a loud, confused voice. "Everyone knows they had sex. It's common knowledge."

"Everyone knows we have sex, too," Xander said, pressing his mouth tightly in his signature *ay-chihuahua* smile. "But they don't really like to dwell on it."

"Why not? It's a pleasurable activity, and our friends care about our pleasure." She smiled at Giles. "I'm glad you found pleasure having sex with Buffy's mother."

Above them, in the loft, Joyce closed her eyes as she belted Giles's thick terrycloth robe and shook her head.

Looks like I'm going to die of embarrassment instead of dismemberment.

Maybe I should have let the monsters kill me.

As she descended the curved staircase, Spike piped up, "I'm wondering if your Initiative has anything to do with all these monsters runnin' amuck."

Riley blinked. He said, "We were disbanded."

Spike rolled his eyes. "I still got a chip, and you had one you didn't know about. Don't have to be bleedin' James Bond to know the government doesn't turn their backs on fancy new gadgets that control people."

"You are not people, Spike," Buffy said. "You are nothing. The reason you still have a chip in your head is because you're not worth worrying about. You bungled your own attempt to get it out, and no one feels like helping you become a homicidal maniac again. Period. End of story." She glanced at Riley, and Joyce detected the slightest trace of worry on her lovely young face. "Riley's fine, and you never were, Spike. And you never will be."

Joyce glanced over at Rupert Giles, who had a thoughtful expression on his face. *Does he think it's the Initiative causing all this?* she wondered.

Then Spike cleared his throat and said, "Any of you dust my girlfriend?"

"Harmony?" Buffy asked, raising her brows.

"Ah." Spike sighed. "I meant Cheryce."

"If I had my powers, I would probably have killed you by now," Anya told him. "You're a terrible boyfriend. Surely one of the vampires you've cheated on would have called upon me for vengeance."

"Well, you aren't a demon, and Cheryce is my . . . is a friend, who is a woman . . . and she . . ." He drifted off. "You seen her?"

"If we had, dusted is what she would be," Buffy said helpfully.

"But she's not," Spike said carefully.

Buffy looked around the room. No one volunteered anything. Joyce saw the look of disappointment on Spike's face and thought, *Maybe he does care for her.*

Giles was studying Spike, and Joyce pulled his bathrobe belt more tightly around herself as she sat back down on the couch.

Xander was getting used to the embarrassment Anya still occasionally—*okay, often*—caused him. *Not growing fond of it, mind you,* he thought, *but becoming accustomed to it. Just another part of life, like doing laundry or scraping gum off your shoes, that you have to endure.*

And the good parts of being with Anya definitely outweighed the awkward parts. So all in all, a happy situation.

But the old gang—not such the happy times, as far as Xander could tell. There was a tension in the air that he didn't like. Anya broke it occasionally with her out there commentary. Even at that, though, since the shadow monster had come, and Buffy had gone to L. A. and returned, things hadn't been right.

Buffy had way too much on her mind, to begin with, and the stress was starting to show on her. Riley tried to help, but that was exactly his problem; all he wanted to do was to protect Buffy, and it didn't seem to sink in that she wasn't really a person in great need of protection. Besides, as much as he liked Riley—and he really did—he couldn't help feeling bugged by the way Riley had usurped his role in the group. He had once been Buffy's right-hand man. Not as close to the right hand as Riley was, but still—that was him. Now it was Riley. Buffy didn't turn to Xander anymore when she had a problem, or when she needed something. She didn't even turn to Willow. It was always Riley.

Which also left poor Giles out in the dark. That man was really adrift since Buffy had moved on. He needed a hobby, a girlfriend, a vacation, or all three.

At first, Xander had just sat back and watched as things shifted, slowly and inexorably, like tectonic plates under the Earth's crust. But sitting here, watching almost all of them gathered—even Buffy's mom, looking way hotter than any mom had a right to—he realized that he needed to do something to fix things. No one else would. *It falls once again,* he thought, *on the mighty Harris shoulders to make the world right again.*

He wasn't sure where to start.

But he'd figure it out.

Los Angeles

Angel walked slowly down the street, watching the faces of the street kids as they watched him. Some of them were sullen, while others tried to hide their fear. But the response that chilled him the most was the numb blankness on many of their faces, as if they had given up expecting to be noticed. As if they were invisible.

I am so not feeling the love tonight, he thought, as he walked past them.

He was looking for information, but every knot of kids he came across refused to come across for him; they were tight-lipped and unfriendly, dodging even the most innocent of questions. He could imagine some of these kids pretending not to see an outstretched hand ready to pull them from a burning building. It was as if they had run away mentally, as well as physically. He understood; he would have, too. He'd been so close.

But then Darla took me, and changed me. . . .

Go home, he wanted to say to the kids. But for some of them, that would be the same as pushing them back *into* a burning building.

A trio of dark young men strode down the opposite street; the one in the center had on a sweatshirt with a hood, which obscured his face. But Angel recognized him by his gait, and began across the street to meet up with him.

"Hey," Gunn said, pulling back his hood. "What the hell's goin' on, man? Kids all over L.A. are scared speechless."

"Disappearing act's not over," Angel said. "You hear anything?"

Gunn shrugged. "Lots of kids are coming into shelters, looking for protection. Most of them think it's either something religious or alien abductions."

"That's what Cordelia thinks. She's the one you guarded in the hospital."

"Gotta meet her sometime, when she's not catatonic," Gunn said. "Seemed like a nice chick. If I'd known that was her under the library the other day I'd have said hi."

"She is nice." His pager vibrated; he looked down. It was Cordy. To Gunn, he said, "Excuse me." He took out his cell phone and called her.

"You are not going to believe this!" she cried, as she answered her phone. "David Nabbit just called. His secretary's daughter is missing."

"Ransom note?" Angel asked automatically. Just because a lot of kids had gone mysteriously missing didn't mean that an actual kidnapping was out of the question. Especially when the victim's mother worked for a multimillionaire. *Or is it billionaire?*

"Not yet," she replied. "But you can just bet that when they send one, they're going to demand a bundle."

"Any leads? Information?" Angel asked.

"No. But he wants you to call him. Probably just to calm him down," she said. "He's pretty upset."

Angel nodded. "Okay." He disconnected. At Gunn's questioning expression, he said, "David Nabbit's secretary's daughter."

Gunn whistled. "What's going on? There have been some high-profile kids snatched, man. And then nobodies. The ones who aren't going to be missed."

Angel looked across the street at the gaunt faces, the hunched shoulders of girls and boys who should be at home arguing with their parents about bedtimes and after-school chores.

"I'm sure someone misses them," he said softly. He turned back to Gunn. "If you hear anything—"

"You got it, man."

They left it at that, Angel walking back the way he came. The kids were still there, still milling, still pretending it was perfectly normal to have run away from home and taken up a life on the streets. As Angel passed her, a girl looked up at him with huge, frightened eyes and said, "Lookin' for a good time, mister?"

He gazed at her. "Is it that bad at home?" he asked gently.

The other kids looked, first at him, then at her.

She raised her chin, gritted her teeth, and struck a pose. "Who wants to know?" she asked coolly.

Angel sighed, and walked away.

Sunnydale

Dawn came, and the weary were no better rested.

Giles had given up his bed to Buffy, Tara, and Joyce, but Buffy spent the majority of the night watching over the others. Anya curled up with Xander on the couch, literally on top of him, which was the sort of thing only people in love could do and still manage to fall asleep. Spike holed up in the bathtub with a blanket spread over it, and Giles and Riley took the floor.

Breakfast was a chaotic affair, consisting mostly of people finding something to nibble on as one by one, they woke up. Buffy was first, and she chose some cheese and crackers, nearly choking when Spike padded in and grumbled, "Who's been stealing sips of my O-pos?"

Giles made coffee and tea, and after a few jolts of caffeine, he set about bringing Buffy and Riley up to speed on what had happened in the brief time since they'd left Sunnydale. The discussion was interrupted several times by various hideous beings flinging themselves against the doors and windows. Most of them, Buffy killed. Riley and Xander took out a fair number, as well, while Spike watched longingly from the shelter of the house, unable to rumble because of the sunshine.

As usual, Sunnydale was pretending that there was a

perfectly reasonable explanation for everything—if it wasn't gangs on PCP or gas leaks, it was gangs from another town wearing rubber masks. Never mind that the shadow monster had been reportedly continuing its murderous rampage, a nine-foot-tall giant had appeared on the commons of U.C. Sunnydale, or that enormous ants had been spotted traveling across the white sands of Sunnydale Beach.

"And what about the fairy-tale creatures?" Joyce reminded them.

They set to work, researching and going on the Net. Giles had a few IM exchanges with friends in other countries. Some suggested sunspots and comets; others went to their libraries of arcana to see what they could find.

"The location of many of the demonic appearances seems to be near the Hellmouth, which makes sense," Giles reported, tapping a white board he'd set up. "But not all of them, which, by the same token, doesn't."

"And not all of them are HST's," Riley said. "Pheromone readings are off."

Everyone took that in. Spike grumbled some more about the missing Cheryce, the "sodding Initiative" and the chip in his head while Buffy decided that, too many monsters on the prowl or no, she had better go check out the Hellmouth.

Riley went with her. And they found exactly nothing. "Is this a problem?" Buffy asked rhetorically. "I mean, maybe it's over. Maybe it was sunspots, or a comet." She looked at Riley.

"Well," he pointed out, "it is daytime. Maybe they come out at night."

"You want to sit around here all day waiting to see?"

"Not me," he said. "You?"

She shook her head. "Although I'm sure we could

come up with some way to pass the time, I don't think that's how we should be applying ourselves right now."

"Then we'll head back, I guess," Riley said. "Report the all clear to Giles."

"Yes, well, they do seem much more active at night," Giles said. "Like vampires, or, um, pinworms."

"But they're not," Buffy said. "Vampires, I mean. Or pinworms, as far as I know. Which, Giles, ewww. So why the nocturnal behavior? I mean, the shadow monster, sure. Shadows in the daytime, not so scary, right? But the rest of them? What do we think they are?"

"That's what I'm still trying to figure out," Giles replied. "No progress so far, I'm afraid. They don't correspond to anything in the books. I'm afraid I'm still at a loss as to what's going on."

"I'll tell you what's going on," Anya said, from the doorway. Xander rushed up behind her, completely out of breath. From his place on the couch, Spike stood.

"Did you find her?" he asked. "Did you see Cheryce?"

"No, I did not," Xander said. "We went to my house. To get fresh clothes and check on my parents."

"Also, to have sex." Anya smiled dreamily. "It was very nice."

"Ann," Xander warned. "Remember what we talked about?"

She looked puzzled and slightly out of sorts. "But that had nothing to do with Mrs. Summers and Giles having sex!"

"Let's get back to the part where you know what's going on," Giles said.

"Yes," Xander pounced, relieved to be off-topic. "We were in my basement, um, loading the washing machine, and this lady comes screaming down the sidewalk that a monster jumped out of a circle of light and started chasing her."

Giles raised his brows. "Did you question her?"

Xander shook his head. "I couldn't get my pants . . . in the washing machine . . . in time."

Anya leaned forward. "We were—"

"Yes, quite," Giles said, briefly shutting his eyes. Buffy was very amused. Also, trying to pay attention to the rambling revelation Xander was about to share.

"She said something about the playground, the one over by Weatherly, so we figured we'd go by on our way back here."

"His parents have not been eaten, by the way," Anya added helpfully.

"Bad luck," Spike said to Xander.

"Thanks, man," Xander replied. "So we went over there, and bada-bing! This weird circle forms, and light shimmers across it, and three really short, sort of caveman-looking things fall out of it."

"It sounds like the Ghost Roads," Buffy ventured. She looked at Giles. "Did you call the Gatekeeper?"

"I did. And he's closed them all. There should be no entrances to any of them at present," Giles said.

"Unless he's not a very good Gatekeeper," Spike drawled.

Buffy gave the pale, white-haired vampire a look. The world with Spike in it was like one of those soap operas, where someone is really, really evil, and does mean things, but the other characters still trusted her—or him—and did all kinds of crazy things like marry him or let him walk unaccompanied into the opened bank vault.

Riley looked at Buffy. Buffy looked back. She said, "Let's wait a bit. See if it holds. When it gets dark, Spike can go with us."

"Hey," Spike said. Xander pointed at him.

"Pull your weight, or it's suntan city for you," he warned.

Spike moved his shoulders like the petulant overgrown baby he was, and said, "Anyone needs me, I'll be in the bathtub."

The phone rang on Giles's desk. Tara said, "I think it's Willow." Giles gave her a nod to pick it up, which she did, and her cheeks reddened. She smiled up at Buffy, who smiled back, figuring it could be no one else other than Willow, to create such happiness and relief on Tara's soft features.

"Hi, Willow," Tara murmured, looping her blond hair around her ear. "What's going on up there?"

Tara listened intently for at least a minute.

Which, when you're listening to someone else listening on the phone, is a pretty long time, Buffy thought impatiently.

"All right. Um, you, too." Tara smiled and hung up the phone.

She said, "You know how Willow did that crow thing?" Everyone nodded. "They want me to try to do it with them. See, you usually have someone transform 'of the wing,' and someone else 'of the claw.' The wing is the one who searches, and the claw protects her. They had to do it without a claw because Doña Pilar had to anchor Willow."

Giles said, "Yes, and I find that most fascinating. So, they want to repeat the ritual with you? Long-distance, as it were?"

Tara nodded. "They've both been having a feeling, as if Nicky were nearby."

"Good. Maybe they can tell him to stop doing whatever he's doing," Buffy said. She gave Tara a thumbs-up. "I say, go for it." Then she grimaced. "Is it very dangerous?"

"N-no," Tara said, then flushed. "Yes. A little."

"And isn't that the way it always goes," Xander riffed. "The best things in life are fatal. Or possibly fatal." He frowned as Anya smacked him. "What was that for?"

"I have not once attempted to take your life," she said. "Therefore, you are not including me on your list of best things."

"Jeez, Ann, lighten up. Don't I always walk around mumbling, 'you'll be the death of me yet'?"

"Are you sure you should attempt it?" Giles asked Tara. His voice was kind and filled with concern. Buffy was touched; only lately had she come to realize just how difficult it must be for Giles sometimes, to send her and her friends out into the field, when he felt rather fatherly toward them all.

"I have to help, if I can," Tara replied. Her flush deepened. *She's scared for Willow,* Buffy realized.

"You are helping, very nicely," Giles countered. "Your wards and protections are marvelous, but they will have to be renewed rather soon."

She shyly ducked her head. Then she said, "I'd like to try the spell with them. I told them I would be ready in about ten minutes."

"Then, by all means," Giles said. "What can we do to help?"

"I need quiet. I need to be alone," Tara said.

From the bathroom, Spike shouted, "Well, you can't have the loo!"

"How about the loft?" Giles suggested. "You can sit on the bed. We'll try to be very quiet."

Anya snorted. "Xander says that every time."

Tara sat cross-legged on the floor in the loft, her hands draped loosely over her knees. She listened to the others trying so hard not to make any noise, tiptoeing around, opening and shutting the refrigerator. Someone had to use the rest room, and Spike sputtered under his breath about it, but even he did it as quietly as he could manage.

After a time, she found her center, and began to block the sounds out, one by one. They became echoes of themselves, very distant. The chilliness of the room—Mr. Giles liked it cool—dissipated, and Tara was enfolded in warmth. Her body became light; she imagined herself rising above the floor, levitating a few inches—

—and then, like a shot, she was hovering high above the earth, with Willow and Doña Pilar on either side of her. They were forming a circle in the clouds, walking among them in glowing, disembodied forms. She looked across at Willow, whose face was filled with light; and then the older lady, whom she had not yet met. She had never felt so calm and happy, and strong, and then—

—She was flying beside a sleek, black crow with a twinkle in its eyes. It was her Willow, and she flapped her wings to keep up with her. They swooped and soared above the streets of Los Angeles, on a bright and brilliant afternoon. Cars and buses clogged the streets; the sidewalks were bursting with busy people, color, and motion. It was a glorious, beautiful day.

"It wasn't like this last time," Willow said; and it was as if, by speaking, she had flown into a different place.

Darkness fell over them like an icy net; Tara flew through thick, cold blackness, syrupy and foul. She looked over, seeking Willow, and saw nothing.

She shivered, hard, and tried to speak. But when she opened her mouth, the blackness filled it. She choked, then spat it out, knowing, somehow, that she must not swallow it, must not allow it passage into her being.

Then someone brushed the little fingers on both her hands; the darkness slid away and she was back in the brilliance, and the love. A sublime contentment filled her and she turned her head, very slowly. All of her moved in slow motion, including her thoughts. She saw eddies and currents of silvery light emanating from her fingertips, and where her heart sat in her chest, golden light flowed outward.

"This is stronger magick than I have ever experienced," Doña Pilar told the girls. She, too, was a figure of golden, shimmering light. "Do you realize how close to the center of the light we are standing?"

Suddenly, alarm pricked along the back of Tara's neck. She said, "Someone's coming."

The three became alert; Tara heard heartbeats—three, no four of them. She listened intently. Three beat in unison; the other was terribly wrong, terribly off.

"There is someone outside the house," Doña Pilar said. To Tara, "Stay in the circle. Flow with us."

They moved through variegated mists; past colors and sounds that were blurs. People and objects stretched and lost shape as the trio wafted past, like phantoms.

A rectangle of brown vacillated before Tara, losing its angles, straightening out, then stretching sideways. It was a door.

It opened.

Tara accompanied the other two witches outside. The sky was a living blue; the grass below her feet thrummed with mystical energy.

Deep, penetrating dread shot through her, making her bones ache with cold. She began to shiver. She held tightly to the hands of the other two witches. The sky tilted sideways, vibrating a strange, flat purple-gray, like a bruise.

A huge, black shape reared up on hind legs and opened

up its maw. Horror and death and evil poured out of it, and Tara began to back away.

"Nicky!" Doña Pilar shouted.

"Don't!" Willow cried.

But the old lady let go of Tara and Willow, racing toward the shadow. She held out her hands, sobbing, *"Mi'jo!"*

The shadow rose up, higher, higher, then rolled over itself, cresting like a wave.

"No!" Willow cried again, grabbing at the woman.

The phone was ringing.

On the floor of Giles's bedroom, Tara jerked out of her trance and grabbed the phone before anyone downstairs could get it first.

"Willow?" she said.

On the other end, Willow was out of breath. "I got her. I dragged her back inside the house."

"Was it Nicky?" Tara asked.

There was a pause. Willow said, "Oh, Tara, I hope not. It was *evil.*"

Tara nodded. "We made strong magick with her, Willow. Maybe we can undo the evil. If it's him." She was exhausted.

"Lie down," Willow said, as if she could feel her tiredness. "Get some rest. We'll try to figure out what happened."

"Please, be careful." Tara gripped the phone. "If anything happened . . . to you . . ."

"I won't let anything happen." Willow's voice was soothing. "Rest now, okay?"

"Okay," Tara said. But as she hung up the phone, she thought, *She can't promise nothing will happen. No matter how strong our magick, it seems like whatever's out there is even stronger.*

Downstairs, Spike groused, "That's all you people *do,* is use the loo!"

"Then find somewhere else to hide from the sun." Anya was indignant.

The voices drifting through her consciousness reminded Tara that she really should go downstairs, let the others know what had happened.

But that would require moving. She tried to move her arm . . . or at least, she thought about moving her arm. Just thinking about it was exhausting.

Frowning softly to herself, Tara drifted off to sleep.

Chapter 7

Moscow, 1983

ALEXIS VISHNIKOFF TRAMPED TOWARD HOME, CLUTCH-ing his battered umbrella as a futile gesture of defiance against the freezing rain. A wind that seemed to blow straight down from the Barents Sea drove the stinging pellets against him, and his feet threatened to slip out from under him with every step. By now, he'd thought he would have a car of his own, if not a driver.

But it was not to be. The American president, Reagan, kept building more and more weapons, increasing the global stakes. The Soviet Union scrambled to keep up. Now Reagan had proposed something called the Strategic Defense Initiative. Americans were calling it Star Wars. It would, Alexis was assured, never work. But there had to be a response nonetheless. And the frustrating thing was that Andropov, in his blindness, didn't see that the People's Project could be that response.

But it was too visionary for him, or at least that's how Vladimir Markov characterized it. Yuri Andropov was not a man of vision, he was a plodder. Amazing he had risen so high in the party to begin with. He seemed constitutionally unable to understand the promise of the People's Project, so he ignored it in favor of new and more powerful missile systems. The Soviets and the Americans both had enough warheads to destroy the world a hundred times over, and still Andropov wanted more. Thinking about him, Alexis shook his head. Icy wind whipped his cheek.

He lived in a flat on the next block over, on Petrovka Street, less than a kilometer from the nondescript office building that housed the People's Project. Andropov didn't understand the Project, but that didn't mean it didn't proceed. Its funding had been established more than a decade ago, and that didn't change. The problem was that there were no increases coming, while the cost of everything else went up and up. The simplest office supplies, paper clips or notebooks, had to be purchased on the black market most of the time. If one of the computers went down, someone had to work on it overnight until it functioned again, as there would be no affording a replacement. But still, despite the hardship, the scientists and researchers who had been working on it continued to work on it. Progress was being made.

If the sidewalks hadn't been so slick, if the wind had been less fierce, if, if, if . . . if anything had been different, he might never have met her. He would have been walking faster, been covering the ground between the lab and home, lost in thought. But as it happened, he needed to pay attention to where he stepped, to peer out beneath the edge of the umbrella once in a while to make sure it was safe to cross the street, watch for puddles.

So he saw her, just a glimpse of blond hair piled up on top of her head, of small round glasses perched on a tiny nose, of naturally red lips and a firm jaw almost submerged inside a huge turtleneck—saw a glimpse of her as she closed the door to her own apartment and stepped down to the street, right before his foot really did fly out from underneath him.

It was, he believed for the rest of his life, seeing her that did it. The brief glance, the moment of noticing her—he turned his head to get a better look, he shifted the umbrella so it wouldn't block his view, and the whole action threw him just enough off-balance so that when his right foot came down on a patch of ice, he wasn't ready for it. The foot skidded and he followed it, into the air and then down with a thump on his rear, his legs and hands immediately soaked.

When he looked up again, embarrassed, she was right there, already kneeling over him with a look on her face that alternated between concern and hilarity. He understood both. He was an important man, a scientist working on a defense project, although she couldn't have known that. But she would know that he was a bureaucrat, a party member, by the way he dressed and carried himself. She wouldn't want to be responsible, even inadvertently, for him injuring himself. At the same time, a grown man falling on his bum in the rain was a comical sight, he realized. He looked away from her, a bit shamefaced, but then looked back with a smile.

"I . . . I slipped," he said. "But I'm fine, really."

"I saw," she responded. She hadn't even opened her own umbrella; it lay on the ground beside her, soaking up water. "Are you sure?"

"Well, I'm wet and cold. But I was wet and cold when I was walking, so the only real difference now is that I'm wet and cold and getting some rest."

She laughed, and the sound was like the chime of a distant bell.

"My flat is right here, Comrade Vishnikoff," she said. "I could make you some tea, let you dry off for a while before you continue your journey."

"No, I'm only—you know me?"

"Of course," she said. Now it was her turn to be shy. She looked away from him, as if suddenly aware that she had overstepped some boundary. "I work for the People's Project," she said. "You would not know me, of course. My name is Valerya Golodkin. I am new there, I just started a few months ago."

"I didn't even know we were hiring any new researchers," Alexis said.

Valerya held out a hand and helped Alexis to his feet. "Please," she said. "Come inside for a few minutes."

Alexis let himself be led into her apartment. Nothing special inside, but she had decorated it nicely with a few pictures she'd cut from magazines and framed, some photographs of Gorky Park and the seacoast, and a couple of pieces of old, well-chosen furniture painted in bright colors. She sat him down at a small kitchen table and put a pot of water on the stove to boil.

As she did, she explained. "I am not a researcher," she said. "I am a subject."

Alexis was stunned. He thought he had been introduced to all the psychics. Most were frauds anyway, he knew—people pretending they had the ability so they could steal a few rubles from the Treasury. But he had never met Valerya, didn't remember even having seen her, and he was sure he would remember if he had. Her appearance was striking. Even here in her small flat, he couldn't stop looking at her.

"I'm surprised we haven't met," he said.

"I think Comrade Markov has been keeping me a bit of a secret," she replied. "We're still doing some testing. He wants to reveal me when he's sure I am what he thinks I am." She scooped some loose tea into a well-used infuser and dipped it into a cup. When the kettle began to whistle, she splashed boiling water over the infuser, and brought the cup to the table. "Milk?"

"No, thank you," Alexis said. "What do you mean, what he thinks you are?"

She sat down across from him at the table. "When I touched you, outside. Helping you up. I had a feeling about you. Would you like to hear it?"

"Certainly."

"Two things, really," she went on. "I'm not sure how they connect, but they do."

"Very well. Continue."

"At your flat, there is a very large painting on the wall. A musical instrument. A harp, a piano, something with strings. You have never played that instrument, hardly ever look at the painting, but it's there."

"A harpsichord," Alexis said. "I have a painting of a woman playing a harpsichord."

"And the other thing, I think, is part of why there is such sadness in you. A fire, when you were very young."

"My mother died in a fire, when I was eleven," Alexis confirmed.

She looked at him, really looked, and he found himself continuing the story. He had never told it to anyone before.

"She had broken her leg and couldn't move fast enough to get out of the house. I wasn't home—I came home from school, as the fire was consuming the house. When I saw the smoke I ran, and when I got closer and couldn't see her outside I knew that she must be inside."

He took a breath. He felt her gaze upon him, and felt strengthened, and warmed, despite his wet clothes and his frozen memories. All his life, part of him had been cold; nothing had ever warmed it before.

Heat had killed his mother; therefore, heat was dangerous.

"I tried to get in," he whispered hoarsely, "but the neighbor next door, he was too strong—he held me, restrained me. He kept me from rushing inside. I probably would have died. Instead, she did."

"And she played the harpsichord," Valerya said, her voice gentle.

"She played piano," Alexis corrected her. "But I never found a painting I liked of a woman playing a piano." He looked at her. She held his gaze, her blue eyes steady and clear. A strand of her yellow hair had come loose, and tickled at the corner of her mouth.

He cleared his throat. "You could have learned all of that from my file at the Project," he said finally. "If you're a favorite of Markov, you would have access to it."

"I could have," she agreed. "But I didn't. And I think you know it."

"What do you mean?" he asked, knowing the answer before he did.

She reached out, took his hand again. "Because you can do it, too," she said. "You can see into me as easily as I see into you. Look."

He felt her flesh, warm against his palm. Their hands trembled a little and he didn't know if it was her or himself. He pushed the question away, trying to blank out his mind, like pulling a clean shade down over a window so the view was obscured.

When his mind's eye looked out onto an empty canvas, he closed his actual eyes and let a picture draw itself there. He saw Valerya, but a slightly younger version of her, barely out of her teens, it seemed. She walked along a seaside, *possibly in Odessa,* Alexis thought, *by the Black Sea.* A tall young man with thick brown hair and piercing green eyes held her hand. Those eyes were turned toward Valerya, and the love in them was unmistakable as he watched her watching the sea. Alexis knew this young man was named Berdy, that he was, at twenty-two, three years older than Valerya, and—as he felt Berdy's hand, through Valerya's perceptions—that he was about to ask her to marry him.

But he also knew that within a year of this moment, Berdy would be dead, shot in the throat and face in a dusty Afghan hamlet. The picture he was watching changed, like a dissolve in a movie, and then he saw Valerya again, sitting in a room not unlike this one, reading the letter from the Soviet military that informed her in dispassionate language that her fiancé had died on the Afghan front. Tears streamed down her face, blurring the paper that she gripped in an unshaking hand.

Alexis let go of her hand, breaking the connection as decisively as hanging up a telephone or pulling a plug. He knew now that she was, in fact, younger than she appeared—that the tragedy of her brief marriage to a doomed man had changed her, aged her in some way. She still looked young, but there were worry lines around her eyes and at the corners of her mouth that seemed to make her look like someone who had been around for a while. A sense of maturity had settled about her like a bank of fog on the Volga. Valerya, he believed, had turned inward after Berdy's death, seeking some kind of meaning within herself, and, remarkably, finding it there.

He believed he came to love her at that moment.

After that day, they were inseparable. Valerya took him by the hand into Comrade Markov's office the following day, and declared in no uncertain terms that Alexis was not to be considered a scientist anymore, but a subject, one who would work with her to heighten perception and increase abilities.

Markov remained unimpressed—until Valerya and Alexis submitted to a test he had devised. They took a standard test—determining cards held in Markov's hand, describing pictures as they were drawn from a stack in another room, selecting numbers that would come up on random rolls of dice. No one had ever scored more than sixty percent on these combined tasks, until Valerya and Alexis tried them together. They shattered every record. They scored in the nineties on every demonstration. Markov's jaw fell in amazement.

From that point on, Markov agreed with Valerya. He relieved Alexis of his laboratory duties, to work exclusively with Valerya, under the watchful eye of Markov himself. The world's most comprehensive and aggressive government investigation into the military applications of psychic abilities had just received an enormous boost in potential, and Markov—with the help of Alexis and Valerya Vishnikoff, as she became when they were married on the three-month anniversary of their meeting—planned to ride that potential to the party's apex.

Los Angeles

Kate Lockley parked her car in the employee lot at Benjamin Harrison High in Los Angeles, leaving a POLICE placard in the window so it wouldn't be ticketed or towed while she was inside. She glanced up and down the rows of cars—Toyotas, Nissans, Ford Focuses, mostly economy cars that cost less and didn't demand much fuel.

Then she looked over at the student lot as she strode up toward the front door. SUVs, raised trucks on huge tires, sports cars, convertibles. The Mercedes, Porsche and BMW brands outnumbered VW Beetles in that lot.

There's something not right about priorities, Kate thought, *when the students have more disposable income than their teachers.* She was a firm believer that teachers and cops did more than just about anyone else to guide and direct the lives of the citizenry, and yet they were near the bottom of the pay scale. She had no patience with police corruption, but she understood, at a fundamental level, how frustrating it was that those who broke the law made more money than those who enforced it. The same principle seemed to hold true here—those who taught were financially disadvantaged compared to those they were teaching. She wondered if wealthy students ever tried to bribe teachers for grades—and if they did, were they successful?

Probably on too many occasions.

As she passed through the school's front door, Kate willed her thoughts back around to the subject at hand. A student had disappeared, a popular cheerleader, and the school's administration had called the police, the press, and the parents almost simultaneously. Kate only hoped she had managed to beat the press here so she could contain the story, or at least direct the emphasis of it. Teens had been disappearing all over the city, but the media only seemed interested in the ones from well-to-do families, like Julie Mazullo here at BHH.

The principal, the cheerleading coach, and Julie's family's attorney met Kate in the office. A pair of uniformed officers was already on scene, one of them here in the office keeping an eye on things while the other took statements from the girls out on the practice field, where the disappearance had taken place about thirty minutes before. Kate shook hands with Vikki Castle, the principal,

Alice Sheldon, the coach, and Henry Martindale, the attorney.

"Are Julie's parents here?" Kate asked.

"They're at home, waiting for any word on their daughter," the attorney replied briskly. He pointedly glanced at his watch. "I'd like to be able to tell them that the LAPD is investigating Julie's disappearance with all due expediency."

Kate flared. "If you mean, are we going to move quickly to solve this, Mr. Martindale, the answer is yes. Our officers were here within ten minutes of receiving the call, I believe. It took me a bit longer because I am also investigating a number of other, similar cases. But I'm here now, so let's get started, shall we?"

Martindale didn't look chastened in the least.

"Very well," he said, crossing his arms. "What do you suggest?"

Kate pulled a notepad out of the pocket of her coat. "I want to talk to the other girls on the squad."

Alice Sheldon spoke up, raising one finger in the air like an old-fashioned school marm chastising a student. "There's another officer doing that right now. I don't want these girls disturbed any more than necessary. We have an important game coming up on Friday."

"I'm not an officer," Kate pointed out, trying to stay patient. Or at least, to sound patient. "I'm a detective. I will read the statements they've given to the officer, but I'm going to need to talk to them myself as well. And I think you can just assume that practice is over for today."

Coach Sheldon let out an audible sigh. A compact woman with close-cropped red hair, she wore a sweatsuit in the school colors of blue and gold. The coach's standard whistle hung around her neck on a white cotton string. Principal Castle gave her an aggravated look, as if her sighing was a fairly regular, and annoying, occurrence. Kate could see how that might be the case—she was annoyed with it already.

"Okay," Sheldon said. "I guess you're right."

"I'm certain of it," Kate replied. "Can you show me where they are?"

Sheldon led the way outside and down a long walkway to a well-kept athletic field. The stadium looked almost as nice as professional stadiums Kate had been in, and probably cleaner. One end of the athletic complex was a practice field for the cheerleading squad, with a small bleacher section for observers. The girls sat on the wooden bleachers, still in their uniforms. One of them stood off to the side, huddled with a uniformed officer who wrote notes on a small spiral-bound pad as they talked. The other girls stayed fairly quiet, for cheerleaders, sitting in stunned disbelief or sobbing outright.

For a moment, Kate thought Coach Sheldon would blow her whistle. But she seemed to catch herself with her hand half-raised, and she held it there.

"Girls," she announced. "This is officer—"

"Detective," Kate interrupted.

"—Detective Lockley of the Los Angeles Police Department. I know many of you have already talked to the officer here, but you'll also need to talk to Detective Lockley. I'm sure she'll try to keep it brief."

She turned to Kate as if for confirmation of her belief.

"Yes, I will do everything I can to make this as easy and painless as it can be," Kate assured the squad. There were about twenty girls. She figured she'd have to spend at least five minutes with each of them. So an hour and a half here, give or take. On top of however long the girls had already been here. *They'll love this.*

As it turned out—as Kate expected, in fact—none of

them could tell her anything helpful. Everyone on the squad loved and respected Julie. No one would want anything bad to happen to her, ever. Each girl managed to shed at least one tear for poor Julie as they spoke. Compacts and eye shadow appeared as if by magic, to touch up makeup after their interviews were complete and the tears dried away.

But none of it meant anything, because no one could explain what had become of Julie. She had been at the front of the squad, leading them in one of the Vegas-style dance numbers that had become more and more important parts of high school cheering sections. This one turned from something resembling a burlesque bump-and-grind into a pyramid, with the stronger girls on the bottom and a tiny waif named Missy Champlain up on top.

Julie had been directing the action, and backing away from the squad at the same time, to get the long view on the pyramid's shape. She was shouting out her orders, walking backward, and then suddenly she was gone. All eyes had been on her. No one approached, no one saw anything happen to her—she was simply there, and then she wasn't.

Which, Kate knew, pretty much followed the same pattern that had happened everywhere else. *Doesn't make it easier to explain, just consistent.*

What Kate found more interesting than the girls' stories was what she could overhear them saying among themselves while she listened to yet another cheerleader tell her how much she'd miss Julie.

". . . always manages to hog the spotlight," one of the girls said. Kate leaned her head in her hand for a moment, so she could surreptitiously steal a glance up at the bleachers. The girl speaking was Heather Jamison, a voluptuous junior who had, only moments before, burst into a sobbing fit when telling Kate about how much she loved Julie and could barely imagine life without her. Kate found herself wishing she could climb the bleachers and yank the hem of Heather's skirt down to a more modest length.

"I know," Dede Micklin replied. "So who do you think Sheldon is going to promote to head cheerleader? You? Or maybe Janice?"

"Janice?" Heather echoed, with audible disbelief. "That cow?"

Dede punched Heather on the thigh. "Cow?" she said. "You're one to talk."

"I'm womanly, not bovine," Heather shot back.

"Sheldon's going to pick Vonna," Dede announced firmly. "No question."

"Yeah, probably," Heather said. She sounded resigned. "Unless someone breaks Vonna's knees."

Kate dragged her attention away from the machinations. She didn't want to hear any more of this. She had begun to feel like she'd need a long shower when this day was over. The girl she was talking to, Carly Fortschen, rambled on about how weird it was that Julie vanished in the middle of the pyramid formation—as if it would not have been as weird had she waited until the end. Kate cut the interview short as soon as she could, and went back to Coach Sheldon.

"I'll get the reports from the officers, and contact the rest of the girls at their homes," she said. "Please make sure they don't talk to anyone from the press about this, if you can. We don't want to alarm anyone unnecessarily."

"Way I hear it," Coach Sheldon said, "kids are disappearing all over the city. Maybe people *should* be alarmed."

"Maybe they should," Kate answered. "But I find it's seldom useful to create a generalized panic."

"I'll do what I can to keep the ladies reined in," Coach Sheldon said, fingering her whistle.

"Thanks." Kate turned away from the squad and left them to do battle over who would replace the recently-departed Julie.

"Cheerleaders?" Willow asked. "I hate to say it, but I'm not terribly surprised."

"Cordelia was a cheerleader," Angel said.

"My point exactly," Kate said. "So this was another nice girl, in a sort of not-really way, but not exactly full of unplumbed depths, if you know what I mean."

"Point taken," Angel agreed.

They talked in an empty anteroom past Kate's office. She had returned to the precinct to find a phone message from Angel, who'd had an idea while talking to Cordelia about Willow. Following his suggestion, Willow had tried to hack into the LAPD's internal system from Angel's computer, but she'd run into a firewall. She had suggested they go to a computer more directly linked to the object of their search. It turned out that the FBI had recently helped the LAPD install a bank of computers for Internet and other searches apart from the officers' desk computers.

That was awesome news for Willow, who had recently figured out how to use those kind of computers without leaving "footprints."

Now Kate stood behind Willow as she bent over the keyboard.

"You're scary," Kate said. "You're not supposed to be able to do this."

Willow beamed. "Thanks." said, loosening up her shoulders and cracking her knuckles. "I'm just grooving on doing it. It's been too long since I played hacker. Especially without worrying about getting caught."

"Getting caught would still be a bad thing," Kate reminded her. She still had second thoughts about this whole idea—second thoughts about anything to do with Angel, really. She didn't trust him for a second. Well, that wasn't really true—she trusted him, she just didn't like him. Or she didn't like herself for trusting him. Something like that. Everything got confusing when he was around. "Especially since that's my computer you're using."

"Oh, it's okay," Willow said, typing fast and furious. "I never *get* caught. I just *worry* about getting caught. Big difference."

"Well, that's a load off my mind," Kate said sarcastically. "Angel, maybe this isn't such a—"

"Ooh—I'm in!" Willow exclaimed. "What are we looking for again?"

Kate checked a list she had written down on a memo pad. "This time, we're looking for Peterson. Bo Peterson. With an 'o.' "

"*Bo* with an 'o' or *Peterson* with an 'o'?"

"Both," Kate said.

"Okay, coming right up." Willow tapped a few more keys, then sat back and waited. She didn't have to wait long. "There you go."

She scooted back, and both Kate and Angel bent forward to look at the monitor. Willow had hacked through the security firewall of the Los Angeles County First Bank & Trust, and then into the personal checking account of Officer Bo Peterson. Peterson's deposits and withdrawals were displayed on the screen of Kate's PC for the world to view.

"Man," Kate said, shaking her head. "He gets direct deposit. I keep meaning to switch over to that."

"Kate . . ." Angel said, hoping to bring her back on track.

"Right, I know," Kate said. "Letting myself get distracted—"

"Kate," Angel said again. He tapped the screen.

Kate craned forward. "Move your finger."

Angel moved it.

"Wow," Kate said. "That's a big one."

"What is?" Willow asked. She had shoved the chair back so far that now Angel and Kate completely blocked her view of the screen. She angled for a better look. Kate stepped to one side to let the girl see. After all, she couldn't have done this without Willow's expertise.

"Deposit," Angel told her. "Fifty thousand dollars. Two months ago."

"Publisher's Clearing House?"

"Somebody named Vishnikoff," Kate answered. "Mean anything to either one of you?"

"Only that it's a Russian name," Angel said. "Which ties in. Maybe he's a member of the Russian Mafiya, paying Peterson off for looking the other way, or doing a job for him."

Kate took the mouse, used it to scroll down farther, watching for big deposits, Russian names, or both. "Here's another Vishnikoff," she said. "Four months earlier. Another fifty thousand."

"But look at his balance," Willow pointed out. "This Peterson person has some big bills to pay."

"Or expensive tastes," Kate suggested. "But you're right, he doesn't seem to keep much of what he makes."

"Those are the only ones that seem out of the ordinary," Angel said. "A few big Vishnikoff deposits. You'd think if they were payoffs, he'd get cash."

"You'd think a cop wouldn't be stupid enough to be crooked," Kate replied. "They always go down. Always. So anyone dumb enough to try to buck the odds would also be dumb enough to take a check for a payoff, I guess."

She shivered and wrapped her arms around herself for warmth. She'd been right earlier, she knew. Between ambitious cheerleaders and dirty cops, there probably wasn't enough water in L.A. for her to scrub the stench of this day off her. She stood back and watched, as if through a rain-streaked window, as Willow and Angel checked the other names on her list.

Chapter 8

Sunnydale

Buffy, Riley knew, was used to not getting much sleep. As the Slayer, she patrolled most nights, then went to school most days. Her stamina was without compare, though, thanks to the powers that came with the title, so she coped. When she did sleep, she slept hard.

So Riley dressed quietly, letting her slumber on Giles's couch, and slipped from the room. She hadn't so much as stirred.

He met Giles and Xander in the cramped kitchen. "You guys ready?" he asked, his voice low. They nodded.

"As rain," Xander said. "No, that's right. Right as rain. I don't know what we're ready as."

"We're ready," Giles put in helpfully.

They moved through the place quietly. Giles's home was not a big place, and there were people sleeping everywhere, the theory being that they were safer, during the assault on Sunnydale, all together rather than being scattered all over town.

Giles, Xander, and Riley had agreed to spend some time looking for Spike's missing girlfriend Cheryce, in exchange for Spike's help fighting the monsters. For Riley's part, he was willing to help find the vampire—as long as he got to stake her once she was found. Spike wasn't holding up his end of the bargain anyway, and, unlike Spike and Angel, Cheryce still fed on humans. She needed to be taken out.

Meanwhile, monsters.

Or not.

The three men walked quietly down Sunnydale's strangely silent sidewalks. The townspeople were pretty much staying inside whenever they could these days, the mass self-delusion—that let them continue to live here when the only sensible thing would be to move far away—slipping a little in the face of constant attacks. But the sun was out now, and in spite of a few daytime sightings, most of the monsters still preferred the cover of darkness.

Cheryce, being a vampire, would be holed up somewhere, waiting for darkness to fall. While there were plenty of places in town a vampire could hide, it would still be easier to find her while she slept than when she was up and in motion.

Xander seemed to read Riley's thoughts. "Do any of us have any, I don't know, *idea* where to look for Spike's squeeze?"

"There are some usual, ahh, haunts," Giles offered. "The cemeteries. Various vampire hangouts."

"Which we can rule out, because those are the places Spike would have already looked." Riley said.

"So all we have to do is figure out the least likely place a vampire might be, and look there?" Xander asked, smiling politely.

"That'd be our best bet," Riley agreed.

Xander half-raised a hand. "Anyone else have the words 'lost cause' floating through their heads?"

"We told Spike we'd look for her," Giles said softly. "We never promised to find her. At any rate, it doesn't hurt for us to be out and about, in case of any other demonic activity."

"Or nondemonic, monstrous activity," Riley added.

"Here's an idea," Xander said. "If you were in a city and you didn't have a place to sleep, where would you go?"

"Umm, a hotel?" Giles suggested.

"Right. You put up the 'Do Not Disturb' sign, and they don't care if you sleep all day."

"That's not bad," Riley said. "Maybe we should check the motels. What do you think, Giles?"

Giles didn't answer. Riley noticed that, while he and Xander were still walking, Giles had fallen behind. He turned.

Giles was a few steps behind them, looking off to his left.

Where, from a postage-stamp sized park, something that vaguely resembled a small tree walked toward them on root-like legs, waving dozens of branches at them threateningly. Its limbs were tree-bark brown, tipped with springtime green, jagged-edged leaves.

"Man," Xander said. "Where's George Washington when you need him?"

Riley gave him a questioning look.

"You know, the cherry tree, the hatchet, and all? Never mind."

"Do you think it's malevolent, Giles?" Riley asked.

"I think it's unnatural," Giles replied. "It doesn't belong here. I don't know that it's genuinely evil or—"

He stopped because Riley slammed into him, knocking him to the side just before one of the tree thing's leaves, fired from the end of a branch like a missile, sliced into the air where he'd been standing. The leaf wedged into the ground behind them, stiff and quivering like a knife blade.

"I'd say evil's a good guess," Xander pointed out.

All three men dodged as two more leaves whistled through the air at them, driving into the ground behind them. One of them skated across the street, kicking up sparks where it struck the pavement.

"Y'know, maybe Paul Bunyan would be more help," Xander breathed.

"I don't think any mythological woodsmen are likely to come to our aid," Giles said. "We've got to deal with this ourselves. And quickly, I should say."

Riley was already on his feet and running toward it. He zigged and zagged, dodging flying leaves the tree thing fired his way. In a flash, he was under the spread of its branches. The thing reared back as if threatened, and it brought its limbs in toward its trunk, as if to trap Riley there.

Got to do this fast, then, he thought, *before it does.* He tugged a knife from a case on his belt and opened it. One of the branches swiped across his face, cutting him, but he dodged the worst of it and pressed on. Blood trickled down his forehead. Behind him, over the rustle of leaves and the creak of the branches, he could hear Giles and Xander. He hoped they were keeping out of harm's way.

Another branch pressed against the small of Riley's back, its sharp-edged leaves slicing into him. This one seemed intent on crushing Riley against the trunk. But since that's where he wanted to be anyway, he went along with it. Drawing the hand with the knife back as far as he could, he drove it with all his strength into the trunk.

The tree shuddered, leaves quaking as if caught in a windstorm.

Riley dragged the knife down, splitting the tree open. Sap ran, red and thick as blood, from inside it.

More branches closed on him now, more leaves cutting him all over. He freed the knife's blade and slammed it home again, higher up this time, opening a second wound in the tree's trunk. The tree writhed and twisted in his grasp, but its own branches kept him close. Again, he sliced downward, both hands on the knife's handle for leverage, making the wound as big as he could. More of the bloody sap flowed from it.

He knew he was bleeding himself, pretty badly, from some of his wounds. *Question is,* he thought, *which one of us can hold out the longest?*

Yanking the knife out, he thrust once more. This time, the tree let out a scream from someplace deep within, a tortured, strangled sound that chilled Riley to his soul. It bucked, its branches fluttering. Riley pushed off from the trunk with hands and feet, breaking the grip of the branches, and threw himself away from it.

The tree did a slow pirouette, branches waving wildly, and then fell over backward on the park grounds. It twitched a few more times and then fell still.

Riley, breathing hard, did a quick inventory of body parts. He seemed to still have everything, though he'd lost a bunch of blood. Giles and Xander came up beside him. Xander clapped him on the back. "Well done," he said. "And can I just say, timber?"

"You can say it," Riley panted. He glanced back toward the tree, and then gestured to something beyond the tree, a shimmering, golden circle that seemed to hang in the air like a painting on a wall. "But can you tell me what that is?"

Giles stared at the circle. He took his glasses off, rubbed his eyes, and replaced them, and then he stared some more. "I daresay I can't begin to imagine what it is," he said at last.

"Well, I'm stumped," Xander admitted. He started toward it. "One way to find out, though."

Both Giles and Riley grabbed his shoulders, pulling him back.

"No," Giles insisted. "No one goes near it until we can do some research, try to figure out what it might be."

"Good call," Riley said. He was feeling light-headed. "Anyway, I think maybe I need to tape up some of these wounds, you know? I'm losing some blood here."

"I thought you were just trying to lure Cheryce out of hiding," Xander joked.

Riley wasn't up to laughing. He looked back at the golden circle again, and as he watched it, it blinked from existence as if it had never been there.

"Yow," Xander said. "Did you guys see that, too?"

"It was there, and then it vanished," Giles declared. "Incredible. Absolutely incredible."

"That's my word for it, too," Xander said. "Without the drama-queen intonation."

Ignoring Xander, Giles put an arm around Riley's shoulders. "Come on," he said. "Let's get you home."

Buffy sat on the couch in the living room of Giles's place, rubbing her eyes and thinking of feather beds. Maybe in a country inn or a bed and breakfast somewhere snowy, with a fire crackling in a deep stone fireplace, Riley Finn's strong arms holding her as she slumbered beneath a down comforter. In her mind's eye, Riley nuzzled her neck and she pushed him away. Sleep was *all* she wanted right now.

When she opened her eyes again, she knew that some time had passed. She looked around for a clock, saw that she'd been out cold for at least thirty minutes, maybe closer to forty. She felt—well, not rested. But maybe not quite as close to absolute exhaustion as she had been.

The rest of the house was quiet, unusual because this house, when the Scooby Gang was around, never really quieted. She figured maybe the others had all dozed off as well. Tara had been working on and off with Willow and Doña Pilar, communicating by telephone and other, less man-made methods, on triangulation spells, and the strain took a lot out of her.

The strain, Buffy thought, *as well as the distance— Tara doesn't like Willow being so far away, and possibly in danger.*

She left her comfortable spot on the couch to make a quick check of the house, to see who else might be around. The thought occurred to her that maybe they had all fallen victim to some sort of sleep spell, which would account for the silence that engulfed the small house. But a tour revealed that this wasn't the case. Spike and Anya sat on the kitchen floor, Anya sipping from a cup of tea and Spike from a cup of blood, talking about old times. To Buffy, of course, old times meant the 1980s, but these two went back much farther, and Buffy had the sense that the eleven-hundred-year-old Anya enjoyed having someone, if not quite her age, at least closer to it than Xander was, to chat with. Not to mention the life experience, or lifeless experience, in Spike's case.

Spike looked up at Buffy as she stepped into the room, and not with an expression that could be construed as welcoming. "Havin' a bit of a private chat here," he snarled. His lips were painted red by his beverage choice. "That is still allowed, isn't it, Slayer?"

"There's no need to get snippy," Buffy said. "I just wanted to see who was around."

"Tara's sleeping in the loft," Anya told her. "Riley and Giles took Xander on patrol with them—I think Giles took Xander because he was afraid we would have sex in his bed if he didn't, although what I really wanted—"

"And my mom?" Buffy quickly asked.

"I'm right here, Buffy," Joyce Summers said. She walked in from behind Buffy, bearing a cup of coffee. "I was just outside the front door, enjoying some sun."

"It's not safe out there, Mom," Buffy warned her, sternly.

"Yeah, Mr. Sun is not your friend, Joyce," Spike chimed in.

"It's not safe anywhere, then," Joyce replied. "So we might as well enjoy ourselves while we wait for whatever is going to happen."

"But—you shouldn't take stupid chances," Buffy pressed on. "You're—you're my mom."

Joyce set her cup down, put her arms around her daughter. Buffy returned the hug, feeling just the slightest bit awkward with Spike and Anya watching them. "And so proud of my girl," Joyce whispered.

The front door banged open then, so they released each other. Riley, Xander, and Giles entered, Riley looking like he'd been through a war.

"Riley?" Buffy asked, all concern and fear. "Are you okay?"

Riley smiled his just-had-the-crap-kicked-out-of-me grin. "Yeah, Buff, I'm fine. Just a close encounter with some overly aggressive foliage."

"Foliage?" she echoed.

"You should have seen it," Xander interjected. "I swear, I'm not going outside again without an ax. Or a lumberjack."

"Ha bloody ha," Spike said sourly.

Los Angeles

Angel and Wesley were waiting inside Bo Peterson's house when he pulled his truck into the drive. He killed the engine and a moment later walked through his own front door. Fortunately for Angel, Peterson didn't know the spell that could uninvite a vampire who had once been invited in. Peterson's mouth fell open with shock when he saw the two men sitting in his living room. Wesley folded the newspaper he'd been flipping through, set it down beside him on the sofa, and stood up. Angel kept his seat.

"Time for us to have another talk, Bo," he said calmly. The calm was a façade. Peterson made him sick. Any cop who used the badge to cover up, or facilitate, his own crimes, was the lowest of the low to Angel. At least, as far as humans went. There were death demons Angel liked better, because at least they were honest about their shortcomings.

Peterson's continued existence on the planet infuriated Angel to his core. When he felt this way, he worried a little—this was Angelus territory, he knew. The kind of emotion he'd been comfortable with, in those days. When one was full of rage, it was easy to unleash it on others. As Angel, he worked to hold that back, to channel it in more acceptable directions. But Peterson brought it all front and center.

Peterson looked questioningly at Wesley.

"Wesley Wyndam-Pryce," Wesley offered. "I can't say it's a pleasure to meet you, considering what I've heard. But it should be an illuminating conversation. I don't believe I've ever spoken with a crooked police officer before."

"That you knew about," Angel put in.

"Quite so." Wesley inclined his head.

"Did I accidentally say something once that made you

think you could come around here any time you feel like it?" Peterson demanded angrily.

"You should have thought of that before you decided to go on the take," Angel observed, barely keeping the fury that bubbled inside him in check. "You don't have a private life anymore. You belong to me."

Peterson looked defiant, but Angel knew the man could be broken. More easily each time, he believed.

"I don't think so," Peterson objected. But his face was pale and his expression shaky.

"You keep thinking that," Angel told him. "But you'll give me what I want."

Now he looked even more uneasy. "And that is?"

"Who's Vishnikoff?"

Peterson blinked. "Never heard the name."

"We know differently," Wesley interjected. He balled his fists and took a step toward Peterson, who outweighed him by about a hundred pounds, most of it solid muscle. "You're going to sing like a canary," he said in his best Bogart.

Peterson looked at Wesley. Wesley looked at Angel. "Not helpful?"

"Not particularly," Angel said.

"Sorry." Wesley stepped back. "Carry on, then."

"Vishnikoff," Angel reminded Peterson.

"I don't know what you're talking about," Peterson insisted, but if he had ever harbored acting ambitions, it was good he had a day job.

"Vish-ni-koff," Angel said again, separating out each syllable. "It's a Russian name, if that helps."

"Why would that help?"

"You trying to tell us you're not hooked up with the Russians?" Angel asked, forcing himself to remain in his chair, his casual, outward appearance belying the barely contained rage he felt. He let his anger color his voice, though. "You going to tell me you didn't sic the Mafiya on me after the first time we talked?"

"The Mafia's Italian," Peterson said. "Not Russian."

"Sicilian, actually," Wesley replied. Angel shot him a look. "Though that's neither here nor there, really."

"This one's Russian," Angel pointed out. "I hear they make the Sicilian one look like a troop of Brownies. Now quit wasting our time, Bo, and don't make me get physical again. We know Vishnikoff has been paying you off. We just want to hear from you who he is and how we find him."

Peterson was still standing just inside his front door. Sweat had started to spring from his temples and forehead, and the armpits of his tee shirt were dark.

"I can't tell you anything about him," Peterson said finally. "If I do my life won't be worth a nickel."

Angel fixed him with a steady gaze. "What makes you think it is now?"

"I'm still breathing."

"That could change. You want to see the face again?"

Peterson shook his head.

"Then who's Vishnikoff?"

Capitulating, Bo Peterson came farther into the room and plopped down heavily in a vacant chair, shoulders slumped with defeat. "You're right, he's a Russian."

"You might try telling us something we don't know," Wesley said. "Unless . . . well, unless you want Angel to get mad at you. It isn't pretty."

Peterson took large gulps of air, like a drowning man trying to breathe. Angel could see the fear that gripped the beefy cop, could smell it on the air, and couldn't help taking an unwelcome degree of pleasure in it. Once again, he felt the old, Angelus part of himself uncomfortably close to the surface. A moment's release, he knew, and Peterson would be meat.

And Angelus, unchecked, would be loosed upon the Earth once more.

He fought it back, controlled it. Let Peterson go on living a while longer. He needed the man alive, needed the information he had.

"He—he's a scientist or something," Peterson said. "He's protected by them."

"By whom?" Wesley asked.

"You know. By the Mafiya. The Russian gangs. They all look out for Vishnikoff, for his whole family. Make sure no one bothers them."

"Why?" Angel demanded. "Who are they?"

"I don't know," Peterson breathed. He looked up pleadingly, and it was just too plain bad that pathetic expressions didn't work on Angel when they were on the faces of dirtbags. "And that's the truth. I just know they're somebody. Somebody big, important. And whatever they do . . ." He paused.

"Yes," Wesley encouraged him. "Whatever they do, what?"

"It's bad," Peterson finally got out. "It's really bad. I don't want anything to do with it, man." His Adam's apple bobbed and his voice became thin and tight. Perhaps unconsciously, he slipped his hands into the hollows of his armpits, protectively huddling in the miserable sphere of guilt he had constructed for himself.

"I haven't been a good cop, I know that. I've taken money, I've done crimes, I'm not proud of that. But whatever the Vishnikoffs are up to, word is that it's a thousand times worse than anything I've ever done, and I don't want to be part of it."

"You don't have to be," Angel said. "It's not too late to change sides."

"Yeah, it is," Peterson argued. His voice dropped to a whisper. "Way too late."

"As long as you're alive, it is never too late to turn a new leaf," Wesley said. Then, glancing at Angel, he added, "Sometimes being alive is not even the deciding factor."

"I turn now, I won't be alive much longer," Peterson said.

"But if you don't, then how many die?" Angel asked him.

Peterson stared past Angel, as if seeing a future there that terrified him. He gripped his own upper arms in a pose that looked awkward on such a muscular man—it was a scared little boy's posture.

"Okay," he said. "I'll tell you what I know. It ain't much. But I'll tell it to you."

He started to talk.

As Peterson had claimed, he didn't know much. But Angel kept up his end of the bargain, delivering Peterson to Kate Lockley at her office. He had his hands cuffed behind his back, and the few cops who had seen them come in had stared with undisguised interest. A few of them had seen Angel around before, but most recognized Peterson as a cop, even though he was out of uniform.

"He wants to confess," Angel said. "He wants to come in from the cold."

Kate held Peterson in a steely gaze. "I'll listen," she said. "But I'll warn you right now, dirty cops make me sick to my stomach. So I won't like it, and I won't have any sympathy for you."

"That's okay," Peterson said dejectedly. "I got enough self-pity for both of us."

She led him into an interview room, and Angel and Wesley headed for the elevator.

* * *

Doña Pilar took Willow shopping.

She grew most of her own herbs, but there were other items she needed to purchase. One could only raise so many newts, and she didn't keep rattlesnakes around at all, so when a spell called for a rattle or a venom sac, a trip to the market was in order.

But these weren't things one found at your standard well-lit twenty-four-hour supermarket. One of the de la Natividads' security guards brought a car around to the front door and picked them up, and then twenty-five minutes later pulled to a stop on a quiet side street in the shadow of downtown. The high-rise financial buildings and fancy hotels were just blocks—and a world—away from this street. On the corner was a *mercado,* its windows papered with handwritten signs in Spanish advertising specials on *manteca, menudo, cerveza,* and other staples. Colorful *piñatas* hung from the eaves, casting odd shadows on the sidewalk.

The store they needed was next door.

Doña Pilar pushed open the metal and glass door, causing the bells tied around its handle to ring. A woman rushed out of a back room, smoothing her skirt down. She was no taller than Doña Pilar, and just as dark-complected, but younger, with pitch-black hair and smooth, unlined skin.

She looked like she'd been crying.

She and Doña Pilar launched into jet-speed conversation in Spanish. Willow could only follow a few words, but it didn't sound good. She passed the time by wandering the narrow, tightly-packed aisles, marveling at the wide array of magickal accessories, herbs, implements and books to be had. It was like the downscale version of Sunnydale's Dragon's Cove Magic Shop, where she'd first been introduced to many of these items—not as well-merchandised, but there seemed to be even more to choose from here.

After a few minutes of conversation, Doña Pilar found her among the shelves. She had a string bag dangling from one arm and a grim expression on her face.

"What's wrong?" Willow asked.

"Her daughter," Doña Pilar explained. "Consuela. She helps here at the shop, sometimes . . ."

"Oh, no," Willow moaned, getting the picture. "Disappeared?"

The older witch inclined her head. "*Sí.*"

"How long?"

"Two days, now." Doña Pilar unconsciously crossed herself.

"I'm so sorry," Willow said. "We have to move faster. We have to find these kids."

"We are moving as fast as we dare," Doña Pilar argued. "It is more important to do it right than to do it fast."

"I know," Willow agreed, letting out a sigh. "It's just so frustrating."

"It is that." She went about her shopping, leaving Willow to examine things she'd only heard about. She was looking at a large glass jar of rat kidneys when she heard Tara's voice.

"Willow?"

"Tara!" She looked around, stood on tiptoes to peer over the shelves. "Where are you?"

"I'm at Mr. Giles's house," Tara said. Willow couldn't see her, but she could hear her as clear as if she were standing next to her. "I found this in a book," Tara continued. "I thought it might come in handy. It's called audial projection."

"Makes sense. Can anyone else hear you?"

Doña Pilar came back around the end of the aisle, staring at Willow as if she'd taken leave of her senses. Willow smiled at her. Doña Pilar shrugged, shook her head, and trundled away.

"Guess not," Willow said. "Do I have to talk out loud, or can you hear me if I just think?"

"I'm talking out loud here," Tara said. "This isn't the same as the mind-links we've been working on together. It's very directed, according to the book Mr. Giles had. I can pick who I send to, and only the chosen receiver can hear me. But if I break the link, you can't talk back to me unless you go through the ritual."

"Is it hard?"

"It's not easy," Tara said. "I'm getting a little worn out here as it is. It's really tough to talk and listen and control my breathing and mental focus all at the same time. While standing on a bed of nails."

"No way!"

"No, the nails part is a joke." Tara giggled. "I miss you."

"I miss you too, Tara. This'll be over soon."

"Promise?"

"It has to be," Willow said. "I can't stay away much longer."

"I'm glad," Tara said. "I'm going now."

"Okay, Tara. Thanks for calling!"

She went to find Doña Pilar, who was at the counter paying for her purchases. "That was so cool!" she exclaimed. "Tara called me! In my head! Audial projection, she said it was."

Doña Pilar and the shopkeeper exchanged glances and smiles.

"Oh, so you guys knew about this all along?"

"There is much you still have to learn, little Willow," Doña Pilar said.

"I know, I know. But I'm picking it up pretty fast, I think."

"You are an exceptional student, Willow. The best."

Willow took the string bag and carried it out of the store for her, still beaming from the conversation and the compliment.

Then she remembered that Consuela was missing, and felt ashamed.

"We have to do more," she said urgently.

Doña Pilar said nothing, only patted her shoulder and walked on.

Nicky de la Natividad felt like a prisoner, and he didn't like it.

His prison was in an apartment upstairs over an auto repair shop. At least, that's how it was presented to the public, but Nicky knew it was a chop shop, a place stolen cars were brought to for repainting, repairs, the filing off of Vehicle Identification Numbers, so the cars could be resold or used by members of the Echo Park gang or other associated groups. One favorite stunt, he knew, was to remove the seats, the engine and the wheels, and then to abandon the carcass somewhere. It would be found, but the car's original owner wouldn't want it in that condition. The insurance company would total it, paying the owner the full value of the claim. The body of the car would be sold cheaply at auction—to a representative of the gang, who would bring it back to the shop on a trailer, where the engine, wheels, and seats would be restored, and a perfectly good car was now theirs legally, complete with pink slip.

Nobody lived in the upstairs apartment. It was a hangout, a place to lie low. It had three bedrooms and one bath, a living room and a kitchen, all filthy. Since no one lived here on any kind of permanent basis, no one bothered to clean up the place or take out the trash.

But it was a prison to Nicky because they held him here—subtly, but unmistakably—against his will. There was always someone coming by to "visit," but each of his requests to leave went unanswered. They had taken away his gun and brought him three take-out meals a day, along with cigarettes he had no interest in smoking. There were always people downstairs, day and night, working on cars or just hanging out. Nicky knew they'd been instructed to stop him if he tried to leave, even though nothing had been said outright. And since they kept his door locked, and the windows were barred, it didn't really matter. He was stuck.

Today a young member of Echo Park named Billy Cruz had dropped by. Billy had been one of the poor kids who went to the same Catholic church as the wealthy de la Natividad family. In fact, it had been Salma who had gone against their snobby parents' wishes and made friends with him.

Of course, Salma had had no idea that Billy was connected to organized crime. But Nicky, who had, hoped for some news of his sister, and of Rosalie Estrada, from whom he hadn't heard since his Night of the Long Knives.

"Hey, Nicky, what's up?" Billy asked. He sat on a foul mattress that occupied one corner of the small bedroom. An ocean of fast-food wrappers hid the floor. Nicky thought of them as an alarm system when he slept—anyone sneaking in would have to wade through the sea of rustling paper.

"I'm getting sick of sitting in here," Nicky replied. "They don't even have cable TV, man."

Billy scrunched up his face. He was good-looking, always had lots of girlfriends. Even Salma had had a crush on him for a while, back when they were all younger.

"That totally sucks, dude," he said sympathetically.

"I know." Nicky spread open his hands. "But every time I try to go, they tell me it's not safe for me out there yet."

Billy nodded. He pulled a cigarette out of a pack in his shirt pocket and lit it. Inhaled. Nicky didn't smoke, but the scent took him back to the oil fields. This was *mierda*. He was *muy macho;* he had risked his life for the Latin Cobras. No one kept him locked up.

"That's what Che says, dude," Billy continued. "Says you and him have ticked off the Russians bad. You went outside, you'd be dead before you went a mile, way I hear it."

Nicky clenched his teeth, pissed off and suddenly realizing he was not going to take this crap any longer. "I'm willing to take that chance, man. I'm going stir crazy here. I read the same stupid magazine ten times already. Anyway, how come Che gets to be out there and not me? He locked up someplace?"

"Che's Echo Park, dude. He's home turf. You're the visitor." Billy took a drag on his cigarette, frowning sadly. "Soon, Nicky. It'll blow over. Give it a day or two."

"Mano, no se." He took the cigarette from Billy, sucked in smoke, thought of Rosalie and wished she, at least, were here. "I don't know, Billy. I think Che wants something from me."

Billy thought for a moment before answering. "Of course he does, Nicky. He wants to know how to become, you know, invulnerable, or whatever it is. Like you was in that oil field. When you show him how to do it, he'll most probably let you go." He crossed his legs and lit another cigarette, gesturing for Nicky to keep his. "What was that about, anyway?"

Nicky's scalp prickled. Billy had confirmed his fears. *They're holding me hostage. They're not gonna let me go unless I give him the secret.*

"I can't do that, Billy. Not for somebody else," he lied. "That's a once in a lifetime deal, and you can only do it for yourself. It's called the Night of the Long Knives, and it's a spell—a combination of spells, really, that makes a person invincible for one night. That's how I was able to set off all those charges in DeSola's oil field and walk away from it."

Billy considered. "But you could teach him how to do it for his own self, couldn't you?"

I gotta keep myself indispensable, Nicky thought quickly. *I gotta get some status, some rank.*

"It ain't like learning how to ride a bicycle or something, man. I was raised by a *bruja.* I got magick in my blood, in my heritage. And even with all that, it was hard for me. Che doesn't have that background."

He drew back his sleeve, showed Billy the wound he'd suffered the other night when the Russian had shot him. "And it doesn't last long. One night, that's it. After that, you get shot, you get hurt. This hurts like crazy, man. It itches."

"You got lucky, though," Billy said, examining the wound. "Six inches over, you're dead."

"Yeah, I got lucky." He rolled down his sleeve. "I got shot, and people tell me I'm lucky. *Orale,* what kind of life is this, *mano?* Is this what we wanted when we were kids?"

Billy smoked for a few seconds. He leaned back his head and concentrated on blowing smoke rings. "It's what I wanted, Nicky. My uncle, my brother, they were both in the Echo Park Band. It's all I ever wanted. But you, man, you got money, you got opportunity. What you doin' here?"

Nicky was silent. He paced the room for a moment, feeling the rotting floorboards beneath his feet. The place smelled like car parts. "I don't know for sure," he said finally. "I been giving that some thought."

"I think you got to try, man." Hunkering forward, Billy dangled his hands between his knees. He looked hard at his *compadre*.

"I think you got to teach Che, you want to get out of here. I mean, you're a Cobra, not a member of Echo Park. Whole reason he hangin' with you is he wants you to be his pal, teach him that stuff."

Nicky moved in close to him, so Billy had to look in his eyes or look away. "Is that something you know, Billy, or something you're guessing?"

"I don't *know* it know it, if you know what I mean," Billy responded. "But I pretty much know it, you know?"

There was a moment, and Nicky realized that Billy was not here as his friend. He was here as Che's messenger.

His guts churned.

No one here gives a damn about me.

"I got you," he said to Billy.

Billy said smoothly, "And if I were you I'd do it as soon as you can."

"What's going down?" Nicky tried to sound curious, but his voice was shrill and scared.

"I don't know for sure, dude. It's probably nothin', you know. But there's a lot of stuff going down out there that ain't good." Billy's voice dripped with sincerity. "People disappearin' and all."

Nicky said carefully, "I heard about some of that."

"Yeah, well, you probably didn't hear that Salma is one of them."

Oh, God. God, don't punish her because of me. I'm the bad one. I'm the one who used Black Magick. Don't let them hurt her because of me.

"That's what I heard, anyway," Billy said, as the silence stretched between them.

"You sure about that?" Nicky croaked.

"Pretty sure," Billy said, tamping out his cigarette in an empty McDonald's container. "I mean, maybe it's nothin', you know. But I thought you'd want to know."

"What about Rosalie?" Nicky asked. "I haven't seen her since that night." They both knew which night he meant: the Night of the Long Knives.

The night he had really blown it, big time.

"I don't know nothin' about anyone named Rosalie," Billy tossed off. "She a Cobra chick? I don't know no Cobras, remember."

"But you hear stuff, right? What about the rest of my crew? Little King, Dom, all those guys? What's the word?"

"Word is, they're just layin' low," Billy said. "That oil field fire, that was a big deal. Newspapers, you know, TV. Live from Channel Five. Sunnydale cops, even some feds, what I hear. So your *amigos* are hidin' out until it blows over."

"I'm going to get out of here," Nicky said evenly. "I got to get out of here. I got magick, don't forget."

"It ain't gonna be that easy to go," Billy warned, sounding very concerned. *You* cabrón, Nicky thought. *Faking like you care what happens to me.* "There's a guard outside, and another one downstairs. Che'll kill 'em if they let you go."

Nicky took another drag off his cigarette, feeling sick and dizzy and so mad he didn't care what he said or did. "Why doesn't Che have the guts to face me himself, he wants something from me?"

"Dude, you know how he works. He'll wear you down first, get you till you're beggin' for him to let you teach him what he wants to know. Then he gets what he wants and you feel like you got what *you* want."

"That don't work anymore," Nicky said, sending the message as clearly as he could. "Not with my sister and Rosalie missing."

Billy shrugged. "Gettin' yourself shot ain't gonna bring 'em back."

Narrowing his eyes, Nicky said, "I want to talk to Che."

"He'll see you when he's ready to, man."

Nicky's tone was determined. "He'll see me *now*."

"I don't think so." Billy's tone was calm, maybe a little sad. Maybe somewhere inside him there was a heart. After all, Salma had liked him, and she was a good judge of people.

Except for me. She looked up to me. Some big brother I've been.

He took a breath and threw it down. "Billy, you ain't going to get in my way, are you?"

"I'm just tellin' you, man," Billy said, "there's guards outside."

"You strapped?"

"Yeah, but—"

Nicky held out his hand. "Give it to me."

Billy shook his head. "Nicky, I can't . . ."

Nicky wagged his hand. "I known you a long time, Billy. I never done you nothing bad." He said, "Salma liked you. My parents, they told her not to talk to you, but she did."

Billy's face reddened. He gazed down at his hands; Nicky saw the gang tattoo in the web of his flesh between his forefinger and thumb.

"Don't make me put a spell on you, man," Nicky threatened.

The other guy reached into the waistband at the back of

his jeans and drew out a small Beretta automatic. He said, "I don't want to see any of the guys get hurt, Nicky, that's all."

"I don't want to hurt them." He meant it. He didn't.

"But I know how important Salma is to you," Billy murmured.

"That's it, Billy." Nicky felt like he had a lasso out, and he was just about to throw it over the head of a wild animal. Too quickly, the coyote was just gonna bolt and run. "I just want to take care of my sister, you know?"

"I know, man." Billy sighed heavily. Nicky wished he was surer of him, but there was no time. "Just don't get in no trouble."

"No such thing as trouble Nicky de la Natividad can't get out of, Billy." He took the little gun from his friend, checked the clip, and shoved it back into place with a satisfying click. Somehow the weapon soothed his nerves, like an infant with a pacifier. He didn't know what he might step into, but he had the feeling that he could handle it. "It's just a matter of playing the angles."

"Nicky." Billy put a hand on Nicky's arm, stopped him. "You gotta—you know, Che would have me capped if he knew I let you go."

Nicky understood. He didn't take time to think it over. With the gun in his fist, he drove a powerful jab into Billy's jaw. His friend collapsed on the bed.

Nicky stepped out of the room.

The dreamlike landscape didn't change as Salma walked, although she had thought for a while that it might, in the same way that a dreaming person might walk from a familiar kitchen into a school hallway and then onto a crowded train, all without proper transition. But that didn't happen here. Instead, it changed only in the ways that a normal landscape did as one passed through it, changing angle of view, coming around a bend and seeing the base of something tall that previously had only towered over trees and cliffs.

It still disturbed her—the colors were all wrong, the sizes seemed not to fit somehow. Things that should have been small, bushes and small succulents, were gigantic here, and where they might have been green on her Earth they were shades of red and blue and purple. Other things had no corresponding objects in her experience—an enormous rock-looking thing that pulsed like a heart, then twitched as if it were a cocoon that a butterfly was trying to escape from when she looked at it. If she looked away, or only looked sidelong at it, the thing went back to pulsing rhythmically. But when she looked straight at it again, it resumed its twitching, and she had to look away for fear that it would erupt at her.

She hurried past it, but there was always something around one curve or the next to make her just as frightened. She began to have a sense of how Alice must have felt after she'd gone through the Looking Glass. She had always wondered, if someone had looked into the Looking Glass closely enough, or concentrated hard enough, would they have been able to see Alice in there? Or was Alice—as Salma believed *she* was—completely invisible to everyone who had ever known and loved her?

When she heard the creak and rattle of mounted riders, she was at first ecstatic. *People!* she thought. *They'll help me!*

But a second thought came, almost on top of the first. *If they're as strange as the plant life, will they help me? Or will I be so different from them that they'll think I'm an animal, or be unable to see me at all?* She hid behind a fallen leaf the size of a Winnebago and watched their approach.

After a few minutes they rode into view.

They looked perfectly human, but like humans from some other time or place, somewhat medieval-looking in dress and attitude. Their mounts were horselike—she thought it might not be inaccurate to call them horses—but they weren't *exactly* horses, the same way nothing else here was exactly like its counterpart at home. Their legs, for one thing, seemed too stout, not thin and graceful like a horse's legs. And their manes resembled falling water more than flowing hair, semiopaque and constantly shifting.

But they were close enough. Salma gathered her courage and stepped out from behind the leaf. "Hello!" she called.

The riders—all men, she guessed, though she tempered that guess with the now-familiar caveat that nothing here was as it seemed—turned in their saddles to look at her. They spoke, but there was no common language, no words or sounds they made that she could understand. "I'm—I'm lost," she said. The men looked at her, uncomprehending. Finally, one of them rode up to her. She was terrified of what he might do, and wanted to run, but fear rooted her to the spot. The man bent over in the saddle, extended an arm toward her.

He wants me to get on with him, she thought. *Should I?* Not for the first time, she found herself wishing that Buffy were here. She had developed great faith in the Slayer's abilities. But Buffy couldn't help her now. She was on her own, with these men she had revealed herself to.

Still, she thought, *if they wanted me dead they could have killed me by now.* She took the man's arm and he hoisted her onto the saddle, behind him. A few of them spoke to one another, and they set off again. She made a couple more attempts to speak, and so did they. But it didn't work, and after a while they gave up trying. Salma felt more alone and afraid than ever.

They took her to a massive stone castle at the edge of a plain, a trip that lasted several hours—she guessed, although she couldn't seem to locate a sun, or any other way to tell time. At the castle they bypassed a number of rooms full of people, men and women, and instead she was taken immediately to a dark interior chamber, lit only by dozens of flickering candles. They closed the door when they left.

Salma was completely alone.

Chapter 9

Moscow, 1991

Everything had fallen apart.

In a few days it would be a new year, and that year
would dawn on a world in which there was no Soviet
Union. Mikhail Gorbachev had gone on television to an-
nounce that the former USSR was dissolving itself, its
member states becoming independent entities. Alexis and
Valerya Vishnikoff and their young daughter Alina were
now Russian citizens, not Soviets.

And it was worse than that. In dissolving the Soviet
Union, Gorbachev and his allies had also destroyed the
power base of the Communist party. The party hierarchy
had been overturned, the KGB thrown out. One day, a
man had been able to know where he stood in the world.
The next, everything was new. It was like starting over.
But Alexis and Valerya had worked hard to get where
they were. The People's Project was finally beginning to
show real results. They didn't want to start over.

They had gone into the lab the day after Gorbachev's

announcement. But there was no work being done. People sat at their desks, stunned expressions on their faces, many in tears. Others ransacked their own work areas, stealing computers, lab equipment, office supplies—one man took the clock off the wall and the wastebasket that stood beside a little table on which there was a coffeepot, a pitcher of milk, and some sugar. No one stopped him, or made any attempt to halt the other thefts. The people who might have, the security guards and KGB plants, hadn't even bothered to come in at all.

Alexis and Valerya huddled together in Markov's office. Markov hadn't shown up either—they would later learn that he had hanged himself from the rafters of his apartment, minutes after hearing Gorbachev's statement.

"It can't be allowed to fall into the wrong hands," Valerya was insisting. "Any of these people could walk out the door with it and sell it on the black market tomorrow. Or deliver it straight to an American agent."

"But what can we do?" Alexis asked her, in an agony of indecision. "It doesn't belong to us."

"To us as much as anyone else on Earth," Valerya countered. She looked determined. "Maybe Comrade Markov, but he isn't even here. Who knows when he will be again? By then it could be too late."

She held out her hands, as if imploring her husband to really listen to her. "If the Reality Tracer is stolen or destroyed, then everything you and I have worked on for the past decade is gone. Worthless. We might as well never have been born."

"Don't say that," Alexis implored her. "We have each other. We have a beautiful daughter."

That was the strongest argument he could have used. Alexis was not religious, but there were times he simply could not believe the exquisite creature they had brought

173

into the world was not an angel. The love that filled him whenever he looked at her—and at her mother—was almost unbearable.

"Our daughter. Who will grow up without ever knowing Communism," Valerya said. "Whose parents will have worked for years to accomplish exactly nothing. What good will we be for her? How will throwing everything we've done away affect her?"

"Then what do you suggest we do, Valerya?" Alexis asked, looking at his wife, gazing at her, remembering a happier time when he had been freezing cold and drinking tea, and telling her about a different catastrophe in his life. "Get a gun and sit in the lab with the Tracer until Markov comes back?"

She looked around to make sure no one watched, and leaned close to Alexis. It was not safe to assume that even Markov's office wasn't bugged, that there wasn't someone listening to the whole conversation. Although, with the chaos at the KGB, he couldn't imagine who it might be.

"We take it," she whispered. "We take it home today, now. And we get it out of Russia, into Yugoslavia, Romania—someplace more sympathetic to our cause."

Alexis tried to disguise his shock. "You're talking treason!"

"Treason against what?" Valerya responded. "A government that no longer exists? A party that has been disbanded? A system that has been overthrown? It would be treason *not* to do something."

Alexis paused. Through the big window of Markov's office, he could see yet another researcher unplugging a computer from its power source and tucking it under his arm. It had only been a couple of years since the Project had acquired desktop computers—if this had happened before that, they'd have had to drive trucks up to the building and lift massive banks of equipment with cranes to steal them.

The whole thing still felt like a bad dream from which he would soon awake. But as he watched the activity in the building, he realized that there was no ignoring reality. Things had changed, overnight. The People's Project—and, in the light of these developments, that name took on a new kind of irony—was only one casualty of the new world order, and not one that most people would ever miss. Very few knew of its existence in the first place.

"You're right, Valerya," he said. He touched her smooth cheek, stroked her blond hair. "As usual, you are right. Let's get to work."

No one tried to stop them. Only a few even looked their way as they disconnected the Reality Tracer from the computers that controlled it, and from the power outlets that charged it. They had made a quick list of the elements they needed to operate the Tracer—the main drive, the database. But the most important factor, they carried within themselves: their own innate abilities. Everything else they needed they could take in one heavily burdened trip home.

Valerya packed while Alexis retrieved Alina from school. The girl was six now, a blond, apple-cheeked miniature of her mother. Seeing her father so early in the day surprised but delighted her. Alexis told the teacher that he would be taking her out for the afternoon, but didn't bother to say that she should not watch for them to return. The teacher would figure it out soon enough, and in the meantime she would not raise any alarms.

Alina, of course, could tell that something was very wrong, but she also knew that she should not let on to anyone else. She smiled at her father and took his hand.

Alexis and Valerya owned a car now, a Citroën they had bought thirdhand from a Hungarian who ran a coffee shop on their street. By the time he got home, through the chaotic streets, with Alina, Valerya was already stuffing the car's boot with clothing, papers, and personal items the family would not want to leave behind.

She tried to pack the car so it would look, upon cursory inspection—in case there was still anyone to inspect it— like that of a family on holiday. But at the same time she didn't want to leave anything behind that might reveal what they had been working on. They couldn't leave any clues as to their destination, for they had no firm plans in mind, just an overwhelming urge to get out of Russia before anyone realized what was missing. Alexis sent Alina to her room to gather some favorite toys while he pitched in with the packing.

They were on the road before dark. By the next evening, they had stopped in Poland. From there, they worked their way down through the former Soviet satellites, into Czechoslovakia, Hungary, Romania, and finally Bulgaria. Associates helped them with border crossings, though the borders, with everything falling apart, were more porous than usual. In Bulgaria, they took an apartment while Alexis found a menial job. Without a lab or any support staff, they continued the work they had begun so long ago.

America was their next move.

The People's Project lived.

Sunnydale

Buffy held the young man's face tenderly in her hands, feeling the roughness of his afternoon stubble, the slightly rubbery quality of his cheeks. She couldn't imagine how things had become so intense so quickly, and found herself wishing for a moment that there was a way to turn back the clock, to restore things to the way they had been. But she knew there wasn't.

She put the face back down on the street where she had found it, and silently vowed to destroy whatever creature had torn it from some unsuspecting victim. Sunnydale crawled with vermin, supernatural beings that seemed to be here only to kill. Buffy was fed up with them.

"Buffy!" Riley called to her from around a corner, his tone hushed and urgent. She sprang to his side. Spike, patrolling with them tonight, was already there.

"What's up?" she asked, ready for combat.

Combat, it seemed, was ready for her.

Four creatures bearing only the vaguest resemblance to anything human, or even mammalian, knelt over a human corpse. Its midsection was split open like a Christmas turkey, and the four were pulling entrails from inside it, shoving them into mouths that hinged open like an alligator's. The fiends had two arms and two legs each, and a head on top of a body, but the body was split into sections like an insect's. *Thorax and abdomen,* Buffy remembered, glad that she could use insect anatomy to distract herself momentarily from the ghastly display of human anatomy before her.

"Reminds me," Spike said. "Gotta have a snack when we get back to Giles's."

"Tell me again why we let you come with us on patrol?" Riley asked.

"Animal magnetism."

One of the creatures noticed them then, glancing over its shoulder toward where she, Riley, and Spike stood. It dropped a length of intestine and made a frantic clicking sound. The others looked up, drawing away from the body into defensive postures. Long, transparent wings on their backs unfolded.

Buffy didn't even glance at her friends. Her rage was boundless now. These things would pay. She threw herself down the street at them. At her attack, their wings began to flutter and buzz. As she ran, Buffy pulled a stake out, knowing these weren't vampires, but a wooden rod through the heart or some other organ would still do some damage. By the time she reached them, one was already taking flight. Buffy launched herself into the air, and caught the creature's spindly legs before it got away.

Her weight brought it down, and they landed in a heap, on top of the others. One of Buffy's boots grazed the corpse, and she drew it away in disgust. She jabbed the stake into the torso of the creature she'd crash-landed.

It let out a trilling, high-pitched wail, in which Buffy took a great deal of satisfaction.

Riley joined the battle, catching another of the creatures as it tried to escape. As Buffy struggled with one, she saw Riley wrestling his, keeping his head back to avoid snapping jaws while trying to break the thing's spine. *Not a bad idea,* she thought. But she took a more direct route, grabbing the wounded one by its head, holding the jaws shut with her powerful hands, and snapping it hard against a building. She heard a crunching noise, and the fiend went limp in her hands.

Spike was trying to get a grip on another one, but it used its wings defensively, fluttering them at him like sword blades, and he couldn't get close. But Buffy was too furious to be deterred. She coiled and released a snap kick that punctured the thing's thorax. It collapsed on the ground, and she followed, driving the stake still clutched in her fist into its head. It shuddered twice and then was still.

"Neat trick, that," Spike said.

Riley had successfully dispatched his, which left only

one more, but for a second, Buffy couldn't see it. Then she heard it, followed the sound with her gaze, up and over their heads. It had been injured when she and the first one had fallen on it; one of its wings was shredded a bit, but it was still able to gain altitude.

Just not fast enough.

"Riley!" she called, and made a quick cradle with her hands. "Boost!"

He understood, which was good. She'd practiced this with Angel, but hadn't really worked on it with Riley. It was really pretty self-explanatory, though. He bent forward at the waist, legs tensed and ready, and repeated the cradle motion. Buffy ran toward him, jumped, and one foot landed in the cradle. As it did, Riley straightened, throwing her into the air, her own momentum furthering the leap.

The fiend fluttered frantically but couldn't get high enough. Buffy, parallel to the second story windows of the buildings, slammed into it. It started to fall, and, her momentum gone, she dropped with it. Pacing it, she drew her right hand back past her left shoulder and backhanded the thing across its long mouth as hard as she could.

Its head swiveled, farther than it could handle. She heard its neck break, and the thing was dead by the time they crashed to the street.

Riley helped her up, a smile on his handsome face. Spike was there, too, helping to dust some of the fiend's body parts off her shoulders.

"Now that's what I call teamwork," he said.

"Funny," she replied. "That's what I call seriously ooky."

Cheryce had always hated the part about having to be invited across a threshold, because usually only friends and allies were willing to do that. Those one wanted to terrorize or kill were the least likely to go along with the program. Sure, there were methods one could employ to get around the technicality, but they were occasionally awkward, and Cheryce preferred to be direct whenever possible.

So when she learned that some Latin Cobras were hiding out in a trailer, less than a mile from where she had lived, she decided to be as direct as possible. She started by banging on the door.

"Hey, come out!" she shouted. "I want some answers!"

Not surprisingly, no one came out.

So she moved on to the next element of the plan. The trailer rested on a low foundation of cinder blocks. It was one of those immobile "mobile homes" that people set up in a mobile home park somewhere and left there. But that just meant it couldn't be easily rolled out on the back of a truck; it didn't mean it couldn't be moved.

Cheryce went to one corner, squatted down, put her hands behind her back, and wrapped them around the bottom edge of the trailer. Then, muscles straining, legs shaking, she stood. The corner of the trailer rose with her. When she had it up as high as she could get it, she let go.

It slammed down, breaking the cinder block wall, and slipped off its mooring. The lights inside went off as it disconnected from its power supply. Unbalanced now, it was easier to agitate. She pushed on its walls, shaking the whole thing like a tambourine.

A moment later, three Latin Cobras spilled out the door.

"Hey, man, what are you—oh, *mamacita,*" one said, looking irritated with her. He had no hair on his head, and none on his shirtless chest. A tattoo of a coiled snake danced on his tight abdomen as he crossed his arms. "You wanted to come and play, why you being so rough?"

"I'm not here to play," Cheryce said. "I'm here for information. Failing that, I'd be happy to just kill the three of you and drink your blood."

Another guy clapped a hand over the first one's shoulder. Shirtless, too, and packing six-pack abs. "Paco," he said quietly. "She messed up the trailer like that by herself, I think maybe we should listen to her."

"Dude," Paco snapped, "she woulda needed a crane or something to pick the trailer up like that. So where is it, lady? How'd you do that?"

Cheryce simply looked at her fingertips. "Damn," she said casually. "Broke a nail."

"What you want to know?" the second guy asked.

"Jorge, I wouldn't—"

"Shut up, Paco," Jorge barked. "You want to take your chances with her, fine. Not me."

Finally, the third guy spoke. "Jorge's right," he said. "We'll tell you whatever you want to know."

"Fine," Cheryce said. "Let's talk about oil fields."

When the conversation was over, five minutes later, Cheryce had a name and a location and a full stomach. *Tomorrow night,* she thought, *I'll boost a ride to Los Angeles and find Mr. Nicolas de la Natividad. I think tonight's been a smashing success.*

She headed back toward her temporary home, to get some rest and dream of revenge—and Paris.

If there was one thing Giles dreaded more than patrolling Sunnydale and finding demons or monsters, it was patrolling with Xander and Anya, and *not* finding demons or monsters. Without the constant possibility of danger, their interminable prattle got on his nerves more quickly than he cared to think about. Either one alone was fine, in small doses, but together, they wore him down.

And, since Anya had become mortal and, more and

more, the effective Mrs. Harris, they had been almost inseparable.

But sometimes there was nothing for it. Buffy, Riley, and Spike were patrolling the west side of town. Tara was working with Willow, on the astral plane, trying to find out what had become of Salma, Nicky, or the other disappeared young people. In such a dangerous period, Giles was loath to patrol alone. So Anya and Xander it was.

At least, he comforted himself, *it was no longer Xander and Cordelia. Now* that *had been a trial.*

At Xander's suggestion, they had been checking Sunnydale's few motels, still looking for Cheryce as they kept their eyes open for further monster attacks. They had just come from the Sleepy-Bye Inn, a seedy construction of equal parts stucco and lost hope, when Anya grabbed Giles's sleeve.

"Look," she directed him. "Isn't that Spike's honey?"

"Cheryce? It's either her or there's a Frederick's catalogue shoot going on in the neighborhood," Xander said.

The six-foot blonde wore what was, for her, a reasonably conservative outfit—a leopard-print dress with a plunging neckline that barely contained her décolletage, the skirt of which actually concealed her entire rear end instead of just the upper reaches of it. It was gathered at the waist by a black patent leather belt, and set off by five-inch spike heels in a contrasting furry gold tiger pattern. Various bracelets and piercings completed the ensemble.

Cheryce sashayed their way, digging a room key out of a pocket. Relatively fresh blood painted her lips. She passed through the light from a street lamp, but hadn't seen them yet.

"I guess she's staying here, after all," Xander whispered.

"I didn't like that desk clerk from the moment I laid

eyes on him," Giles said. "Seemed remarkably haughty for someone working in a place like that."

"Well, he knows all the classy people," Anya offered.

"Now what?" Xander asked. "Do we dust her? Or take her back to Spike?"

"We promised Spike!" Anya insisted.

"Yes, we did," Giles agreed. "But-but look at her. Clearly, she's been feeding on human blood."

"Could be lipstick," Anya said.

"Only if it's also chinstick," Xander said. "She looks like she's been dunking in it."

"No, I'm afraid we have no choice," Giles said. "She's a threat to all humanity."

Anya gripped his arm. "Spike will be furious," she declared. "We told him we'd look for her, not that we'd kill her."

"Already dead, remember?" Xander suggested with a smile.

Anya didn't return the good cheer. "I can't believe we'd betray him like this."

Xander took her shoulders in his hands. "Anya," he said. "Do I have to remind you? You, human. Giles, human. Me, human. Cheryce, vampire. Spike, vampire."

"Just because someone's a vampire doesn't mean they're all bad," Anya argued. "Well, okay, usually it does, with a few well-known exceptions. And I grant you, she does come under the 'bad' category. But a promise is a promise, no matter who you make it to."

"The question may be moot," Giles said. "She's seen us."

Cheryce stopped a dozen feet away and stood, hands on her cocked hips, watching them. She snapped her gum. "Aren't you guys the Slayer's little friends?"

"Yes," Xander said. "I mean, not so little. But yes, we are friends of the Slayer."

"And of Spike," Anya added. "Remember him? The vampire who loves you?"

"Spike doesn't love me," Cheryce said. "Spike loves himself. Anyone else just gets his leftovers."

"That isn't true, completely," Anya huffed. "He's very sensitive."

"Anya, you may be spending a little too much time with Spike," Xander pointed out. "I think he's hypnotized you."

Anya frowned at Xander and turned back to Cheryce. "He really misses you."

"He misses the good times we've had, and he misses the fact that I won't help him get his chip out. And he thinks I'm too dumb to know that's why he hangs around."

"I'm sure you're wrong," Anya continued. "You should hear how he talks about you."

"Whoa. Whoa, whoa, whoa," Xander said. "What about the chip? You know something about the chip?"

"And if I do?" Cheryce said, posing. "Because why—yikes!"

All three turned, though Giles hesitated, in case it was simple misdirection. But the look of concern on Cheryce's face looked genuine, so he followed her pointing hand. Behind them—but closing fast—was a monster that looked somewhat like a charging bull. Its head and shoulders were enormous, and lowered at them as if to ram into them. Powerful haunches drove it forward at high speed. It was all black, as if made from the very stuff of shadows. For a horrible moment Giles thought it might be the shadow monster that had plagued the town for a while, but this wasn't how it had been described, and it hadn't been seen for several days.

Before any of them could move, Cheryce dashed forward, putting herself between them and the onrushing form. She spread her arms. It ran straight into them, and she closed them around its substantial bulk. The thing's speed and momentum lifted Cheryce off her feet and carried her backward a dozen yards, until she was able to plant them again and get some traction.

Once she did, though, she was able to outmuscle the beast. She flipped it onto its back, locking its neck in a death grip. She bent close to its head and said something. Giles couldn't hear the words, or even make out the language, but the appearance, from where he stood, was that she was interrogating it in some way. Then, apparently not satisfied with its answer, she broke its neck. When she stood, she was winded but uninjured.

"What was that about?" Giles demanded.

"Nothin'." She transformed into vamp face. "See ya."

She turned on her heel and melted into the night.

"Bloody hell," Giles muttered.

"Okay, that was weird," Xander said. "What does she know about the chip? Is that why Spike's been so hung up on her?"

"It's a new development," Giles agreed. "I suggest we find Spike and demand to know what's going on."

"Last I saw of him, he was lounging in the tub and swigging microwaved blood," Xander said. "Slacker."

But the road home was a crowded one; the trio collided with a few other vampires trying to take advantage of the general panic to feed on those few humans still out on the streets, plus a random assortment of monsters, though nothing quite as creepy as the insect-things they had dispatched.

"So, what's up with the chip, Spike?" Buffy insisted, when everyone gathered back at the apartment. "What's your scheme this time?"

"Said she knew how to get it out," Spike said flatly. "Obviously, she lied about that to get me into bed."

"Oh my God," Buffy groaned dramatically. "I'm going to be sick."

"Not in my loo, Slayer."

"It's not your loo." Buffy held out her hand. "Xander," she piped, "give me a stake. I've had it."

"She saved you from that monster thing," Spike said to Xander. He'd stood with his arms folded, listening to the three discuss the beast and wonder why Cheryce had saved them. Tara had offered that the monster sounded very like the one that had lured Doña Pilar outside the de la Natividad home.

"Yeah, well, so?" Xander threw back at Spike.

Buffy left them to it. She was more exhausted than she had realized. Within minutes of her head hitting the pillow, she was out.

And a few minutes after that, she dreamed.

She knew she was dreaming, as she frequently did. She watched herself as if at a distance; there was a remove, a dissociation, between Dream-Buffy and Buffy herself, almost as if she were watching an actress playing herself on a television show.

Like that would ever happen.

Dream-Buffy walked slowly through a long corridor, lined on both sides with immense doors. She couldn't even see the tops of the doors—they were shrouded in darkness or hidden behind clouds, she couldn't tell which. They were miles tall, and maybe eight feet wide, and ornately carved with indistinct figures that blurred and shifted under her gaze. She gave up trying to look at them; Dream-Buffy reached for the knob of the nearest one, but there was no handle on it, no knob of any kind that she could distinguish, so she got a grip on some of the carvings and pulled.

It swung surprisingly smoothly, as if on well-oiled hinges or ball bearings.

A silhouette stood surrounded by a void; a person, or something in human shape. There was no detail on the person, not gender or age or even a real sense of size, because there was nothing behind the person to give scale. The door opened onto a vast plain of nothingness, not dark, not smoke, not a screen of any kind—merely the absence of anything at all.

Ghost Roads, she thought, but it was wrong for that, somehow; though she watched Dream-Buffy standing before the threshold for what could have been hours, or seconds, there was no transition to another plane, as there would be on the Ghost Roads—the void would then eventually find form and substance, revealing phantoms journeying on the pathways of the dead.

But here, there was nothingness, except for the figure, which appeared to be gazing out the door—not at Dream-Buffy in particular—just observing what was before it.

"Huh," the figure said, in a voice that was neither male nor female. "Nobody's home."

It pushed the door shut in Dream-Buffy's face.

She moved to the next door, the features of which were equally unreadable. She tugged it open. Again, she encountered a field of emptiness and a dark figure standing in the doorway.

"Hmm," the figure said. "Nobody home here."

And the figure closed the door in her face.

Dream-Buffy continued. Door after door, figure after figure. Each one waited in front of an impossible nothingness, and each one failed to see her as she stood there looking in. Each spoke a phrase that was very similar, if not identical, to the one before it.

None of them could see her.

She couldn't find a voice to speak to any of them.

And, finally, she ran out of doors. The corridor dead-ended. The futility of it all overwhelmed her, and she woke up feeling like a thousand-pound weight pressed on her heart.

She shook Riley awake, told him about the dream.

They sat up in bed, and he caressed her arm as he spoke. "I don't know if it really means anything, Buff, except that you've been under a lot of pressure."

"That's it? Pressure? You were the TA for a psych teacher, not me."

"Okay, then." He stroked a nonexistent goatee. "In my best Freudian interpretation, I'd say you're feeling invisible in some way. You're upset because people can't seem to see you."

"Maybe," she admitted. "But I think there's more to it than that."

"Like what?"

"Something about the doors. Remember that thing you guys saw, when you fought the tree?"

He was listening. She loved that he listened, really listened to her.

"It wasn't really a tree. It just looked like one."

"Whatever. You said there was a shimmery gold circle behind it. Like the one in L.A. that Angel almost followed Sleepy Ramos through."

"Pretty much just like it, yeah."

"If they're here, where things are coming into our world from who knows where, and they're there, where people are vanishing from our world . . . what if they're some kind of doors?"

"Could be," he agreed.

"I think we need to check it out."

Riley looked at the bedside clock. "Are you sure you want to go now? I could go out and have a look. You haven't had much rest, Buffy, and it's oh—"

"Don't," she interrupted. He would do it. He'd be perfectly willing to go out there and face who-knew-what so she could have a few more minutes of rest. It was sweet, it was ingratiating . . . but Buffy felt somehow oddly confined by the knowledge. "I know you military types use the phrase oh-dark-hundred to describe what time it is, but we civilians use actual numbers. And I don't really want to know what number it is right now, so let's just go without looking at a clock."

Riley put his feet on the floor and started looking for clothes. "Okay, then," he agreed. "Let's check it out."

Fifteen minutes later they stood in the little park where Riley had conquered the tree-beast.

"Nothing now," Riley said.

"It was here," Buffy insisted. "Maybe there's some kind of trace energy from it that we could measure, or—" She stopped in the middle of her sentence and watched, wide-eyed, as a tiny glowing dot appeared before her, and expanded to the size of the one they'd seen in Boyle Heights. "Or it might come back."

The golden light bathed Riley's features as he stared into it, or through it. Buffy walked to its edge, peered around it. Just Santa Ysabel Street, on the other side of the park. From this side, she couldn't even see the shimmering circle. "There doesn't seem to be a side on this side."

Riley started to reach for the circle.

"No," Buffy warned. "I wouldn't do that. We have no idea what's inside."

Riley withdrew his hand.

"It's kind of pretty, though," she said.

"Pretty like a shark," Riley said.

"Sharks aren't pretty. They're vicious-looking and they have those little dead eyes."

"Okay, pretty like something else that's as deadly as a shark, but prettier."

They fell silent, scrutinizing the circle. Then Buffy cocked her head as she heard a faint sound. "Did you hear something?"

"Yeah."

They both stood still, and listened. After a moment it came again, soft and distant yet perfectly distinct.

A female voice calling Buffy's name.

"It sounds . . . it sounds like Salma," Buffy said slowly. She started toward the circle.

Riley grabbed her arm, yanked her away. "No. Research, Buffy. Never a bad idea."

"Sometimes it slows things down," she said, frustrated. She was a Slayer and Slayers didn't research. Slayers acted.

"She's in there, Riley," Buffy said. "That much we know."

Riley shook his head. "And Sleepy Ramos went in there, or somewhere like there, and didn't come back out again. Think about it. It might be a one way trip.

"We find out more, Buffy. First."

"Find out more," Buffy echoed. "And then maybe it's too late?"

"And maybe by waiting, we don't die, or kill her by accident." He had on resolve-face, and in her sinking heart, Buffy knew he was right.

"You got it. Let's get help."

As they walked away from the glowing circle, they heard it again, more clearly than ever.

"*Buffy . . .*"

* * *

Buffy . . .

Angel dreamed, but in the dream, what he dreamed was real.

He was the only vampire on Earth possessed of a soul, and he was the only being on Earth who remembered a day . . . and a night . . . that had been lost.

Buffy . . .

She had come to Los Angeles to take him to task for "spying" on her in Sunnydale. He had understood her pain, and her confusion, known exactly why she had been so upset: she still loved him. She still wanted him.

Buffy and Angel were soul mates; no matter how many times he had lost his soul, and regained it, it was the other half of hers.

He had a beating heart, in Buffy's chest.

He walked in the sun, when she did.

Buffy . . .

He had become mortal, after the blood of a demon had touched him. For one day, he had known Buffy as a man knows a woman; he had loved her as a man, fully, desperately. What they had had before had been nothing compared to that twenty-four hours; heat and passion, yes, but the deepest of connections, the truest intimacy he had experienced—a connection that could not be severed, ever . . .

Except by his choice. Knowing full well everything he was losing, he asked the Oracles to take that day away; he sacrificed his mortality to save Buffy from a vendetta that eventually would kill her.

Buffy . . .

The scent of her, the smoothness and velvety warmth of her; the innocence and the courage and the deep love of her. She had forgotten it all; for her, at least consciously, the connection was severed when the day disappeared. She didn't remember it, any of it. She did not know that they had finally crossed all the bridges spanning the chasm between them.

He alone, bore the memory.

In his uneasy slumber, Angel wept.

And dreamed.

In Sunnydale, Buffy Summers felt a deep, strange tugging at her heart. For less than a heartbeat, she almost thought of something.

Then it was gone.

And the Slayer went on with her life.

Chapter 10

Sunnydale

IT HAD BEEN A WHILE SINCE GILES HAD PHONED ANGEL, and he hadn't known about his office blowing up. He got the new number from Buffy and dialed it. The phone rang twice before a female voice answered.

"Hello?"

"Cordelia?" he asked, smiling. "Is that you?"

"Well, given the Grand Central Station nature of my apartment lately, it could be me or it could be one of about a hundred other people. But I think I still know who I am, and I look like me from the neck down, which is pretty much all of me that I can see from here, so I'll venture a guess. Yes, it's me. And, judging by that very British stuffiness, and the fact that Wesley is sitting on my favorite part of my couch swilling all the tea in the building so it's not him, I'll venture another guess, and say, hello, Giles."

Same old Cordelia, he thought. *Never one to use a single word when a hundred or so might be applied.* "Um, hello, Cordelia. I trust you've been keeping well."

Unseen

"Oh, you know. Fighting demons and hanging out with the undead, what could be better?"

"Yes, right. The, um, Los Angeles social scene makes it into the Sunnydale newspapers, you know, so . . ."

Cordelia paused. "Giles, was that a joke?"

"Well, yes, as a matter of fact."

"I can never tell with you. Maybe if they were ever funny it'd be easier."

Giles changed the subject quickly. "Speaking of Wesley, is he available?"

"In the sense of not hooked up with anyone, or in the sense of can he come to the phone?"

"The latter, please."

"Here you go. Don't get him talking about the Queen Mum or anything, because I hate it when he gets all emotional on me."

"Thank you," Giles said, but he was talking to empty space. He heard a moment's shuffling, and a sound very much like a cup of tea being placed on a table.

"It's Giles," he heard Cordelia say. Buffy, Joyce, and Riley went out the front door to forage for something to eat—grocery shopping not currently a priority, given the siege state of Sunnydale—and to hazard a trip to the Summers's home for fresh clothing and to see if the monsters had destroyed it completely. Xander, Anya and Spike had set out to see if they could trace Cheryce. That was the stated objective at any rate: Giles had actually asked the couple to keep tabs on Spike, in case he was up to anything.

The house was empty, for the first time in weeks.

It's absolutely heavenly, Giles thought.

"I couldn't help overhearing," Wesley said. "The Queen Mum is an emotional topic for every Brit, Cordelia."

"God, you people are strange."

Giles could hear breathing over the phone, and Wesley's voice—the first time he had heard it in quite some time. There was a certain amount of mixed emotion about that. The two Watchers hadn't always agreed on things— or had they ever agreed on things? But each had, in his own way, the safety of his Slayer in mind at all times. "Hello, Giles. How're things?"

"Hello, Wesley, and God save the Queen." Giles replied, feeling a bit awkward. He didn't want to let on just how bad things were in Sunnydale, as if it would reflect poorly on his own abilities. "Things, um, could be better, I imagine. And you?"

"Well, the same, I suppose. Could be better, I mean." Giles supposed Wesley felt the same, wanting to downplay anything going on in his city.

"Right. Young people are still disappearing, then?"

"More than ever, I'd say."

"Quite the opposite here in Sunnydale, though. Things are . . . appearing, right and left. Manifestations of all sorts. But we don't seem to be having the disappearance problem that you are there."

"That's very odd," Wesley said. "That it's so localized. Almost as if the two were connected in some way. Like, like . . ."

"An intake and an outlet?" Giles prodded.

"Yes, precisely."

"I've begun to think along those lines as well," Giles said. He switched ears, moving the receiver around to the other side of his head. This would not, he believed, be a brief conversation. Talks with Wesley seldom were, he recalled. "Buffy swears she heard Salma de la Natividad calling her name through a . . . a portal of some kind."

"Really," Wesley said. "That *is* interesting."

"Buffy dreamed about doors," he added.

"Doorways. Portals. Entrances and exits," Wesley mused. "Yes, that would make sense. As much sense as anything else, at any rate. We're no closer to finding Nicky up here, either. Perhaps Buffy's heard his voice?"

"No." Giles pushed on his glasses. "Let's assume there's some route of passage—into or out of where, we haven't any idea. But your disappearing people are going somewhere, and our creatures are coming from somewhere. Possibly the same somewhere, possibly a completely different one."

"Perhaps our disappearing people are being transformed into your monsters."

"Certainly something to consider," Giles said. He realized that, in some ways, he missed having Wesley around to talk to. They had enough of the same life experience—for one thing, they were both on the outs with the Watchers Council—to have quite a bit in common, even beyond the England connection.

"The portal or whatever Buffy saw," Giles said. "She and Angel also saw one like it, there in Los Angeles. She kept him from going through it."

"Good girl," Wesley said. "We'll continue our work up here, then. Put on the pot and boil up some tea."

"Oh, yay, more tea," Cordelia drawled in the background. "Don't you *have* a bladder?"

"Right," Giles said.

"Tara's audible spell is quite useful," Wesley added. "You . . . you've a good grip on the situation down there, old man."

Old man. Yes, I suppose I am old. And feeling rather redundant these days.

"Thanks awfully," Giles said, without a hint of irony.

They said their good-byes and hung up. The house was dead silent.

Giles strode to his books and began running down the titles, as he always did.

"Purpose," he said wistfully. "Direction. Tea."

He got down to it.

The girl's name was Jacquee Anderson and she was crying so hard she slid to the floor. As she lay helplessly against the wall, Gunn turned to Angel.

"So you're saying, that dude in Sunnydale thinks they go in here and come out there?"

"Giles." Angel was looking at the girl. Her boyfriend, Marcus, had disappeared one block down from the American Legion Hall in Hollywood, where they had gone to a big charity event. Marcus worked with the Make-A-Wish Foundation, and he had gone ahead to get his Taurus.

Then, *poof!* He had vanished from sight.

Gunn owed Marcus, big time. Dude had gone to the mat many times for Gunn's people. Jacquee, who owned a small catering firm, had provisioned them more times than he could remember.

And with great food, too.

"Jacquee, I'm getting him for you," Gunn said.

Angel looked sharply at the man. "You're not going to Sunnydale."

"I'm getting her man for her," Gunn replied. "I'll do whatever I have to."

By nightfall, Giles had made progress. Doors and portals in myth and legend had limited significance, primarily serving as entrances or exits to some sort of Underworld. Even the Hellmouth right here in Sunnydale fell into that category, and nearly every belief system had something similar, whether it was the Christian Hell, the Hades of the ancient Greeks, or the sipapu of the Anasazi Indians, the opening that allowed them to move to this earth from their underworld, and presumably back again when they vanished from the planet centuries before.

Giles had nearly given up when he spotted a thin monograph he had almost forgotten he owned, half-hidden on the bookshelf between two larger volumes. "Within and Without: Being an Examination of Passageways Between the Realms of Light and Dark" had been written by an Italian named Tessitore, somewhere around 1650, and translated by two Welsh scholars named Roach and Collins in 1879. There had been a private printing of this version, of which fewer than a hundred copies were believed to exist. Giles owned one of these copies.

He sat down on the couch and began to read.

He had almost finished an hour later when Anya and Xander returned. He grunted some sort of greeting at them, and remained immersed in the monograph. A while after that, Buffy and Riley came in. Spike followed shortly after. The house took on the level of noise and chaos to which Giles was, sadly, becoming accustomed, but he tuned it all out.

He found the monograph fascinating. He was sorry he'd never taken the time to read it before.

Tessitore had postulated that all of the various underworlds and afterlives of myth and legend were real, though not necessarily located in the specific spots their believers had placed them. Hell was not necessarily beneath the crust of the Earth. Valhalla and Heaven were most likely not ensconced in the clouds above. But these places existed, and one could travel to them if one could only find the right doorways. Giles supposed that, had Tessitore been living in the beginning of the twenty-first century, he might have referred to his doorways as "wormholes," since they seemed to share some properties in common with that modern scientific theory. The very fabric of space/time could be folded in upon itself, so that one might move an incredible distance in space, time, or both in the blink of an eye, just by stepping in at one end and climbing out at the other.

Giles suspected that Tessitore might have had some inkling of the Ghost Roads, although probably he had never traveled them. But they might have fit into his theory—or they might have been solely responsible for the theory, and the portals with which they were now concerned wouldn't even enter into the discussion.

Impossible to tell without looking deeper, he thought.

And quite likely, the only way to look deeper was to go inside. Giles sat amidst the din, debating whether or not to even tell Buffy what he thought. If he told her, she might want to have a glance inside one of them, and if that happened, he might never see her again.

If he didn't, hundreds, maybe thousands, could die.

He agonized over the decision.

Finally, he told.

As expected—and feared—her response was to leave the house within moments of receiving the information. She tugged on Riley's arm. "We have to check this out," she insisted.

"Buffy," Giles said. "You will be—"

"I'm always careful," Buffy countered.

Giles touched his glasses, looking at her over the tops of his lenses. So deceivingly frail-looking, he realized. "Yes, but—"

"Carefuler I shall be," she assured him. "More careful than usual. Riley will be there to observe my carefulosity."

"That's fine, Buffy. Go. Hurry back."

"Thanks, Giles," she said. She gave his arm a quick squeeze. "Bye."

And then they were gone again, leaving him to his scholar's role. His Watcher's role.

I am the exposition, he thought. *She, the action. It's been this way ever since the Council of Watchers was formed.*

My job is to guide her, provide her with tools. That's what I do. That's who I am.

Then Spike swaggered in through the front door, gave him a contemptuous look, and began to pass by him on the way, Giles surmised, to the kitchen.

Giles grabbed his arm. Spike paused, looked down at Giles's clenched fist around his forearm and said, "Why, Rupert, time for schoolboy games, is it?"

"My Slayer is out there," Giles said through clenched teeth. "You are alive only through her deference to your helplessness. But you can still kill monsters."

"Been out all evenin', doing just that," Spike protested.

"I'm not sure what you've been doing," Giles said. "But if you don't go back out there, find Buffy, and help her, I will stake you next time I see you." Giles glared at him. "And that's a promise."

"Well." Spike moved his shoulders. "At least let me get something to drink out of the fridge."

"Nothing. Nothing for you while she's out there."

"Cheryce?" Spike asked hopefully. "Oh, you mean, the Buffs. Got it, mate." Spike shrugged off Giles's grip. "Cut off my circulation."

"You have none. Get out," Giles spat.

"Feeling a bit o' the ol' Viagra, eh?" Spike said. Then he went back out the front door.

Giles picked up a book, stared down at it, stared back at the door, and sighed.

Los Angeles

The business was called Got Game Card Room and Casino, and it purported to be open to the public, for poker, 21, and general games of chance. Members of the general public who wandered in, however, soon found out that they were neither welcome nor wanted, and no one ever went in more than once.

Unless they belonged.

The real reason for its existence was as a hangout—and money laundering front, since it was a cash-only business—for a Hispanic gang called the East Side Kings. The Kings had a close relationship with the Echo Park Band, and in fact Che's older sister had married a leader of the Kings in a big Catholic ceremony in Echo Park a year before.

Tonight, there were about a dozen Kings in the place, and a handful of Queens, their "women's auxiliary." They played cards lethargically, downed beer, joked and laughed. It was too hot outside to go out, and at least Got Game was air conditioned.

Just after midnight, three cars pulled up outside the club. They had covered the last block with no headlights on, and the dome lights inside the cars had been turned off as well. Anyone inside would have to have been listening closely to have heard the cars, since there was no light and the club's huge plate glass windows had been painted over, for privacy. But the air conditioning was blowing hard, music played, people chatted. No one inside noticed the cars.

Until the muzzle bursts from the car windows lit the night, and plate glass shattered and crashed in on the people sitting near the front windows. Bullets screamed through the casino, scattering chips, shredding green felt tabletops.

When the cars sped away, seven Kings and two Queens were dead, nine others wounded or cut by glass or flying debris. They hadn't even gotten a shot off at the cars.

Everyone inside knew the attack was a declaration of war.

Nicky de la Natividad didn't know about the attack on the casino.

He had an agenda of his own. He had a sister to rescue, and he had a city full of gangbangers who were, no doubt, after his hide by now.

He'd been down on Olympic. There was a *carniceria* down there where he knew the butcher. Nicky had done the guy favors now and again, and he'd returned the gesture when he could. Nicky had met him on shopping expeditions with his grandmother; she hated supermarkets, and would rather go from store to store to store gathering what she needed than set foot in one. But Nicky had overheard enough conversations between his grandmother and this butcher that he knew the butcher knew where his grandmother liked to buy the ingredients for some of her spells. Nicky knew the general neighborhood, but he couldn't remember what street it was on, or the exact name of the store. It wouldn't do to go into the wrong place and ask for scorpion pupae, for instance. Especially for a hunted man.

So he walked up to the *carniceria,* intending to just go inside and ask a couple of questions and split again. But before he reached the door, he saw two guys stroll around the corner and head his way. They wore baggy jeans and tee shirts, and one of them had a headband around his thick black hair. Both had dark shades over their eyes.

Nicky had seen these two before. Both were strapped. The tall guy carried his snug against the small of his back, in a little holster. The shorter one kept his in an ankle holster, invisible under those wide-legged pants.

There was no guarantee that they were looking for him. But there was no guarantee that they weren't.

Nicky made a quick one-eighty, on the chance that they hadn't recognized him yet, and ducked inside a laundromat up the block. He went to a dryer in the back and opened the door. With his head inside, he watched through the dryer's window as the two passed by the front, not even looking inside. When they were gone, he slammed the dryer shut.

There was a pay phone inside the laundromat, but a woman in a halter top and hot pants—a woman who, in Nicky's opinion, was spectacularly unsuited for either—was talking on it about her kids, her parents, her aches and pains. After giving her the evil eye for a couple of minutes, and being ignored, he walked right up to her.

"Look, lady, I got to make an important call."

"I'm sorry, I'm not finished with my call," she said.

"Yes, you are."

"No, I absolutely am not. No, Carol," she said into the phone. "Just a very rude young man who wants to use the—"

Nicky reached past her and put his finger on the disconnect. "Sorry, ma'am," he said sweetly. "But I guess you're done now."

She humphed at him and walked away, head high, shoulders up, as if he was something beneath her notice. He didn't care. He checked the coin return out of habit, and fed a handful of coins into the slot. Then he dialed a Sunnydale number.

In three rings, someone answered.

"Yeah."

"Little King? That you?"

"Yeah, hey, Nicky? Man, where you been, dude?"

"Here and there, you know? L. A."

"Everybody wants to know what you up to, Nicky. You coming back, or you joining up with Echo Park, or what?"

"I don't think I'm joining Echo Park," Nicky told him.

"Yeah, I don't think so either."

"What do you mean, King?"

"Oh, you know, man, you hear stuff, you don't ever know it's true or not."

"What have you heard?" Nicky demanded.

"Heard you're a marked man, Nicky. You got a price on your head. Echo Park wants you bad. What'd you do?"

"It's what I wouldn't do, King. Thanks for telling me, that's what I wanted to know. Got to know how hot I am."

"Hey, Nicky," Little King said. He paused for a moment, as if trying to find the words, then went on. "Hey, I wouldn't come home, either, I was you."

"What, the Cobras don't want me either? After I blew up that oil field for you?"

"Well, you know, man. We have an arrangement with Echo Park. So any enemy of theirs . . . you know what I mean."

"Yeah. Yeah, I guess I know," Nicky said. *The man without a country,* he thought. *No place to go. No place that's safe.* "Hey, can I talk to Rosalie, King? One last time, you know?"

Little King hesitated again.

"What is it, man," Nicky asked him.

"Umm, Rosalie's dead, Nicky."

Nicky felt the world fall away from beneath his feet. "What happened to her?"

"I don't really know. Like an accident or something."

Nicky knew Little King was lying. He also knew the man wouldn't tell him anything more. He was done with Nicky—the Latin Cobras were done with Nicky.

I did it for you, he thought. The whole Night of the Long Knives thing—his one night of magickally induced invulnerability—had been for the Cobras. He'd blown up Del DeSola's Sunnydale oil fields to enlist Del's help smuggling drugs on his ships, a partnership that would have made the gang millions.

And it all blew up in his face. Rosalie dead. Salma missing. He, Nicky, a wanted man—wanted by the cops, by the Echo Park Band, by his own *compadres* in the Latin Cobras.

How could it have all gone so wrong?

He stumbled from the laundromat, blinded by tears of rage. *Someone has to pay,* he thought. *Someone has to pay.*

Sunnydale

"Are you sure about this, Buffy?" Riley asked her when they had arrived back at the park by Santa Ysabel Street.

They looked at the portal, which had appeared again in the dark of night. It seemed to wink in and out of existence without notice, one moment not there at all, the next spanning the width of the roadway. As usual these days, the streets were virtually deserted, so its presence here didn't really qualify as a threat to the passing motorist or pedestrian.

Except that, in this case, the street was only devoid of humans.

Monster-wise, it was an outright population explosion.

They had turned onto Santa Ysabel four blocks away from where the portal had been seen before. Two blocks away from that, the monster throng began. It extended from there back to the portal itself, filling the street and overflowing onto the sidewalks. It looked like a creature convention, and more of them seemed to be emerging from the portal at every moment. They were unpleasant-looking beings of every description—large, small, tentacled, toothed, furred and finned—and every color imaginable, from pure white to deepest black to one of a beautiful iridescent blue, who seemed to be basically a seven-foot long centipede with as many fanged mouths as it had legs.

Riley had stopped the car and killed the lights. They still sat in the dark, discussing the questionable wisdom of wading into that bevy of beasthood. Buffy thought Riley seemed unusually cautious.

"Giles needs us to test it," Buffy urged. "Reading about them in books is all well and good, but he says we need some hands on—or at least hands close by—information, about the portals, since it seems like they're the focal point of all the activity."

Riley indicated the mass of monsters before them. "Yeah," he said. "No kidding. But I don't see how we're going to get close to it with all those things in the way."

"On the other hand—" she began.

"There's another hand?"

"Maybe a few. But this one says that we can't exactly just walk off and leave all those things there to terrorize the populace."

"I suppose not. But can we take on that many demons?"

Buffy looked at the two blocks of spookage before them. "We've faced worse odds."

Riley looked at her in the dim light of the car's interior. "When?"

Buffy shrugged uncertainly. "I think we have, anyway. Or, maybe not. But I don't think we have any choice."

Riley shook his head. "We could use the Initiative here."

"That'd be handy," Buffy agreed, "except that they're

scattered to the four corners. And we don't know how many of them we could really trust, even if they were around."

"Well, there's that."

"Anyway, we have to try to do something," Buffy continued. "What if there's some way of closing the door before more of those things get out? If there is, we need to find it. Fast."

"It could be dangerous," Riley observed. "You wouldn't just walk up on the Hellmouth without checking it out thoroughly first, would you?"

"If there were demons gushing out of it like a broken hydrant, I might."

"That's what I thought," Riley said. "Well, we have stakes. Swords. An ax or two."

Buffy attempted a confident smile, knowing even as she did that it wasn't coming off right. "On the bright side, it doesn't look like they're armed, really."

"Just teeth and fangs," Riley agreed. "And sheer numbers."

"They got us there."

Buffy leaned over and kissed Riley. "Let's do it," she said. She opened her car door—right into the face of the vampire who stood outside, watching through the window.

"Hey!" Spike shouted. "Have a care. That's my nose you just slammed your door into. I might need it again someday."

"What are you doing there, Spike?" Buffy demanded without preamble.

"I got back to Giles's place and he told me you might be needin' some assistance," Spike said. He shrugged, in his usual black leather trenchcoat. "I may not be able to prey on humans, but there's nothin' says I can't beat the

207

snot out of a bunch of interdimensional uglies, or what-ever that lot is. Lookin' forward to it, in fact."

"We can use the help, Spike," Riley said as he emerged from his side of the car.

"I'm not doin' this for you, soldier boy," Spike said.

"I don't care why you're doing it," Buffy assured him "Just that you're here."

"What are we standin' here jawin' for?" Spike asked, bouncing a bit and shadowboxing. "We're gonna do it, let's do it."

Riley passed out weapons. Each of them tucked some stakes into handy spots in their clothing. Spike tried to refuse to have anything to do with stakes at first, but quickly saw the wisdom of carrying a few, just in case. He also took a double-headed battleax. Buffy and Riley both settled for swords with broad, flat blades, sharpened on both edges.

"Let's kill some," she said through clenched teeth.

"I'm with you," Spike offered. Riley was silent.

The three of them started for the monsters.

They had closed to within less than a block when one noticed them, a green, dripping thing that hopped rather than walked, on powerful hind legs not unlike a kanga-roo's. It let out a piercing squawk, pointing at them with its three skinny arms.

"They're onto us," Riley observed, hefting the sword in his hand. "Here we go."

They braced for battle, and they heard someone behind them call out, "Guys! Hey guys! Buffy!"

Buffy turned. Anya and Xander ran toward them. Anya had dressed for battle in a yellow floral sundress and san-dals. Xander wasn't much better prepared in his orange and white hockey jersey and khakis. "What are you doing here?" she asked.

As soon as Xander began his answer, she knew what he would say. "Giles thought maybe you could use some help."

"He was wrong," Buffy insisted.

"He was right," Riley corrected. "Buffy, we can use every hand we can get."

"Riley, they're—" She looked at Xander and Anya. Xander looked crestfallen at her ready dismissal of his usefulness. Anya wouldn't care one way or another, but Xander really did mean well, she knew. And he had been helpful in the past, and brave, and very very loyal. *He is,* she thought, *most of the Boy Scout oath rolled into one slightly accident-prone guy, excepting perhaps the reverent part.* "Weapons are in the car!" she shouted. "It's open!"

Risking a glance over her shoulder, she saw Xander handing a crossbow to Anya and holding an ax for himself. She turned back, ready to do battle.

By now, of course, the creatures had prepared for them. But they were caught off guard when Anya's crossbow bolts began sailing over their heads into the creatures' midst. A couple went down, and general alarm sounded in a variety of monster tongues.

Buffy steeled herself with the memory of the face she'd found on the street earlier, and the knowledge that these creatures wouldn't think twice about killing all of Sunnydale if it suited them. They had shown no mercy, and they had terrorized her town, leaving dozens of corpses in their wake.

They would die. Simple.

She charged into them, blade swinging in a furious arc. It bit into creature flesh, and thick green blood spattered her forehead. The first monster, a gangly many-tentacled squid-looking thing, fell before her assault. As soon as it dropped, there were two more, snapping and reaching for her with clawed appendages. She lowered the sword blade and swung up, slicing one of those appendages off. It sailed backward, into the monstrous throng. Another grabbed at her, snagging her long-sleeved black tee with one of its claws. Buffy squirmed from its grasp and spun the sword around in her hand, bringing it up with an underhanded grip to slice the beast open from the bottom up.

Over the top of a basically cat-shaped creature with battleship gray scaly skin, Buffy caught a glimpse of Riley. He swept his own sword at head-height, carving a swath around himself. Heads flew and monster blood jetted into the night air. On the other side of him, Spike worked with his ax like a carpenter driving nails, arm pistoning a steady rhythm. Something almost like a smile danced about his lips, but his eyes were hard.

Buffy went back to paying attention to her own situation. A tall, powerfully built humanoid thing came at her, pushing away smaller creatures in its mad desire for what she could only assume was her blood. A line of spittle connected its upper teeth with its lower, and its mouth opened wide enough to swallow a football whole.

She braced herself for its attack, holding the sword in both hands, against her side. When the beast came in range, she thrust it forward with all her might. The blade tore through its armored flesh.

The creature stopped in its tracks, glared down at the sword that penetrated it, and grabbed the weapon by the blade. It tugged the sword from its body and threw it to the ground, then looked at Buffy, its yellow eyes gleaming.

She didn't like what she saw in them.

Instead of letting it take the offensive, she took a double step forward and leaped into the air, lashing out with a strong right foot at its throat. It brought a hand up to block her, and managed to catch her heel and overturn her in midair. She hit the ground hard, on her shoulder. As it doubled over to reach for her, she shoved off, sending both feet directly into its chin. Taken by surprise this time, it wasn't able to block her, and the blow sent it staggering backward. Buffy regained her balance and kept up the attack, with a swift combination of punches and kicks. Its razored teeth grazed her knuckle once, drawing blood, but she jerked her hand away and replaced it with a booted foot. She felt teeth crumple beneath her heel, and when she drew her foot away, blood ran from its nose and that huge mouth. It seemed unsteady on its feet now.

But as she spent her time on it, other creatures were surrounding her. She felt hands grasping for her, heard their moans and grunts and growls close to her. She needed to finish this guy off in a hurry. She feinted another kick, and he fell back. She dove for the sword, still on the ground where he had thrown it. When she got her footing again, she feinted one more time, this time flicking the blade toward his gut. His arms went down to protect it, and she brought the blade up, driving it straight into his throat. It came out the other side, coated in his thick blood. Still, his strong hands clutched at the blade, so Buffy turned it forty-five degrees before she drew it out.

At last, the monster fell. Buffy wasted no time swinging the blade in a semicircle around herself, and the other creatures fell back. A couple fell from bolts fired by Anya's crossbow, and when she hazarded a glance back she saw Xander battling one with his ax. His opponent fell, and Xander unleashed a war whoop.

Then she sensed Riley beside her, breathing heavily. With bits of monster stuck to his face and clothes, he smelled like an open sewer, but his presence there was comforting.

Then a fresh swarm rushed them both, slamming them both to the ground. Buffy shouted, "Riley!" but she couldn't see him past leathery legs and taloned feet. Something stepped on her back and something else stepped on both her hands. She was pinned.

She gave herself a moment to collect her wits, then worked hard to push herself up. No good.

A human shout of pain sent Slayer adrenaline to her Slayer muscles and she gritted her teeth together as she pushed up again.

Then something grabbed her hair in its teeth and started yanking.

She heard another human shout, and then gunshot.

Whatever had her hair in its mouth toppled to the ground, landing beside her with a heavy thump.

A hand gripped her upper arm and hauled her to her feet.

"Slayer?" asked a good-looking guy she didn't recognize. "Gunn."

She gave him a nod, and they got to work. Gunn was good, and it was clear he was on board with the fighting. They slammed and punched and kicked their way to Riley, got him free, and everybody got down tonight.

Finally, there was a bit of a break, and Buffy found herself next to Riley with nothing to hit.

"They're on the run," he panted.

She looked up, and he was right. Their number had been decimated, and the survivors raced for whatever protection the portal might offer them. Spike, dripping with sweat and ichor, chased after them, ax swinging like a mad woodcutter chasing runaway timber.

"Let's go," she said. She and Riley took off after Spike.

He had made it almost to the portal itself when they caught him. Buffy risked the ax's backswing to catch his shoulder, just before he jumped into the portal after a retreating reptilian-looking beastie.

"Don't do it, Spike," she warned.

He shook her hand off angrily, spinning around and raising the ax before he really focused on who was there. When he saw Buffy he relaxed, lowering the weapon to his side.

"Guess I got a little carried away with the Conan bit," he said. "Gotta say, it felt good to spill some blood again, even if most of it came in funny colors and stank like old cabbage."

Riley picked off a bit of brain that had adhered to his forehead. He examined it briefly, then threw it into the portal. "Yeah," he agreed. "It's a messy business, isn't it?"

"Guess that's why Martha Stewart's not a Slayer," Buffy offered. She gestured to the newcomer in their midst. "This is Gunn."

He nodded. They nodded. Much with the nodding.

Gunn said, "Is that a portal, like Jowls told Angel about?"

Spike snickered. "Jowls," he repeated. "So what now? We just leave 'em in there?"

"Not much else we can do," Buffy replied. "As long as they're not making trouble for Sunnydale, they're no concern of ours."

"Of yours, maybe," Spike said, rubbing a triple-gash on his forearm. "One of them clawed me, and I never got a chance to rip his guts out."

"Chances are he'll be back," Riley suggested. "In the meantime, we have to do an experiment while the portal is still here."

"That's right," Buffy said. She dashed off into a nearby

yard, and returned bearing a small branch with leaves on the end. "This ought to do."

"Giles said as long as it was organic," Riley pointed out. "I think he was kidding about using a cat on a string."

"You can never be too sure with him," Xander said. He and Anya approached from the direction of the car. Xander balanced the ax over his shoulder, and Anya still carried the crossbow, loaded, as if more monsters might appear at any time.

Buffy held the branch at one end and pushed it through the portal. There was a moment's resistance, almost like trying to pass through water, or maybe Jell-O. But once it crossed beyond that initial film, it went in easily, the part inside the portal disappearing the way Sleepy Ramos had when he went through, back in L.A. She held it there for a moment, then brought it back out.

It didn't look like the same branch that had gone in. The leaves were gone, the wood splintered and smoldering. Something violent had happened to it on the other side, and Buffy, holding the end, hadn't felt a thing.

"Glad I didn't go in there," Spike said.

"No kidding," Anya agreed. "You'd look disgusting all chewed up and set on fire."

Spike gave her a look. "Thanks."

"You're welcome," she replied cheerfully.

Gunn looked frustrated. "So, there's no one going in, no one coming out, huh?"

Buffy tossed the mangled branch away. "You care because?"

"I got some people disappeared," he said simply.

"Did Angel send you here?" Riley asked. His voice was controlled, and probably no one but Buffy realized it cost him something—in pride, if nothing else—to ask.

Gunn shook his head. "Man didn't want me to bother. Looks like he might have been right." He looked at Buffy. "What's the plan?"

"I guess we should go tell Giles. I wonder if that's what he was expecting." As they walked back toward the cars, Buffy glanced over her shoulder at the portal, which seemed to be fading from sight again. Like Spike, she was happy that she hadn't had to go through.

And that I kept Angel from doing it, she thought. *Guess he owes me one.*

Chapter 11

Los Angeles

"TELL ME AGAIN WHAT WE'RE DOING HERE, ANGEL?" Cordelia asked. *But,* Angel thought, *her asking sounds more like pleading.* "I mean, I know this is the kind of place you hang out at night, but it's not, you know, really my preferred sort of evening activity."

They were in downtown Los Angeles, walking up and down the streets of a neighborhood that was, according to the beat cops, controlled by the Russian Mafiya.

"We're looking for clues," Angel said, trying to be patient with her. He knew she was afraid, but he wanted more than one set of eyes to be on the lookout, and Wesley was on research duty for a while—and anyway, there was always the likelihood that some people would rather talk to a pretty girl than to a vampire. Working with Buffy, that had proven true a number of times. He pushed that thought aside, though—he didn't want to be thinking about Buffy right now. He wanted to be alert, ready for whatever might come up.

Anyway, he also knew that Cordelia was plenty brave—he had seen her act with unconscious courage that surprised everyone who knew her—but that it wasn't really part of how she saw herself. Cordelia believed herself to be a coward who would rather hide from confrontation than face her fears.

But that was a flaw in her self-image, not a fact of who she was. She had proven herself to be one of the bravest people Angel had ever known in his long and strange life. When he had asked her to come along, she had done so without a moment's hesitation, only asking once they were in the car what they were setting out to do. He'd explained that they were going to hunt down Vishnikoff.

"Why do we want Vishnikoff?" she had wanted to know.

"He's up to something bad," Angel replied. "I don't know what. But he's somehow a link between the Mafiya and those crooked cops I told you about, and whatever it is he's working on is enough to terrify L.A.'s finest."

Cordelia chuckled insincerely. "You're being sarcastic, right? Quote marks around the 'L.A.'s finest' part?"

"That's right. But dirty or not, those guys are cops—and probably killers. If they're scared of Vishnikoff, then he must be pretty scary."

"They're scared of *you*," Cordelia pointed out.

"That's what I mean."

Now they walked the streets of this neighborhood, and she had a look of some concern on her face. "Maybe I'm missing something," she said, "but how are we supposed to find clues out here? Aren't they, like, in the den with the candlestick? Shouldn't we have a magnifying glass and a really funny-looking hat?"

"There are two ways to look for clues, Cordelia," Angel informed her. He understood her concern, intellectually. But he found walking night streets as natural as most people did breathing. He had spent the centuries on them, in one city after another, from continent to continent. "You ask people questions, and then when you get their answers, that gives you more questions to ask of the next people, until you find someone who knows something."

"Sounds boring," Cordelia said.

"Generally. But it's how most police work is done."

"You said there were two."

"Right. The other way is to stir up trouble in the bad guy's backyard. Eventually, he'll find you."

Cordelia looked at the tall, dark buildings around them. An empty cab cruised slowly down the street, passing them and turning at the corner. "And this is Vishnikoff's backyard?"

"We don't know yet where his backyard is," Angel said. "So this is mix-and-match. We'll stir up trouble until we find the people we can ask questions of."

"How very scientific," Cordelia observed. "You know, I could be in the safety of my own apartment right now."

"Doing research in some of Wesley's dusty old books."

"Point taken. Where are those pesky Russian gangsters, anyway? Let me at 'em."

They reached a corner, made a right turn. "They're around," Angel said. "They just haven't wanted to be seen yet." Then he stopped short and touched Cordelia's arm, pointing to a shadowed doorway up ahead. He thought he'd seen some kind of movement there.

"Hang back a little," he whispered.

Cordelia nodded, but her idea of hanging back seemed to mean hovering six inches from Angel's back. He thought she'd be safe enough there, so he left her alone and approached the darkened doorway. It led into an office building, but the offices were closed and the doors presumably locked, so whoever or whatever he had seen going in would probably still be there. Unless, of course, they had a key.

He hoped for Russian gangsters, someone who might be able to supply an address for this Vishnikoff, whoever he was. But when he stepped into the entryway, he saw two frightened girls, younger than Cordelia, huddled together against the glass doors. One of them was tiny and black, with a build like a figure skater or a gymnast. The other was blond and a head taller, but also thin as a rail.

"Sorry," he said. "Thought you were someone else."

"Jean?" Cordelia asked from behind him. "Nicole?"

"We didn't do nothing," the blond one said. Her voice was piercing; Angel figured anyone working late in any of the buildings on the block could hear her protestations.

"Yeah, so just leave us be," the black girl added.

"No problem," Angel said. He looked at Cordelia. "You know these girls?"

"No," the loud blonde insisted. "Nobody knows us."

"They're friends of Kayley Moser," Cordelia said. "They're some of the library girls I told you about. You know, the vampy wannabes."

The girls remained huddled in the corner of the doorway. Cordelia approached them. "Don't you remember me, Nicole?" she asked. "Jean? I'm Cordelia Chase? I bought you food, and saved you from the vampires."

"We never seen you before," Nicole stated flatly.

"That's right," Jean agreed. "Don't know what you're talking about."

"This is them," Cordelia told Angel. "I'm not wrong."

Angel led her away from the girls. "They're scared of something," Angel said. "Terrified. I don't think they'll admit to knowing anyone."

"But . . . but I was good to them."

"Maybe they're just not used to that," Angel suggested. "Let's leave them alone. They don't want our help."

"Are you sure?"

"He's right," Nicole bellowed. "Can't anybody see us anyway. Just go on and leave us alone."

"What, they think they're invisible?" Cordelia asked.

"They might as well be," Angel said, "as far as the rest of the world is concerned. It's probably safer for them that way."

Cordelia gave in, and Angel continued down the sidewalk in the same direction they had been going. *Still no Russians,* he thought. *Which is probably just as well, since those girls back there look like prime victim material.*

When he was almost to the next corner, he noticed that Cordelia was no longer beside him. He turned, and saw her leaning against a building, holding her head in her hands. Clearly in pain. He hurried back to her. Her face had gone alabaster white and a line of perspiration had broken out along her hairline.

"Vision . . ." she managed. "Head splitting open . . ."

He held her for a moment, until the pain subsided. "Better now?"

"Better," she breathed. "I may not chop my head off, after all. This time."

"What'd you see?" he asked her.

"Not much to go on," she said. "A boy. Teens, maybe twenty. Thick blond hair. Nice build. I'd date him."

"Cordelia, what's his problem? How do we find him?"

"No idea, and ditto. All I got was the picture of him, and his name. Mischa."

"That's a Russian name," Angel said.

"So it is." Cordelia nodded. "Oh. Okay. Russians. Got it."

Sunnydale

Back to HQ: Gunn got introduced; the mangled branch got discussed; and Giles's response was a measured "Hmmm."

Buffy and Riley wanted to head back out to see if the monsters they'd fought were an isolated bunch, or if tonight was a particularly bad night for them.

"Just because we chased a bunch of those ghoulies back into their hole doesn't mean there aren't others around," Buffy said.

"Or vampires," Riley reminded her.

"I'd almost forgotten about them," Buffy admitted. "Doesn't seem like we've heard much from them lately."

"I don't think they get along with those interdimensional thingies," Spike said. "I know they give me the heebie-jeebies."

"Well, that's a plus," Buffy said. "We'll have a look around and see what's out there."

"You do that," Spike said. "I've got to get back out and . . . fight, fight, fight."

"Okay," Anya volunteered. "We can do that, too."

"Ann, we just fought half a million monsters," Xander complained.

"There weren't more than forty or fifty," Anya countered. "And Buffy and Riley fought most of them. You probably didn't kill more than half a dozen."

"Still . . ." Xander pouted.

"Yeah, and I helped, didn't I?" Spike said. "I held up my end of the deal."

"Yes. And Mr. Gunn, too." Anya smiled at the new guy. "Okay, Xander, you don't have to come. I'm going, though. And I'm sure Giles will."

Giles had been rubbing his eyes, his glasses held

loosely in his left hand. "Hmm? Oh, certainly. I mean . . . yes, I can do that."

"It's settled, then," Anya said. "Are you coming, or not, Xander?"

Xander gave in. "I guess so."

Buffy and Riley left before the conversation could turn back into an argument.

Gunn said softly, "I'm in," and trailed after the duo.

As expected, Sunnydale seemed quiet, almost somnolent—the way it was on good nights, before the sudden influx of monsters from who-knew-where. There were nights that Buffy spent dusting one vamp after another, and there were nights when her patrol was nothing more than a good brisk walk through a sleeping town. This night seemed like the latter. The kind of night, she remembered, when she and Angel had just walked and talked all night long—okay, the occasional pause for kissing, but then back to the walking and talking. In a way, those already seemed like long ago days, when she'd been much younger and more innocent.

Just the difference between high school and college? she wondered. *Or something more?*

"So this is the famous Sunnydale," Gunn said. "Doesn't seem so bad."

"Looks can be deceiving," Riley replied.

"You got that right." Gunn was doing a good job of surveillance, and Buffy was glad he was along.

Passing through town, they spotted Willy's Place, and from the number of cars and motorcycles parked in front, it looked like it was doing a banner business. Riley looked at Buffy, who shrugged. "Worth stopping in, I guess," she said.

He agreed, so the three made their way through the cars and into the front door.

There were a couple of clutches of demons drowning

their sorrows at tables, imbibing whatever kind of brew Willy concocted for them. Random solo drinkers, maybe human and maybe not, stood at the bar. But at one table sat eight Hispanic-looking guys, tense, shoulders hunched, some talking, some sitting in silence with glum expressions. Their clothes were a mix of denim, plaid, and white cotton. Empty bottles filled their table. A couple of the men had tattoos on their muscular arms that said "L.C."

Buffy nodded toward them, and whispered to Riley and Gunn, "Latin Cobras."

"Wonder what brings them here."

"Not a celebration," Buffy observed.

Willy had spotted Buffy and pals coming in. He rolled his eyes and ran a hand through his dark hair, the very picture of exasperation. Buffy set her sights on him and made a beeline for the bar.

"My favorite Slayer," he said ruefully.

"Save it, Willy. What's up with the Cobras? They look like they just came from a funeral."

"Only they don't know yet whose funeral it was," Willy said.

"What's that supposed to mean?" Riley asked.

Willy glanced nervously at the Cobras, then bent over the bar and spoke in hushed tones. "War," he said. "The Russian gangs and the Mexican gangs in L.A. have gone to war. So far, it's mostly confined to L.A., but the Cobras have associations there, a treaty with a gang called the Echo Park Band. They might have to go over to L.A. to help out—or the Russians might come here. Either way, blood's gonna spill."

Buffy frowned. She'd left Angel back in L.A. to deal with things there—well, Angel and Willow, to keep working with Doña Pilar.

I'd better check in on them ASAP.

It was only then that the other aspect of what Willy had said sunk in. A gang war in Sunnydale, on top of the bizarre demonic incursion already taking place, could be catastrophic. Her influence over the town was mostly limited to dealing with supernatural assault, but she didn't want to see its streets overrun with ordinary human violence, either.

"Do me a favor and don't hassle 'em," Willy continued. "They're on edge. You start tryin' to rough 'em up, bullets are gonna fly, and you know that's bad for business."

"I won't touch them," Buffy promised. "But what do you think—are the Russians really going to come to Sunnydale?"

"I'm going home," Gunn said suddenly.

"Home?" Buffy asked. "You barely got here."

"I know," Gunn said. He didn't look happy about his decision. "And I need to bring Marcus home, for Jacquee. For myself. But my people, they live on the streets, you know? There's a gang war in the making, people are going to get hurt. My crew, they'll be in the target zone. Anything happened to them while I was out here in the burbs, I'd never forgive myself."

Riley nodded at him. "We'll keep in touch. If we find something out about the portals, we'll call immediately."

Riley held out his hand. Gunn took it.

"Not if," Gunn said. "When."

They locked gazes, two soldiers.

"Right."

Gunn turned on his heel.

"Welcome to Sunnydale," Del DeSola said, "and the home that oil built." He held his arms open expansively as his guests filed into his den. A butler had met Teodor Nokivov and seven soldiers at the door of the palatial home and invited them inside, where two armed men had frisked them. Nokivov told his troops to give up their weapons. He assured them that they would be safe inside DeSola's house.

"Thank you, Mr. DeSola," Teodor Nokivov said as he shook his host's hand. "It's a pleasure to be here."

"Getting out of the city is always a pleasure," DeSola responded. This was how he liked to receive guests—when they were expected and came in properly escorted—not after first killing his guard detail, the way Cheryce had done. He was still waiting to hear from her, see what kind of progress she was making for the cash advance he had given her.

"I rarely do," Nokivov said. "First Moscow, now Los Angeles. Apparently I'm not comfortable away from large cities."

"I hope you'll be comfortable here," DeSola said. He ushered Nokivov to a chair. Before he sat, Nokivov excused the soldiers, except for one, a big man with a deeply lined face and long hair pulled into a tight ponytail, whom he introduced as Karol Stokovich. Stokovich took a seat behind Nokivov, who sank into a rich leather recliner. DeSola sat across from him on a leather sofa. Before him was a modern glass coffee table with a clear drink on it. DeSola rattled the ice cubes in his glass.

"A drink?" he asked. "Vodka?"

"Nothing for me, thank you," Nokivov replied. Stokovich didn't answer and it was clear that he didn't really count. This was a meeting between DeSola and Nokivov, with Stokovich here only to watch his boss's back.

Nokivov studied DeSola as he drank from the crystal tumbler. Wealthy people look different from the rest of humanity, and DeSola was clearly wealthy. In his sixties, he was powerfully built, as if he spent a lot of time in the gym with a personal trainer. His handsome face had probably been lifted once, Nokivov thought, and his hair had been darkened to hide the gray. Only the weariness and wisdom of his sad brown eyes belied his age. He wore a two-thousand-dollar suit by Perry Ellis, cut a little youthfully for his actual age but appropriately for the age he pretended to, and boots that Nokivov recognized as Prada.

Smacking his lips, DeSola set the glass back down on the coffee table. "We have something in common, you and I," he said.

"We do indeed."

"The Latin Cobras and the Echo Park Band, among others, have taken something valuable from both of us. They cost me an oil field, and now they are harassing my warehouses."

"And they cost me my son," Nokivov said.

"My understanding is that this is not the case," DeSola told him. "I have it on good authority that your son was not killed by my countrymen at all, but by four police officers—the ones who arrested the suspect who was later released by the district attorney."

Nokivov was stunned by this revelation. "Are you sure about this?"

"My sources are good," DeSola said. "I have interests in several communities. This is the word I get. I would not say this just because I also am from Mexico—if anything, the assault on my interests by my own people has soured me on those criminals even more."

Nokivov sat in silence for a moment. He looked at Stokovich, who shrugged almost imperceptibly. Stokovich knew as well as he did that those four police officers were on his own payroll; though the checks had the name Vishnikoff on them, it all ultimately came from the same source. Nokivov was the chief "fund raiser" for the effort in southern California—he ran the rackets that brought in the money. He had to be kept at a remove from the dispensation of it. But if this was the case, if the police officers were at fault, then a lot of blood had been spilled for nothing.

In the past week, a state of all-out war had broken out between the Russian and Mexican crime interests. In Culver City, a safe house operated by his people had been compromised and a dawn attack, with automatic weapons and hand grenades, had cost the lives of nine valued soldiers. In Hermosa Beach, the Russians had retaliated against a Mexican restaurant known as a hangout of some of the upper-echelon Mexican leaders, burning the place to the ground on a busy Friday night. In both Russian and Mexican neighborhoods, drive-by shootings had become commonplace.

"If what you say is true," Nokivov said, "then I have much to answer for. I have declared war, in the name of my son, against people who had nothing to do with his death."

DeSola shook his head. "You have declared war against people whose business interests run counter to your own," he said. "You were at an impasse—business could not continue to grow as long as they controlled the neighborhoods and the industries that they did. You need more than insurance fraud, extortion, banks and heroin. You need marijuana, cocaine, prostitution, the automobile trade. True?"

Nokivov inclined his head. "Yes, of course."

"Then war was inevitable," DeSola said bluntly. He spoke with his hands. "The final trigger doesn't matter—it had to happen. And now that it has, it must be won."

"And your interest in this is purely revenge?" Nokivov asked, settling back into his chair, as if he anticipated a long conversation.

"Not purely," DeSola said, shrugging. He waved a

hand to indicate his lavish home, then leaned forward as if he were about to take Nokivov into his confidence. "I am a legitimate businessman. Oil, shipping, real estate—I don't need the criminal activities that they do. They believe that since I am a Mexican, I should be on their side."

He grunted and shook his head wearily. "In fact, having them running all over the landscape committing crimes puts me in a worse position—it casts an unfavorable spotlight on all Mexican and Mexican-American business activities."

Nokivov said, "The same as with the Italians."

"Yes. I have ships delayed all the time because DEA agents are searching them from stem to stern looking for drugs. People in my employ are stopped by INS agents because of their skin and hair color, when they're trying to get to work or running errands for me. I pay my people well, and it's insulting to them and to me to be treated this way."

"But you do not seek redress within the Mexican power structure?"

"Neither within it, nor outside of it," DeSola countered. "I understand the historical forces at work here, and the economic ones. My people have come to California for generations, seeking fortune, a better life." He looked pensive for a moment, perhaps remembering his own family history. Nokivov respected his silence, and waited for the other man to continue.

"They don't always find it," DeSola said softly. "They move into ghettos, or purely Mexican neighborhoods. There are turf wars. They are unemployed, or underemployed, and they turn to crime to feed their families, to put bread upon their tables. Their fathers, their uncles, their brothers were in these gangs, and they grow up in them."

"As with the original Mafia," Nokivov asserted again.

"I understand it," DeSola went on, "but I don't like it

and I want to see an end to it in my lifetime. This is where you come in. There has never been a criminal organization like yours in the United States. You have the potential to break the back of the Mexican gangs once and for all— to liberate my people from generations of servitude." He'd thought about this a lot, and had come to the conclusion that the criminal gangs would continue as long as there was profit to be gained. He wanted to cut into that profit, to make it more expensive to stay in a gang than to get out of it and go into legitimate business. If that meant that the Russians controlled the nation's criminal interests, that was all right with him. He knew somebody would. He just didn't want it to be his people. "I want you to do this," he said.

"It will mean that many will die," Nokivov promised him.

"That many more will live free of this scourge," DeSola said firmly. "It's worth it to me."

"How do you propose to help us in this action?"

DeSola rose and crossed to a large safe that stood on the floor behind his desk. He spun the dial quickly, and opened it. He removed a large canvas bag from inside it, brought the bag back to the glass-topped coffee table, and unzipped it.

It was filled with hundreds.

"This is a million dollars," he said. "Consider it a down payment. I have forty-nine more bundles like this, set aside. Fifty million dollars cash. With that money, I expect that you can buy the best weapons, and soldiers to use them. Information. Intelligence. The law. The courts. I don't care if they die or go to jail—I just want them gone. Echo Park, the Latin Cobras here in Sunnydale, the Inglewood Raza . . . all of them. You can start with the Cobras, though."

"You understand that I do have an agenda of my own,"

Nokivov said, intrigued by this man's proposition . . . and by his money.

"Of course." DeSola gazed at him. "I believe that your agenda complements my own. I don't think there's anything you want that would inhibit you from acting toward what I want."

Nokivov thought. He didn't think DeSola was wrong. And he could certainly use DeSola's money. The industrialist was right—fifty million could buy a lot of help, and he saw a certain poetic justice to taking it from the hands of a pure capitalist.

He accepted the bag from DeSola's hands and forced it closed around the bulging stacks of cash, zipping it tight. It was heavy—ten thousand hundred-dollar bills had real weight.

"We have an agreement, then," he said. He extended his hand, and DeSola accepted it.

With this kind of backing, the war might be brief indeed. And when it was over, Teodor Nokivov would be the undisputed crime boss of southern California.

Then the real work could begin.

Chapter 12

Los Angeles, 2000

ALINA VISHNIKOFF SCRUBBED HER FACE, DRIED IT ON A
fluffy towel, and then left the bathroom. She had her own
bedroom and her own bathroom, and while these rooms
didn't look like the rooms she'd seen on television, she
understood from her parents that this sort of luxury had
been virtually unknown when they had grown up in the
Soviet Union. She had complained, saying that the rooms
on TV shows were much more colorful and lively, filled
with posters and pillows and stuffed animals, and why
couldn't she go shopping for some of those things? Her
father had responded by taking the television out of the
house altogether, and telling her she had work to do.

Alina always had work to do. It was, in many ways, the
only life she had ever known. She knew that other six-
teen-year-olds went to school. She never had. Her mother
and father had taught her what they thought was important that she know—Russian and English, Soviet history,
mathematics and science. This had all taken place in the

house here at Mount Vernon and Fairway—her memory of life before coming to America, of living in Bulgaria in that tiny, cramped apartment above a butcher shop, was limited to brief flashes that rose in her memory now and again.

Before she went into the lab this morning—now that her mind had been set down this path by the fluffy richness of the towel, one of the few capitalist luxuries her parents allowed themselves—Alina returned to her room. All of the necessities were there, but little else: a bed, a closet for her clothes, a dresser for other things, a bookshelf for her textbooks, a desk at which to study. In the desk there was a drawer, and on the bottom of the drawer—underneath the bottom, so she had to pull it out, empty it, and turn it over—she had taped a photograph. Alina knew enough about American teenagers to know that most of them would have taped a singer or an actor, a celebrity of some kind, there, if one were going to tape anything. But celebrities meant nothing to Alina Vishnikoff—even when she heard the names, she had little idea who they were or what they represented.

The picture Alina had taped there, torn discreetly from a magazine that some visitor or worker had left in the house, was of a place. This place was called, according to the magazine, the Grand Canyon. The Grand Canyon, she gathered, was a special place to Americans, and she could see why. It was an amazing sight—a vast rip in the fabric of the Earth, a mile across and immensely deep.

In this photo she couldn't see the whole thing; it clearly extended beyond the photograph's borders in both directions, and the bottom wasn't even visible. There were some gnarled evergreen trees in the foreground, and then the earth just dropped away, and across the enormous expanse there was a far wall, with striations of red and pink and brown and white.

She had studied enough geology at her parents' direction to know that she was looking at a geologic record of the planet itself, each band of color representing some era in which sediment piled up atop the last layer. She suspected the whole thing had been revealed over the eons by the river cutting through the middle of it—a powerful river indeed, if it were true. That, or an earthquake of impossible magnitude, were the only forces she could imagine would have torn the Earth's crust in that way.

In addition to the purely geological spectacle the picture represented, and the evidence of incredible forces beyond any control of humankind, there was a third aspect to it that drew her—there were no people in evidence. Certainly one had taken the photo, and the assumption she gathered from the bits of the article she had seen was that the Grand Canyon was much visited by people from across the globe. But there were no human habitations present.

Alina had never been—except crossing the ocean in an airplane, a trip of which she had little memory—in a place from which one could not see the houses of others. She had never stood on a spot where all you could see in every direction were the works of nature instead of man. *Someday,* she thought, *I should like to stand there, just there where the photographer stood, and turn in a circle and see nothing, nothing at all, that was built by people.*

As she dreamt about it, her gaze happened to fall on the simple dial clock that stood on her desk, and she realized she was perilously close to being late to the lab. She hurriedly replaced the drawer and tossed the contents back into it. She'd reorganize them later.

She shut the drawer and rushed across the house to the lab, which was downstairs in a room that would once have been a dining room. The upstairs was family space, but the downstairs had been transformed over the years into a warren of offices, file rooms, computer rooms, and the lab. From the outside the house looked like any suburban ranch house, but on any given day more than a dozen people worked inside it.

Today, she had been told, would be the beginning of something big. The People's Project would—finally, her father said with a beaming smile—reach fruition.

She was late, and her parents were waiting for her when she got there. But the occasion was too momentous, too joyous for their anger to last. She bowed to them both and took her place behind the Reality Tracer. This version of the machine—about the size of a toaster oven, all stainless steel and illuminated control panels—was warmed up and hummed softly. Her mother came forward and attached electrodes that dangled from it on cables to Alina's forehead and temples, and wrapped a cuff around her upper arm, like a blood pressure test, except that this cuff was also connected to the Tracer. It was tight, but not uncomfortably so, and Alina nodded to indicate that she was ready.

She had been told the full history of the People's Project since childhood—since it became apparent, at least, that she was the missing piece that could make it work. She knew that Soviet scientists, monitoring schizophrenics in insane asylums across the Soviet Union, had noticed a surprising similarity to many of the so-called visions they saw and voices they heard. They catalogued these similarities, and then the study was expanded. People who saw things, or heard things, but were not institutionalized, were included in the study. Then writers and artists, poets and musicians—people who pulled images and ideas seemingly from the ether—were drawn in, when it became apparent that some of their ideas resembled the visions in intriguing ways. Fictional characters, fairy-tale images from great paintings, all seemed to have doppelgängers in the lunatic ravings of the insane.

And so the theory was put forth: what if these people weren't seeing specters from the depths of their own imaginations, but were instead tapping in somehow to other worlds, other realities where these things were real?

As the study was enlarged further, theoretical physicists got into the act with their own concepts. One of these, which quickly earned wide acceptance, was parallel universes. In some way, this theory claimed, whenever a person made a life-changing decision, a new reality was created in which the decision was made in a different way. The result was an infinite number of alternate realities, some in which evolution itself progressed down remarkably different paths.

There were universes, it was hypothesized, in which monsters ruled the world and people were enslaved to them, or prey, or had ceased to exist altogether. There were other universes in which people had developed amazing powers, either physical, mental, or both. Whatever could be imagined by humans existed somewhere, in one of those realities.

And if people could see and hear fragments of those realities, or "alternities," as some began to call them, then people could travel to them, through them.

Which was where the Reality Tracer came in.

If travel to these alternities was possible, then a device of some kind could theoretically be developed to open the doors. The military applications were immediately apparent—monsters or unlimited numbers of soldiers could be imported into our world to fight wars; enemy soldiers or unfriendly politicians could be dispatched easily into other worlds. And there were peaceful uses to which the

Tracer could be put as well, extending the scope of human knowledge, curing disease, putting an end to the fear of death.

The only problem was, the machine couldn't be made to work.

They got closer and closer. They learned how to create portals, but they couldn't get anything to go through and come back. Experiments showed that when they did put things through, they were changed, distorted horribly. It seemed impossible to pass through in the same state as one left one's own reality. No one dared test it on humans, since the results were likely to be so grisly.

But the Soviets spent decades on the problem, and gradually made progress. Someone named Markov, with whom her parents had worked, made the final connection—positing that since the people who had first exposed the existences of these other realities achieved mental connections with them, then the power of the mind had to be brought into the overall equation. So he tapped the USSR's most powerful psychics and hooked them up to the Tracer to direct its field mentally.

Still, no luck, although there seemed to be marginal improvement in the generation of portals.

After the disintegration of the Soviet Union, and the birth of Alina to parents who were both gifted psychics, her mother Valerya had thought to test Alina's own psychic abilities. What they found astonished both of them. Her powers far outstripped their own—as an accident of her birth, Alina was perhaps the most powerful psychic the Soviet Union had ever seen.

So from a young age, they had worked with her, developing her abilities, hooking her up to the Tracer to test and retest their theories. They had come closer and closer to this day, the day that practical application of all they had worked on would come into play. There were still limitations, grave ones, but they couldn't be fully explored until the system was operational.

For instance, there was a distinct geographical limitation—the Tracer couldn't be made to pluck the president of the United States out of his existence, unless it was located within a few miles of the White House. And even then, the Tracer's "aim" was inaccurate. Alina could direct it at, say, politicians, but the chances of snagging the president were no greater than of capturing the president of a high school class.

These difficulties could be overcome, her parents believed, with trial and error, with practice. Live, online practice, not continual testing. She had to be doing it, for real.

So it would begin. Once begun, her parents feared, the world would soon know of the Tracer. The United States had been the ideal place to work, its much-vaunted privacy laws allowing them to function free of government interference. But once the officials knew what was in their midst, the Vishnikoffs were sure, they would swoop down and take it away. There was only one place that the Reality Tracer would be safe, one place where the Vishnikoffs would be valued and allowed to continue their work.

A Socialist Soviet Union.

Restored to its former, pre-Andropov glory.

It could happen—it *would* happen. But it would be expensive.

Only one nation had the money to rebuild it, to allow Russia to recover from its current economic blight, and draw together the satellite states that had split off from it. The United States had the capital. The Vishnikoffs, and their supporters, including Teodor Nokivov and his arm of the Mafiya, had the will and the inspiration.

So the Reality Tracer's first job would be blackmail.

Beginning today, Alina would begin snatching the youth of Los Angeles. When public terror and concern had peaked, the Vishnikoffs would demand billions, and assistance, and acceptance for the new Soviet state.

The Americans would have no choice but to agree, or continue to lose their teens one by one.

A youth-oriented culture like the West's would never stand for that. Without teens, the economy would grind to a halt. They would discuss it for a few days, but they would give in.

Alina set to work.

As her captors bathed her, Salma de la Natividad still didn't know if she was a princess or a prisoner.

She had been alone in the big room for almost an hour, she guessed. Finally the doors had opened and people had begun to spill in. They chattered with each other, and made conversational sounds at her, though she couldn't understand a word of it. They seemed to have no interest in learning her tongue, or teaching her theirs. It was almost like she didn't really matter, except as a way to pass the time.

Now, nine lovely young women in sky-green robes held Salma's arms behind her back. When she tried to struggle free, they only held her more rigidly, laughing amongst themselves at her efforts. An army of muscular men in loincloths, their heads and bodies shaved, brought in tank after tank of hot water, which they poured into a large, hammered metal tub.

The tub full and steaming, the men left the room and the young women stripped off Salma's clothes. One of them sprinkled petals from a large yellow flower into the tub, and Salma found the fragrance as they struck the warm water sweet and calming. Salma tried to break free again, convinced that she was being somehow drugged

by the flower petals, but she couldn't break their grips
and she gave up after a moment.

She allowed the women to place her into the tub and,
still holding her arms fast, they sponged every inch of her
with the scented water and soft, caressing cloths. This was
the part where she began to wonder if she was in fact a prisoner, or perhaps some kind of royalty being prepared for a
ceremony. What they did felt so good, and the soporific effect of the flower petals floating on the water soothed her
fears and quieted her heart. No more tears flowed, and she
found herself smiling under their tender ministrations.
Through all of it, the silent women worked seamlessly together as if they had done this a thousand times.

When she was clean—and so relaxed, she felt as if she
were bathing inside a cloud—they helped her from the
bath and dried her with thick green towels. The nine
women carefully dabbed every part of her to ensure that
she was dry, and then two of them went to work on her
hair, combing it over and over again, massaging her scalp
in the process. She almost fell asleep as they worked.
When they finished, they helped her into a yellow robe,
much like their own except for the color. The soft, rich
fabric felt heavenly against her clean skin.

She thought about trying again to communicate with
them, possibly through sign language of some kind. But
something warned her that such an attempt would lead to
further frustration and would negate the comfort and
peace that she now felt, so she didn't bother. Instead she
sat, silent and compliant, as one of the women dotted her
forehead, cheeks, and chin with some kind of scented,
musky oil.

That done, all nine of the women came before her in
turn. Each one knelt down before her and touched the dot
of oil on her forehead. Salma thought maybe they were

worshiping her, or marking her for some reason. But the narcotic effects of the bath lingered, and she didn't pursue any line of thought for very long.

When each woman had performed this task, they helped her to her feet and took her through a series of hallways to a massive door. Four of the women, straining together, could barely muscle it open. Beyond it a narrow staircase wound down and out of sight. Torches burned in sconces on the staircase walls. The women led Salma to the staircase, and started her down the stairs.

When the big door closed behind her, Salma's heart skipped and a brief flurry of panic overcame the flowery drug. But it passed, and she continued down the stairs, one part of her wanting to see what new wonder would be discovered below, even as the rest of her just wanted to be home again.

At the bottom of the long, steep staircase she found another door. She pushed against it and it swung away easily, almost like an automatic door at the supermarket. As she passed through it, it closed behind her with a determined clang. When she glanced back at it, the door had vanished, melding totally with the wall of the tunnel in which she found herself. So there was no going back, no way out except to move forward.

Into the dark unknown.

Sunnydale

Xander had just about had it with Spike. He could only take so much of the guy in the first place—always mouthing off, always putting others down. *Especially me,* he thought. *Like I'm his personal whipping boy.* And it bugged him that Spike and Anya seemed to have so much in common; their age, their demon pasts, the fact that both of them had been, for all intents and purposes, defanged. They had long talks, serious talks. When Xander tried to have a serious talk with Anya, they usually ended up in bed. *Which, not complaining,* he thought. *But still, sometimes a guy just wants to cuddle and converse.*

He and Anya walked ahead of Spike, who, despite his insistence that he wanted to whomp some demon, um, butt, seemed determined to investigate every shrub, every Dumpster, every spot that could possibly hide a person of Cheryce's size. Xander's personal theory was that she wouldn't hide in someplace so mundane—she was flashy, outgoing, a show-off.

As they walked the dark streets, Spike stopped now and again to peek into trash cans.

"Stop it," Xander warned. "I'm getting hungry."

"Bite me, Harris," Spike snapped.

"You'd like that, huh? Since you can't bite me?" There was, Xander realized, at least some pleasure to be had, taunting Spike now that he couldn't possibly hurt anyone. Of course, in the back of his mind, he realized there was a possibility that situation wouldn't last forever, in which case, his would probably be the first neck Spike targeted.

Xander and Anya turned a corner, a couple of blocks from the business district in a mixed commercial/residential neighborhood, and there she was. Spike's ticket to chipless land. Cheryce held the head of a young man in her hands—*fortunately,* Xander thought, *it's still attached to a body.* The man looked like a gangbanger, in his baggy pants and plaid shirt. He was sobbing, and Cheryce had her face very close to his neck.

"Let him go," Xander said. He pulled a stake from his pocket.

Cheryce laughed. She sauntered up to Xander, and then, when she was near enough, her face changed, fangs elongating. Xander thrust the stake over his head and down, but she grabbed him before he could follow through.

"Hey!" he shouted, trying to struggle. Her grip was too strong.

"You leave my boyfriend alone!" Anya demanded. "Spike!" She drew a stake of her own and jumped onto Cheryce's back, but the vampire simply hurled her off with one hand, slamming her into a wall. The stake clattered on the ground.

"Not him again," Cheryce sighed. "Don't you ever hang out with interesting people?" She lowered her face to Xander's neck. "Oh, well. Won't matter anymore."

Xander felt the teeth graze his skin. He closed his eyes, trying to prepare for the inevitable.

And a sudden force knocked them both flat on the ground.

Xander opened his eyes. Cheryce was on top of him, which under other circumstances he might have found pleasant. On top of her, though, was a multilimbed, copper-colored humanoid. Its two legs kicked in the air, while its six arms wrapped around Cheryce's torso and clawed at her face. She tried to buck it off, but it was too strong, and had too many solid grips. Finally, she managed to slide off of Xander and then throw herself back against the same wall she'd slammed Anya into. The creature, between her and the wall, took the worst of the blow. It let go of Cheryce, but only for a moment, and then it flailed out with all of its arms, pummeling her with half a dozen fists. Some of the blows connected, and she dropped to the sidewalk.

Spike came running around the corner now, alerted by Anya's shouts and the sounds of struggle. He saw what was happening and launched himself at the monster. It caught him in midair, whirled, and flung him down the street, where he landed in a cursing skid.

The thing turned on Anya, who had rushed to Xander's side when he and Cheryce went down. "No!" Xander yelled, trying to push himself to his feet. But the creature only smacked him back down with two of its hands, and grabbed Anya with the others. It wrapped a couple of big hands around her head, as if meaning to tear it from her neck.

Then its disgustingly humanlike face went slack. Cheryce had come up behind it and attacked it somehow. As it turned on her, almost in slow motion now, Xander saw that there were two holes in its back—hand-size holes. Black blood flowed from them, and Cheryce's hands were coated with the same thick ooze.

She had saved them. He wondered if she realized it.

But as he watched, the monster lunged for her, apparently not down yet. Two of its hands caught the front of her shirt, and another grabbed one of her arms. It yanked her off-balance, and she tripped, landing back on the sidewalk again.

From behind them, Spike ran toward her, his mouth open in a silent cry. He had already seen what Xander hadn't noticed yet—one of the thing's other hands had scooped up Anya's fallen stake. They all watched, unable to reach Cheryce in time, as the monster drove the stake home into her heart.

Cheryce exploded in a puff of dust.

The monster keeled over, dead.

Spike dropped to his knees and shouted, "Dammit!"

Anya shot Xander a look. He couldn't read it, exactly, but he knew that he should just keep his mouth shut. She went to Spike's side, kneeling beside him. He buried his head against her and wept.

"There, there, you'll find someone else," she cooed.

"Yeah, but will she know how to get this bleedin' chip out of my head?" he wailed. "I'm doomed. Bloody doomed!"

Los Angeles

Wesley looked up from a laptop computer he'd plugged into Cordelia's phone line. It rested on her kitchen table, and he had been sitting in front of the screen for what seemed like hours. "There are dozens of Mischas, perhaps more than a thousand, in Los Angeles," he said. "I'm afraid we need something a little firmer to go on."

"Angel's out looking for clues," Cordelia said, glad he was actually speaking. She'd already alphabetized the contents of her pantry, which, to be fair, hadn't taken that long since it was pretty bare. She had thought that reading a magazine while he searched the Internet would be rude, then decided she didn't care, and it beat looking into her empty pantry again to see if maybe pea soup should be under "S" for soup instead of "P" for pea.

Or "C" for can?

She closed *Vanity Fair.* "Actually, I think he's looking for people to beat up. Only they have to be the right people. He's past the point in his life where he just beats people up for fun; now he only does it for information. Soon as the sun went down, he headed out, trying to find someone he could beat up for a lead to Vishnikoff, or Mischa. Or both."

"At least it's narrowed down to people who know something about Russians," Wesley said, stretching his arms over his head. Cordelia could hear his shoulders pop. "That's something."

"Makes me feel better," Cordelia said. "Only I feel

bad, because when I had my head in the pantry, thinking about all the yummy foods that weren't in there, I remembered something about the Mischa-vision I had that I didn't tell Angel. It just didn't make any sense at the time."

"What is it?" Wesley asked her.

"I was trying to remember names, places, faces, that kind of thing. So I ignored this smell, but maybe it was important, after all."

"An odor? What kind?"

"Sweet," Cordelia replied. "Doughy. Like a bakery. Cakes, cookies, bread, that kind of thing."

"That narrows it down," Wesley said glumly. "There can't be more than a thousand bakeries in the greater Los Angeles metropolitan area."

"Russian bakeries?" Cordelia asked. "I mean, it's not necessarily a Russian bakery, but several aspects of this case seem to point to Russians, so maybe . . ."

Wesley turned back to the computer, started tapping keys. "Good point," he said. "Let's check."

Visiting every Russian bakery on the list was proving to be a time-consuming operation. There were more than one might expect, to begin with, and they were scattered over a much greater geographical area than one might hope—if one had hopes of hitting them all in a single day, that was. Given the sheer square mileage that Los Angeles encompassed, Cordelia figured she should not have been so surprised, but when she saw the sun going down before they were done with their list, she was.

The first nine bakeries they stopped at had no Mischa. The tenth had one, but he was in his fifties, grizzled and gray, with an enormous belly that looked like he had swallowed a beach ball. They thanked him, bought a cookie, and left. Wesley had insisted it was only polite to buy a small something for the trouble to which they were putting the bakers.

"If this keeps up," Cordelia said as she munched the cookie on the way to the car, "we'll look like him by the time we find the right Mischa."

The eleventh, twelfth, and thirteenth bakeries had no Mischa either. There was one who worked at the fourteenth, in Baldwin Hills, but he was not working that evening. Cordelia described him, and the elderly woman at the counter blinked behind thick-lensed glasses and nodded her head.

"That's him, that's Mischa," she said. "He's a good boy." But she refused to give them Mischa's last name, address or phone number.

They made another purchase, and Cordelia gave Wesley a thumbs-up on the way outside. "Now all we have to do is wait here until Mischa shows up. Can't be more than a few days."

"Unless the trouble he's in is lethal," Wesley observed. "In which case—"

"Yeah, I get it. So maybe we're no better off than we were."

"In fact," Wesley pointed out, "we may be far worse off."

Cordelia followed his gaze. There was a crowd of people standing around their car—a crowd of men, all in their mid-twenties, rough-looking. As Cordelia and Wesley walked toward them, they spread out across the sidewalk, standing in the circle of light cast by a streetlamp.

"I don't like the looks of this lot," Wesley whispered.

"No one's asking you to date them," Cordelia replied. "Let's get out of here."

They turned to walk in the opposite direction, but two more men emerged from a doorway they had just passed, cutting off retreat. "Blast," Wesley said.

"You looking for Mischa," one of the men said as they surrounded Cordelia and Wesley. It was not phrased as a question, and Cordelia didn't think that was because of any unfamiliarity with the intricacies of the English language. He was well over six feet tall, probably two hundred pounds. His shirt barely contained his muscles. His English carried a Russian accent. "Why?"

"We, uhh, heard he was in some trouble," Cordelia said. "Just hoping we could help out."

"Trouble?" the man asked. "What kind?"

"Umm, he . . . won something. And we're supposed to deliver it. Money, I think. Lots of it."

"Do you even know Mischa?"

"No, not at all," Wesley said, with a short little laugh. "She's kidding. We just heard that he worked at the best Russian bakery in all of Los Angeles." He hefted the small white bag in his hand. "We thought we'd pick up some rugelach."

In support, Cordelia smiled and said, "And, boy, is it yummy."

"What I hear, you've been looking for Mischa all over town," the man continued, glowering at Wesley. "Probably you are interested in trouble, not rugalah."

"If we were interested in trouble," Wesley said politely as he adjusted his glasses, "I have no doubt that you could provide it. However—"

"However," another voice joined in, "I'd recommend that you back off and let them go."

"Angel?" Cordelia said. She spun around. Sure

enough, behind them on the sidewalk was Angel, fists clenched, coming toward them.

"And how are you involved in this?" the Russian man demanded.

"You're eight guys, picking on two people who just bought some rugelach," Angel said. "Seems a little unfair to me."

"Kill them all," the man commanded his cronies.

Angel moved faster than anybody else as well as everybody else. He dove into the center of the men, feet lashing out. Two men dropped immediately with broken knees. Angel spun and caught another in the belly with his own knee, finishing him with a quick chop to the back of the neck.

Two more rushed him simultaneously, and he dropped both of them with jabs to their chins. Another couple of men ran away then, and Angel turned toward the apparent leader of the group, the one who had been threatening Cordelia and Wesley.

"Looks like you guys weren't as tough as you thought," Angel said.

"You have not tried me yet," the man replied.

"Somehow I don't think you'll be a problem," Angel said calmly. He touched his own chest. "I'm just getting warmed up. My heart isn't even racing yet. Want to check?" He went vamp-faced as he spoke.

The man backed away a step. The confidence on his face had been replaced by something that looked to Cordelia a lot like terror. Angel moved forward, keeping the distance between them even.

"You saw what I can do," Angel said, still in his calm, low voice. "You haven't seen the worst of it, but you saw a demonstration. I don't want to hurt you, but I will unless you tell me what I want to know."

The man didn't answer.

"I want Vishnikoff," Angel said. "Take us to Vishnikoff, or take us to Mischa."

"I-I cannot," the man stammered. "It would not be safe."

"You're beyond worrying about safe," Angel said. He took another step forward. The guy tried to move back but he was against a wall. His eyes were huge and he swallowed repeatedly. Angel reached out one hand, gripped the man's biceps, and began to squeeze. "You're at the point where you have to wonder if I'll kill you or just cripple you, unless you tell me what I want to know."

Angel scared Cordelia when he was like this. She knew he was overplaying it, trying to scare the overgrown thug. Or not trying, just scaring. But it seemed to come so naturally to him, like he was playing a very familiar role, reciting oft-spoken lines. She was glad she was too young, by a couple hundred years and change, to have known him in the old days.

The scaring part worked. The Russian wrote out an address for Angel. Angel warned him that he'd be back if the address wasn't accurate, and the Russian swore— moisture beginning to fill his eyes under the pressure of Angel's squeeze—that it was.

The address was over in Hawthorne, a house at the intersection of Mount Vernon and Fairway.

Chapter 13

Los Angeles

THEY SAT IN ANGEL'S BELVEDERE GTX CONVERTIBLE, top up, looking the house over. It looked pretty much like all the other houses on the street. Two stories, built in the postwar housing boom when L.A. had suddenly sprawled, filling every hill and valley as far as the eye could see and then some. This one was painted a pale yellow with brown trim. It was uphill from the street, its driveway sharply slanted.

A wide expanse of lawn led from the sidewalk up to the house, and a paved walkway split the lawn down the middle. The paint job was faded, a few years old, and the lawn was tended, but not lovingly. Some of the houses around here were occupied by people who loved them, and some were just occupied. This was one of the latter.

There were a few cars parked around the house, almost as if there were a party going on. Lights burned in the downstairs windows. But no party sounds, not even the hum of conversation, issued from the silent dwelling.

"What do we do, Angel?" Wesley asked. "Do we break in? Just knock on the door and see if Mischa can come out to play?"

"It's a house," Angel said. "You might be able to get in, but I need to be invited."

"Good point," Wesley agreed. "So we need an ally on the inside."

Angel nodded.

Just then, Cordelia pointed to a car pulling to a stop at the corner. A young man stepped out of the passenger side, with thick blond hair. A tight blue tee shirt with a surf logo barely stretched across his football player's broad shoulders. "How about Mischa?" she said. The car pulled away as they spoke, and Mischa headed up the sidewalk toward the house.

"That him?" Angel asked.

"Looks like him to me," Cordelia announced. "And since it was my vision—"

"Talk to him," Wesley urged. "Quickly."

She glanced at Angel, who nodded again.

She left the car and hurried up the walk toward Mischa. When she knew he was looking at her, she tripped. "Ohh!" she called as she hit the grass. "My ankle. I think I sprained it."

Mischa quickly turned from his path and came to her side. He knelt down and took the ankle in his hands.

"Does it hurt?" he asked her.

"Very much," she emoted, hoping she wasn't overdoing it. *Not like I needed those acting classes to attract a male,* she thought. *But it's nice to get some use out of them.*

"I can get some ice from inside the house," he said. "Ice is good for that, isn't it?"

"Ice? Ice is good for pretty much everything, the way I hear it. Except maybe a broken heart, and I don't have one of those. Just this old ankle sprain." She made a little-girl pouty face, then allowed it to blossom into a smile. "If you'll help me up, I think I can walk."

He held out his strong hands and helped her to her feet. She walked with a pronounced limp, holding onto his arm, up the sidewalk to the house. Mischa seemed nervous, and she couldn't tell if it was about bringing a stranger inside or something else. But then, she remembered, she'd had a vision about him, and that meant he was in some kind of serious trouble.

So nervous is maybe not a bad way to be, after all.

As soon as he opened the door, she realized this was not the normal house they had believed it to be from outside. There was a foyer just inside the door, but within it, an antique desk like one at which the concierge at an upper-crust hotel might sit, crouched on slender legs. No one sat there now. Instead, a video surveillance system watched the foyer and doorway.

On the wall by the desk, there was a check-in board with names and pegs to keep track of who was on the premises. Mischa's name was on the board, and he moved a peg to the spot next to his name to indicate that he was here. On top of the desk was a row of mail slots big enough to put letters or messages in, and a multiline telephone.

Beyond the foyer, the entire downstairs had been reconstructed. Cordelia saw what looked like a maze of carpeted hallways, painted gray, extending in both directions, with closed doors everywhere. She heard muted voices behind some of the doors. It looked like someone had built a miniature office building into a private home, and did it with a minimum of style.

"I'm going to take a wild guess that this is not just somebody's house, is it?" she asked.

"No, it's not," Mischa replied. "But please do not ask any more questions. I can tell you nothing." He led her down the hallway to the right, which brought them to a kitchen that looked mostly like a kitchen, except that its huge stainless steel refrigerator and range and coffee urn revealed that it was used to cook for more than just one small family.

Inside the kitchen, Cordelia closed the door and turned to her host. "Mischa," she said. "My name's Cordelia. I know you're in some kind of trouble. I can't really explain how I know—it's long and complicated and involves this demon, or half-demon anyway, named Doyle, and—well, never mind, I said I couldn't explain it."

He stared at her, mouth open a little. "How do you know my name?"

"I know more than just your name," she said. "Haven't you been listening? I know you're in trouble, and I know that we can help you."

"We?" he asked.

"My friends, Angel and Wesley, and I." She tried to appear calm, but inwardly, she was saying, *C'mon, c'mon, just believe me.*

"How can you help?" he asked. His voice was shaky as he glanced around. She could see in his eyes, and in the tiny lines around them, the bags underneath them, that he'd been living with fear for a long time. "How can anyone?"

"I can't really answer that until we know what the trouble is," Cordelia explained patiently. "But if you invite them in, we can talk about it and figure out what to do. You're worried about something, it's all over your face. We're the people who can fix it. Is it safe to talk here?"

"There is no place safe to talk," Mischa said. Worry

furrowed his brow. "You are right, there is trouble. It's Alina . . . but I do not know what I can do for her."

"Don't tell me," Cordelia said, holding up her hand. "Save it for Angel. He can do something. Trust me."

"How can I?" he demanded. "I don't even know you."

"How can you not?" she retorted. "Alina's in trouble. You're in trouble. There's no one here who can help you, is there?"

Mischa shook his head. "They've made her go too far," he said. "Too many people lost . . . how will she ever get them back?"

"Mischa," Cordelia said firmly. "Let's bring Angel in. Now. He can help, really. You don't have any other choice. Angel's right outside, and he can help if you let him. If you don't let him, he'll find another way. So you might as well cooperate."

Mischa blinked, and then nodded his head slowly. He and Cordelia went to the front door, and she summoned Angel and Wesley from the car. Cordelia warned them about the video camera, but they decided there was no time to worry about that. At Mischa's invitation, Angel was able to enter, and they all returned to the kitchen.

"Okay," Cordelia said. "Start from the top. Who's Alina, and what has she gotten involved in?"

It took the guy a minute to pull himself out of whatever fugue state he had fallen into. It was his moment of decision, his last chance to play it safe or open up to Cordelia and the others. She literally sat on the edge of her seat, willing him to spill. If she had read him right, he would. He had been surviving on a precipice overlooking a chasm for some time, and now there was finally someone on solid ground, extending a hand. He'd take it.

He did.

"Alina is the girl I love," Mischa began. "She's Vishnikoff's daughter. And she's the one making teenagers disappear all over Los Angeles." He shifted his attention to the three of them, looking at each of their faces in turn. "You know about that?"

"We know," Wesley said. "It's Alina's doing?"

"Yes," Mischa replied. "She didn't want to. Her parents made her. But something went wrong, some kind of interference. She thinks it's magickal. So the portals are out of her control, and operating in both directions."

"Portals?" Angel repeated carefully. "Maybe we should talk to Alina."

"Yes, all right," Mischa agreed, bobbing his head. He was frightened. "I'll see if I can get you to her."

He led them out of the kitchen and back through the twisting maze of narrow corridors. Reaching the desired door, he held them back with one hand while he opened it and peered inside. Satisfied, he motioned them in rapidly.

They were in a small, sterile room with empty white walls. A machine dominated it, all shiny steel and plastic, with dangling cables trailing toward the floor. Curtains presumably covered a window to the outside, but they were heavy and closed.

A young girl, fifteen or sixteen with fine, dainty features, sat in a straight-backed kitchen chair next to the machine. Her blond hair was drawn back into a severe ponytail. Her blue eyes opened wide at this unexpected intrusion. "Mischa?"

"Alina, these people say they can help us," he said quickly. "I think we should trust—"

He stopped, cut off by a sound from the corridor. Footsteps, walking quickly toward them. Then the doorknob rattled and began to turn.

Sunnydale

As soon as he had arrived back in Los Angeles, Teodor Nokivov had put together a revised war plan with some of his most trusted lieutenants. Feeling that an immediate demonstration of his appreciation to Del DeSola was in order, the next evening Karol Stokovich returned to Sunnydale with a carload of troops, to pay a visit to the Latin Cobras. Informants in L.A. had told them where to look and who to look for, so finding the gang's headquarters was no problem at all.

A lookout, posted on the street corner opposite the house the Cobras were using as headquarters, spotted the car full of men and began to whistle, loud and long. A burst of fire from a MAC-10 stopped him before he could get out much of it, though.

Once the ice had been broken, the Russians turned their attention to the house itself, spraying the doors and windows with lead. After a few moments, they jumped from the car and rushed the house. Halfhearted return fire failed to discourage the Russians. Within five minutes, the Mafiya soldiers had stormed through the house, finishing off everyone they found inside. A couple of Cobras escaped out the back as soon as the fireworks started, and were presumably still running.

Karol Stokovich himself walked through the house, room to room, kicking back doors with his automatic rifle at the ready. He found bodies in almost every room, it seemed, and sprays of blood had painted most walls. Acrid smoke hung heavy in the air. Stokovich breathed it in contentedly.

When he got back into the car, he felt like he had done the job right. The Cobras had been sent an unmistakable message, and when DeSola heard about it—which he would—he would know who had delivered it.

Los Angeles

Nicky de la Natividad crept along the shadowed alleyway behind Che's crib. A streetlight at the end of the alley threw a circle of light about halfway down, so until he cleared that he stayed close to the wall. Beyond the light's reach, he felt more free to move rapidly toward Che's back gate. Che had a small fenced yard, mostly dead grass and old playground equipment that had been there when he rented the place. Nicky had been over for barbecues a couple of times on trips to L.A., so he knew what to expect when he approached the gate.

He also knew that Che didn't have guards back here, but had a lookout in front. Or at least, he didn't think Che had a guard in back. There hadn't been any during the barbecues. But then again, during the barbecues everyone had been in the backyard, so maybe that didn't mean anything at all. Suddenly he was not so sure about this plan.

This had not been one of Nicky's better weeks, even though it had started out so well. The Night of the Long Knives had been an incredible experience, but since then he had realized, in a most painful way, that the sense of power he had then didn't last. He'd been shot—his arm still burned from the Russian's bullet. He'd been imprisoned by his own friends, his gang's associates here in this city, and he'd had to rely on an old buddy to escape. It was a good thing Nicky was from L.A.—if he'd just been another Cobra from Sunnydale he'd still be holed up in that filthy apartment, or dead.

But he was, so he knew how to get around in the city.

He had two powerful ambitions now: he wanted to get to Che, who he figured he owed for having him held prisoner; then he wanted to get home, to find out the latest with Salma. If she was really missing, someone would pay, big time. After that, he'd put this whole gang thing behind him for good—there was just no percentage in it for him. He didn't need the money, and the respect turned out to be too highly priced.

When he got to Che's back gate, he stooped low and tried to peer through the space between two boards. He couldn't see anything in the dark yard. Drawing the Beretta he'd taken from Billy Cruz, Nicky jacked a round into the chamber and tried the gate's handle. It opened. He pushed it in, lifting it slightly in case it started to squeak. At the same time, he shoved the Beretta through the narrow opening, ready to pull the trigger if anyone 'fronted him.

But the yard was empty. It looked just as he'd remembered it—rusting playground equipment off to the side, a couple of barbecues on a concrete patio, and a back door that led into Che's kitchen. A few lights burned inside the two-story house, although not in any of the rooms facing the backyard.

With the Beretta gripped tightly in his fist, Nicky ran across the yard and flattened himself against the kitchen door. He froze there, listening for signs that anyone inside had heard him. He stayed there for a minute, willing the hammering in his heart to die down. By now it was hard to even hold the gun steady in his quivering hands.

The kitchen door opened easily. Nicky went inside. Che was probably upstairs, but Nicky didn't know for sure where, or how many were here with him. Rather than go searching through the house and maybe get shot for his trouble, Nicky decided he'd let Che come to him.

He turned on the kitchen light, then tugged open the refrigerator door. He found a beer inside—to be truthful, there wasn't much except beer inside, he realized. A carton of milk, a couple of eggs in a plastic egg-tray, and a Tupperware dish covered in plastic wrap that strained mightily to contain something that looked like moss. Nicky screwed the lid off, slammed the refrigerator door and put the bottle down on the table with a bang. He opened some cupboards, and slammed those doors as well. He tried the garbage disposal, which made a grinding noise that didn't sound healthy. Nicky knew that the disposal shouldn't be turned on without water running, so he turned the water on full blast, shut off the disposal, and left it that way. Then he sat down at a yellow vinyl-topped table and waited.

After a minute of this racket, Che ran into the kitchen. His hair was in sleepy disarray, and he wore only a stained white muscle shirt and blue checked boxer shorts. A roadmap of scars marked Che's arms and shoulders, prompting Nicky to feel, at first, that complaining of his one bullet wound indicated weakness. Then he thought better of that, and felt a flush of embarrassment that he had a bullet wound to begin with. His father and his grandfather had managed to go through life within the law, and neither had ever been shot at. What was wrong with him, he wondered, that he couldn't do the same?

Che shut off the water and stared at him through narrowed eyes. "What's goin' on in here?" he demanded angrily.

Nicky pointed the Beretta at his heart. "Have a seat, Che. Let's talk."

"Nicky? Man, what's up, dog? What you doin' in here?"

"Came to see you, Che. You wouldn't come to see me at that pit where you were holding me."

Che shook his head from side to side. "No, you got it all wrong, *hombre*—"

"I don't think so, Che," Nicky said.

"*Pues,* look, man, put that strap away, you want to talk to me here in my own house."

"There anybody else home, Che?" Nicky asked. He didn't move to put the gun down.

"Just my old lady."

"No guards?"

"*Orale.* There's one outside, in front, in his car, that's all. Look, man—"

Nicky cut him off. "You wanted something from me, Che, all you had to do was ask. You wanted to be invincible, to have your own Night of the Long Knives. I can't give you that. You want to take the time to study, to prepare, you have a grandmother who's a witch can help you with the hard parts, that's cool, you can do it. But without those things, forget about it. There are no shortcuts, Che. Not to that."

Che started to sweat, rivulets running down his temples. He pushed a hand through his thick dark hair. "You don't need that gun," he said.

"I think I do," Nicky countered. "You have the power here. I'm on your turf, in your house, and you're the leader of the Echo Park Band. One word from you, I'm a dead man. Hell, I'm already a dead man, since you already put out the word."

"That's true even if you're strapped," Che said.

"Not if it's pointed at you."

"Look, what do you want?" He ran his hands through his hair and dropped them in his lap. "I screwed up, okay? I didn't know if I could trust you, and I wanted to know how to do what you did. If you just told me what you did now, that you couldn't teach me, that woulda been the end of it. Now you've made everything worse. Now we have to kill you."

Nicky narrowed his eyes. He was getting angrier by the

minute. "Way I heard it, you weren't taking no for an answer. Because I was saying no, and wasn't anybody coming to cut me loose."

"I was gonna come tomorrow," Che said feebly.

"Don't lie to me, Che. That just makes it worse."

"Well, what can I do now?" He jutted his chin out and threw back his shoulders. "You just want to shoot me? That make it better somehow?"

"No, Che," Nicky said. "I don't want to shoot you. I did. That's why I came here. But sitting around waiting for you to come downstairs, I realized that's not what I'm all about. I just want you to know I'm not someone you can mess around with that way, you know? You see what I'm saying?"

Che nodded eagerly. "I got you, man."

"Some people you can treat like that. Not me."

"Okay, I'm sorry, *mano*," Che said, exhaling. He looked levelly at Nicky, then dropped his gaze. "I didn't know."

"*Orale.* Now you do." Nicky kept the gun leveled at Che. He had never killed anyone, but he realized that he could, and would, if he had to. It was a realization that made him feel both powerful and kind of sad.

"Now I do." Che took a deep breath and tapped the table. He shifted his weight. He was scared. "So what else? What I got to do to get straight with you?"

"Someone said my sister is missing. Salma. You heard that?"

Che looked solemn. "That's what I hear. I don't know where she is, man. I swear it."

"I'm going to find her," Nicky vowed. "If I need your help, will you be there?"

"I'll be there," Che assured him. "We all will be."

"All right. Take the price off my head. I need to be able

to move around without watching my back, until I find her."

"Done," Che promised.

"One more thing," Nicky said. "I took this gun off Billy Cruz. I don't want him hurt."

Che hesitated. "Uhh, too late for that, *chico*. We heard you escaped with his gun, we punished him."

"Punished how?"

"Let's just say he won't be losing any more guns, where he is. Unless it's to a fish."

Nicky blew out a breath and swore softly. The urge to ask Che about Rosalie rose up in him, to see if the Echo Park boss knew anything about what had happened to her back in Sunnydale. But he pushed it back down. Chances were, Che had never heard of Rosalie—the Latin Cobras were basically small time compared to the Echo Park Band, at least until Nicky had taken out Del DeSola's oil field during his Night of the Long Knives. And a dead gang girl wouldn't mean much to him.

Che must have noticed his hesitation. *"Sí, hombre?"*

"No," Nicky said, blowing out a sigh. "I feel okay having you in front of me, Che," he said. "But I sure don't want you at my back."

Chapter 14

As Salma stepped out into the tunnel itself, she realized that things were very different down here. The walls and floor and ceiling were smooth rock, as if worn by the erosion of water or wind over a period of centuries. No torches or lights burned here, but the surfaces glowed with a kind of blue phosphorescence. And when she felt the walls, she found them slick to the touch.

Same with the floor and, she presumed, the ceiling, though try as she might, she couldn't reach it. Walking on the slippery surface was difficult, and she often had to balance herself with a hand on the unpleasantly slimy wall. The tunnel smelled damply organic, like freshly-turned earth, but with an undercurrent of something else, something sour and decayed.

The drug was beginning to wear off. As she continued to go forward, through the blue-lit maze of tunnels, her hands shook and despair welled inside. She broke into a run at one point, from one tunnel into a branching one, and then around another corner. But all the tunnels looked the same; she might be back in the original one or she might have traveled for miles. And running was dangerous when the footing was so awkward—she had fallen a couple of times already, skinning her knees and the palms of her hands.

The tears came again. Salma stood, hunched over, hands on her knees, and sobbed as they rolled off her cheeks to splash on the gloopy stones. The sobs racked her body, wrenching her again and again until her ribs ached and her throat burned. Finally, she sat down in the slime, determined to just stay here until someone came along or she died of starvation.

And in the sudden silence after she stopped crying, she heard it. A rushing noise, like water moving through a pipe. But it wasn't water, it was something more solid. It seemed to travel at subway speed, and from the sound of it, it passed through one tunnel after another after another, all around her. At one point, the glow from a cross tunnel ahead seemed to dim, and Salma pressed herself flat against a wall, heart pounding so loud she thought it would give away her location.

Something—she could not put a name to it, nor would she want to try—flashed through that tunnel, passing in front of the opening to her own tunnel so fast she could not even get a real sense of it, except to know that it was enormous.

And it seemed to be hunting. . . .

Sunnydale

Buffy and Riley stood to the side with the rest of the spectators. Flashing lights from the ambulances and police cars parked helter-skelter on the street and driveway

around the Cobras' ruined headquarters strobed the surrounding houses and bathed the watchers in alternating
red and blue and yellow. A pack of about fifty people,
kept at bay by yellow police tape and a couple of officers,
watched the process.

Paramedics brought bodies, zipped into black bags, out
on gurneys and deposited them into the waiting ambulances. As soon as the ambulances were a block away
from the crowd—even though they were still in view—
the lights and siren were cut. Speed meant nothing to
these people now.

A separate clutch of reporters stood on another part of
the block, watching or speaking into microphones with
the blasted house as a telling backdrop. The assault on the
quiet suburban house—though everyone had known gang
members lived there—was big news locally. Buffy had
even overheard one neighbor telling a reporter that the
gangsters there kept the neighborhood safe—that they
didn't cause trouble so close to their headquarters, and as
long as they stayed, no other troublemakers dared to venture in.

But trouble had come, and, unlike the supernatural type
that Buffy confronted on a regular basis, this kind, born of
flame and lead, was fair game for public speculation.
Everyone saw the news from Los Angeles, of course, and
knew that war had broken out between the Russian and
Hispanic gangs in that city. It required no great intellectual
leap to postulate that, since the Latin Cobras had an association with L.A. gangs, the Russians had staged this attack
as a response to events that had transpired there. Reporters
solemnly intoned this theory into the TV cameras.

After they watched for a while, Buffy turned to Riley,
who stood close by, hands in his pockets. "Do we have
anything to gain by sticking around?" she asked him.

"Think there's anything we can learn here that'll help us deal with things?"

He gave the answer she expected. "No," he said. "They're just bringing out bodies. They'll work over the house, but all they'll find are bullets that can't be traced from guns that can't be traced, and the fingerprints of the guys who lived there. If there were any witnesses, they'll keep quiet, or they'll say they saw men they've never seen before or since get out of a car, shoot the place up, and get back into the car. No one's going to identify the shooters."

"You sound so certain," Buffy said.

"That's how these things work," Riley replied. "That's how the cycle continues. Eventually someone will talk, word will get back to any remaining Cobras or their families or friends, and the same thing will happen to a Russian gang headquarters somewhere. They'll think of it as taking care of their own problems, when really it's just extending the violence over more time."

He sounded tired. "It's the Hatfields and the McCoys all over again, only instead of happening in Appalachia somewhere, it's the southern California version."

They turned away from the spectacle and walked down the block, beyond the range of the spinning lights. They were quiet for a moment. Riley put his left arm around Buffy's shoulders and she pressed up against him, sliding her right around his waist and holding him close. Their hips bumped as they walked.

"You're pretty smart," she said after a block or so. "I wish so much of what you knew didn't have to do with violence, but I still like that you know it."

"I could say the same about you," he responded. "The knowing part, and the violence part."

She stopped, and Riley stopped with her. She turned to face him, still holding onto his waist. She put her other hand on his other side, and he brought his left hand up and put it on her right shoulder. She looked into his blue eyes, though in the dark under the overhanging trees she couldn't make out the color.

"They say cops and soldiers have a hard time making relationships work," she said. "Too much time away from home, too much danger, too much stress. High divorce rates. Do you think that's true?"

"That's what they say," Riley agreed.

Her eyes were huge. Her nervousness, huger. "Then we—do we stand a chance? Should we even be trying?"

"Buffy, I—you have to try. If you don't, you're defeated before you even start, right?"

And there was that smile, that Riley, dimpled smile that was so kind, and so understanding, and so strong. She relaxed into it, and loved him for it.

"Makes sense." She smiled. "Maybe I just needed to hear you say it."

"I don't like losing," Riley said frankly. "And I don't like being beaten. So you can be certain that anything I try, I have a pretty good feeling I'm going to succeed at." The smile was there again. Riley smiled at her a lot.

He smiles more in a day than Angel did in all the time I loved him. . . .

She moved against him, encircling him with her arms, enjoying the sensation of his arms wrapping around her. She pressed her face to his sweater-clad chest.

"Optimism," she murmured. "That's something else I like about you."

What she left unspoken, though she understood it, was that optimism had never been one of her strong points. She thought of herself as a realist—a common trait, she acknowledged in moments like this, of pronounced self-honesty, among pessimists.

267

Riley seemed to pick up on it without her saying anything. He pressed his lips to her hair. "Optimistic enough for both of us," he said softly.

You'll have to be, Buffy thought. But she kept quiet and relished the feeling of his comforting bulk against her, and found herself wishing she would never have to let go.

Los Angeles

"What is it?" Alina called out. She used her high, little-girlish voice to full effect, speaking in a singsong tone and drawing out the words.

"It's your father," Alexis Vishnikoff's gruff voice spoke from the other side of the door. "Unlock this door at once."

Mischa had already crossed to the curtains, thrown them open, and slid up the window. Angel helped Cordelia, then Wesley, out and to the ground. He hesitated before going out himself. Alina watched as she headed for the door.

"You sure I shouldn't stay?" Angel whispered.

"No, go," Mischa said. He patted the pocket where he had put the business card that Cordelia had given him on her way out, with the old address and phone number crossed out and her apartment information written in by hand. "We'll find you."

Angel dropped to the ground as Mischa pulled the curtains closed. Alina heard him land softly outside, and then she flicked the knob lock and opened the door for her father.

Even though he was a gifted psychic, her father could not guard his own thoughts at all times from his more talented daughter. She had seen into his innermost being many times. She knew that his physical appearance—gray and lined, with a sparse beard and sad eyes—did not match the way he thought of himself. He still pictured himself as the young man he had been back in the USSR, when he and his bride worked around the clock on the People's Project and set aside everything else in life in deference to the importance of their task. Those had been his favorite days, full of young love and intellectual challenge, feeling like he contributed something worthwhile to the party and the State.

As he stormed into the room, rage purpling his face, Alina knew that she resented her own knowledge. Her father's favorite times, she thought, should include his only child. He remembered fondly the days of her infancy, when he doted on her. But as she grew older, as her psychic skills matched, then exceeded, his own, he had changed. It was as if her coming along had somehow precipitated the end of things, rather than being a new beginning. Alina believed he was jealous because she had been able to make the Tracer work where he couldn't—that he accepted her powers because they enabled him to continue his precious work, but otherwise would just as soon not have a daughter at all.

"You are never to lock this door," he sputtered. "And you—" he pointed to Mischa, "—what are you doing in here with her?"

"We were talking, Father," Alina said. Mischa stood by silently. "Just looking for a moment of privacy to talk about things, that's all."

"You have no privacy," he declared. "You are not an individual, you are a component of the People's Project and a servant of the Soviet Union."

"I am a sixteen-year-old girl," Alina argued. "And sometimes I need privacy."

Alexis stomped around the room, drawing back the curtain, looking into the corners. "I thought I heard other voices in here," he said.

"Only Mischa and me," Alina replied steadily.

Alexis stopped and stood still for a moment, as if contemplating that answer. "And your work?" he asked.

"It's very late, Father," she said. "I'm tired. I want to stop for the night."

Alexis Vishnikoff glared at her. "You stop when I say you can stop. Your mother and I didn't work our fingers to the bone for decades so that you could quit whenever you're a little weary."

She frowned back. "It's not working right. We know that now. It's taking people we don't mean it to. And it's backfiring, letting things in. I don't know why or how, but it's creating portals in other places. I've been hearing things—"

"You're not to pay attention to any of that." He whirled on Mischa. "Have you been filling her head with this nonsense?" he demanded.

"Alina doesn't need anyone to fill her head," Mischa replied. "She is quite capable of accumulating information all on her own."

"I suppose so," Alexis Vishnikoff said. His fury had ebbed, but the gruffness remained in his speech and his combative stance. "We cannot afford to quit now," he urged. "We have come so far, we are so close to victory."

Alina crossed her arms and took a step away from her father. "I'm afraid. I feel like I'm losing control of it. And if that happens—"

"If it happens, it happens," her father said bluntly. "The Americans should have never demanded that we disband our Union."

"It won't affect just America if things go really wrong," she ventured. "Even Russia—"

"A chance we'll have to take," Alexis said, dismissing the subject with the imperiousness of a czar. He went to the door and turned the knob a couple of times. "Never lock this door unless your mother or I are in here with you," he instructed. "Never."

He stomped out and shut the door behind him.

Alina turned to Mischa. "He's going to check the security video," she whispered in a rush. "He didn't believe us, about there being no one else here. He thought he heard unfamiliar voices."

"What do we do?" Mischa asked frantically. "Cordelia and Angel and Wesley are certainly on the tape. I could have explained just Cordelia, but not us going out and getting the others and bringing them all in here."

"Why did you?" Alina asked him. She made a conscious effort not to go prying into Mischa's head, as the best friend—really, the only one—she had, she felt she owed him that courtesy.

"They said they could help," Mischa explained, sounding earnest and uneasy. "They seemed to know a lot—that I'm hooked up with the Mafiya, and that your father is as well. That I am in some kind of trouble."

That caught her attention. "What trouble?" she asked.

"Not my own trouble," he said. "But yours. I know you've been worried about the Tracer malfunctioning, and I've been worried about you. Terribly worried. About what might happen to you, or . . . or what you might do."

"You mean, that I might commit suicide as a way to shut it down?" she asked.

Mischa's cheeks reddened and he looked away.

"I would never," Alina assured him. "I have considered it, and decided it's not worth it. Better I learn to control it more effectively."

"Thank you," he mumbled.

"But I'm touched by your concern, Mischa." She put her hand on his shoulder and flashed him a quick smile. Then she let her hand drop and clenched her hands in front of herself, like a double fist. "That doesn't help us with the immediate problem, though. My father will look at the tape, and when he does, he'll be back in here for you."

"Then I should leave?" he asked, heading for the window.

"I think so," she said. She held out a hand to him. "For that matter—we both should."

"Do you mean it?" Mischa asked. "You would run away?"

"I can't stay here," Alina said. She slumped and pressed her fingertips against her temples. Her lips quivered. "I can't continue to work at their whim. What they're doing—it's just wrong. I can't be part of it any longer."

He reached for her. "We'll go together, then."

"Not together," Alina said. "Not yet, anyway."

Mischa's face fell. "Why not?"

"My parents are both powerful psychics," Alina reminded him. "If we go together, they'll be scanning for us and we'll be easy to find. If we split up for a while, we'll both be more difficult to locate, and we'll stand a better chance of reuniting after a little while."

"We need to pick a meeting spot, then," he ventured. "Someplace safe, where they'll never find us."

"I know just the place," Alina said. She brightened, filled for the moment with a kind of insane hope that they might both actually survive what was to come. "It's called the Grand Canyon."

Chapter 15

Los Angeles

"YOU HAVE TO FIND HER, GRANDMOTHER," NICKY SAID.
Doña Pilar sat on a sofa in the house's big living room,
where everyone had gathered upon Nicky's return. Her
feet didn't quite reach the ground.

Nicky had pulled up to the house driving Che's Boxter.
The clan had gathered for an impromptu celebration,
complete with lots of hugs and kisses from family and
household staff, but spirits were still muted by the fact of
Salma's absence. Now, Nicky was left alone with Doña
Pilar and Willow.

"Finding people, I guess I am not so good at," Doña
Pilar said. "I looked for you for days, and *nada.*"

"Well, it wasn't a total *nada,*" Willow reminded her.
"As the crow flies."

"I was a special case," Nicky said. "I did a hiding spell,
specifically so no one would find me. And I had my Night
of the Long Knives—no magick could touch me then."

Willow watched Doña Pilar's face when he said that.

She looked heartbroken—the fact that her grandson would involve himself in such dark magicks clearly dismayed her. At least, Willow thought it to be a dark spell, from what little she'd heard about it. Doña Pilar had not talked about it in the days they'd been working together—but then, they'd been pretty focused on trying to find Nicky and Salma and, oh, save the world from whatever threatened it this hour.

There had been plenty to do.

"I've got some *compadres* searching for her on the ground," Nicky continued. "If she's in the city, we'll find her. My concern is if she's not in the city."

"We do not know where any of the missing children have gone," Doña Pilar said. "Willow," and here she inclined her head toward where Willow sat in a straight-backed chair, rather graciously, Willow thought, including her in the effort, "and I have been trying to find some clue, some hint. We know there are doorways, and the young people are going through them. But the doorways come and go, and they do not seem to respond to any of our magickal attempts to control them."

"Does that mean they're not magick, or that they are?" Nicky asked. He surprised Willow—she thought of Nicky as a gangbanger, a thug, forgetting that as Salma's brother, he was probably extremely bright. The perceptive question cut to the real heart of the matter, the thing they had been trying to figure out ever since they'd become aware of the portals. Even the research that Giles and Wesley were conducting hadn't answered that one yet.

"We do not even know that," Doña Pilar admitted. "If they are of a scientific origin, then they will respond to a different set of laws and rules than if they stem from magick. We need to determine that one way or another before we may begin to influence them."

Willow squirmed in her chair. "Umm, I have a question," she said. "Nicky. When you were missing, and you did your spells—that was around the same time, I think, as when the first kids started disappearing in L.A. Is it possible that what you did somehow got mixed up with whatever was going on with the doorways? Could that explain why Sunnydale is having portals appear, too? Maybe that shadow monster was only the first one through to our side."

At the mention of Sunnydale, Doña Pilar shivered and crossed herself. "*Boca del Infierno*," she said. "Brrr."

"We get a lot of that brrrness," Willow agreed. "But do you think there's a connection?"

Nicky deferred to his grandmother.

"It is possible, I suppose," she said. "You did your spells in Sunnydale itself, Nicky?"

He nodded gravely.

"Then anything could have happened," Doña Pilar said. "That makes as much sense as anything else we have considered. Sunnydale is a bad place, and magick is not to be used lightly there."

"So the things that are appearing there might be tied to the kids disappearing here in L.A.?" Willow asked. "That was Wesley's theory, I think. Or Giles's. One of them. You know, those Watchers all kind of sound alike after a while. Or maybe you don't know. Probably you don't. Not being, you know, Slayers, or anything." She sat back in the chair, as far as one could sit back in such an uncomfortable construct.

"That's a scary idea," Nicky said. "But I wasn't thinking of that when I did the spells in Sunnydale. Guess I was stupid."

"No," Doña Pilar said, warming as she looked at her

grandson. "Not stupid. Impulsive, perhaps. You did not know what might happen."

He exhaled, blowing dark strands of hair off his forehead. "That's right, I didn't."

"So what do we do now, to look for Salma?" Willow asked.

Doña Pilar considered. "We go back to work, you and I," she said finally. She smiled at her protégée. "You never knew magick was such hard work, did you?"

Willow shook her head. "No idea."

Los Angeles terrified Alina.

She had lived there since she'd been a little girl. But she never went out alone. Always, a parent or one of the other people who worked for them on the People's Project drove her wherever she needed to go. And since she was educated and worked in the same house, and her parents didn't shop, go to movies or museums, or eat out, there was precious little reason for her to go anyplace. She had been driven through different parts of the city on different, widely-spaced occasions, but she had never acquired a real, working knowledge of its landscape or its inhabitants.

She was getting one now. And she didn't like it.

She and Mischa had left the house together, through the window. He led her down from the suburban house to a restaurant in the shadow of the freeway, and there they had found two taxicabs. He gave her two hundred dollars cash and put her in one, while he took the other, since they were convinced that by now, her absence would be noted and her parents would be mentally scanning for her presence. He told her driver to take her to the downtown Greyhound station, and he would meet her at the Grand Canyon's south rim in three days' time. He would not be traveling by bus, he said, but by some other route to avoid detection.

At the last moment, he reached back into the cab and gave her Angel's card. "If you get into real trouble, call him," Mischa told her. "I don't know who he is, really, but I believe he can help you." She thanked him, and then he was gone.

With no clothes but those she wore, nothing in her hands but the Reality Tracer, she went for her first taxi ride.

And on the way, she "heard" the cab driver's thoughts.

He kept looking in his rearview mirror at her. At first, she thought that he considered her pretty, which disgusted her, but which she could have lived with. But his thoughts were even worse than that, and he made no attempt to hide them. He planned to drop her at Greyhound, then rush right back to Hawthorne, figuring that whoever searched for her would still be around. He'd sell the details of where he'd left her, and she'd be picked up before morning.

So she told him, as they cruised the nighttime streets of downtown, that she had changed her mind. She wouldn't be going to the bus station after all, but would be staying in town. When they passed a place called the Avalon Hotel, she told him to stop and let her out there. That would be home, she said, at least for a while. She paid him and got out of the cab, and he turned around to find her parents and tell them where the Avalon Hotel was.

As soon as the cab had rounded the corner, she turned and ran in the other direction. She reached out to people's minds as she passed them, probing for clues as to the direction of the Greyhound station. She still needed to get out of town as quickly as possible.

Alina worried about Mischa as she went. He was not just crossing her father—he was crossing the Mafiya, his own organization. He was practically a newcomer, just working his way up the ranks, and certainly no one important yet. He didn't even carry a gun.

But he was on his way, and he had known that with hard work and a little luck he would be a rich man someday. He had talked to Alina about these dreams, of striking it rich and taking his money back to Russia someday to live there like a czar.

Alina had laughed at him—his goal was so contrary to her own, which had been instilled in her since infancy by her father, of remaking the Soviet Union as the Socialist state it was meant to be. She knew her father used the Mafiya to protect his operation, used its illegal activities to fund the People's Project, and used its muscle, and its hired police officers, to keep the world at bay while he, her mother, and Alina worked on it. She had met Mischa because he was a driver, at times, for some of the higher-ups in the organization.

But even though she could find no nobility in Mischa's stated goals, she liked the boy himself. He was funny and gentle and kind to her, and she wasn't used to people being kind to her. So she came to look forward to his visits, and she knew—as she always knew—that he had come to look forward to them, too. He liked her, a lot.

Too much.

Just sixteen, while she knew many girls her age were interested in boys, she had no experience at that kind of thing. She studied and worked from morning to night, and didn't see how dating or having a boyfriend could possibly fit into her world. So she kept Mischa at arm's length, enjoying his visits but never letting him think that anything more could come of them.

And then this. Running away from home in the dead of night, stealing the Reality Tracer so they couldn't continue trying to use it and maybe making things worse into the bargain. Finding herself alone on the mean streets of downtown Los Angeles, where the homeless and the desperate and the dangerous looked at her like wolves eyeing a stray lamb. The sidewalk smelled like garbage, and worse.

She *had* to find that bus station, and soon.

Cradling the Reality Tracer in her arms like a baby, Alina dashed from one streetlight to the next, hurrying across the dark stretches as if something sinister might be hiding there.

She "heard" them before she saw them. They had seen her, though, and were practically screaming their thoughts in her direction. And they meant her no good.

Despite their jumbled, chaotic thoughts, she determined that there were five of them. But what was strange, possibly more frightening even than what they were thinking, was the fact that she could only read two of them. The other three she knew existed because of the thoughts of the first two, but their thoughts, their minds, were closed to her. She didn't know who could do that, except for a few powerful psychics she'd met.

They hung a little more than a block behind her, moving carefully in the shadows, hiding in doorways or behind parked cars whenever she glanced back. Following her.

She looks like money, they thought. *And that computer or whatever she's carrying, ought to be able to pawn that for something. And anyway, she's kinda cute, you know. Might be a tasty little bit.*

And more graphic thoughts, which Alina pushed away. She didn't want to "hear" what they would do to her, she just wanted to be able to keep track of them while she tried to figure out how to escape.

On streets they knew, where she'd never been.

At night.

Alone.

She sauntered, almost casually, to a corner, and as soon as she rounded it she broke into a dead run. Across the street, and into the mouth of an alley there. She entered the alley, still running flat out, the Reality Tracer still clasped to her breast.

And stopped.

Because the alley was a dead end, a high brick wall closing it off, the back of a store, it seemed. No doorways faced this side, just a few windows on the second and third floors of buildings, up ladders that folded so they didn't reach the street.

She could "hear" them behind her. They'd made the corner and were coming this way. The very fact that she was out of sight had tipped them off that she knew about them, and was making a run for it. So they spread out, moving quietly, alert for anything.

One of them thought about the alley. He spoke to another one, and the two of them headed that way.

Trapped.

She turned, ready to face them when they found her. She didn't want them to see her back, no matter what. If she had to fight or die, she'd do it looking them in the eyes.

The two men stopped in the alley's mouth. Looked at her. One whistled, and the other three came running. They started to smile, to laugh. And, once they opened their mouths, she understood why these three had been unreadable to her.

Vampires. Their long fangs gave them away. Vampires weren't human, and she could only read humans. She knew most kids her age wouldn't even be willing to accept that there were vampires, but most kids didn't have her life experience. She'd encountered her first one in Hungary, more than a decade ago. She feared and hated them, but she did not disbelieve.

"Hey, sweetcheeks," one of them said. "You found us a nice private spot, huh? Guess you're in the mood."

"Just hand me that computer," another one demanded. He lunged for the Tracer, knocking it from her hands. It hit the street with an unhappy crunch. "I seen one of them once at RadioShack, I think."

"I'm first," a third said. "I'm so ready for this."

Over their words, she could still "hear" the thoughts of the two who were still human, could barely begin to block them out, they were so loud in her mind. And on top of all the images of what they wanted to do to her, one thing stood out.

What they really wanted.

They ran with vampires. They wanted to become vampires. To persuade these vampires to turn them, they had agreed to prove their worth.

Even though they were still human, these two wanted to taste blood.

Her blood.

Alina braced herself.

And a *thwipping* noise cut the momentary silence, followed by a *poof* as one of the men exploded in a cloud of dust. The other four whirled to find a group of raggedy-looking young people facing them, wooden stakes and crossbows in their hands.

At the center of the group stood a handsome African-American man in a hooded sweatshirt and baggy pants, a stake in each fist. He smiled. Alina found the smile friendly-looking, but at the same time understood how her attackers might not consider it so.

"Only thing worse than a buncha vamps is a buncha lowlife criminal vamps," the young man said. "Tryin' to boost this girl's stuff and drain her."

"Gunn," one of the attackers growled.

"Got that right," the one called Gunn said. He signaled with a nod, and his crew burst into action. "Looks like L.A. needs me more than Sunnydale."

The fight was over in seconds. It ended with the three vampires gone, all disappearing in puffs of dust like the first one had. The two still-humans ran, screaming, into the night.

When it was done, the man they had called Gunn smiled at her. She was right, it was a friendly smile. "You'll be okay now," he assured her.

"Thank you, Mr. Gunn," she said. She was reeling from all that had happened. She felt almost as afraid of him as she had been of the vampires, and only because he was a stranger.

I'm so handicapped, she thought. *I'm like a little baby.*

"No prob." He cocked his head. "What's that accent, Russian?"

"Yes." She swallowed hard, wondering if she should have divulged her nationality.

"Long as it ain't Transylvanian, we'll be okay," Gunn said.

"No, you were right," she assured him, not certain if he was teasing, not understanding why he didn't like Transylvanians. "It's Russian."

Gunn's thoughts were guarded, but she probed a little, wanting to make sure that he meant her no harm. She didn't believe he did, but had just learned the value of being extra cautious.

And she saw something familiar there.

She had to know.

"Excuse me," she said. "But, do you know a man named Angel?"

* * *

"I wanted you to hear it from me," Kate said. "Before you see tomorrow's morning paper."

"Angel's not big on the morning edition," Cordelia pointed out.

Kate looked at her.

"Sunlight," Wesley added.

"I got it," Kate said brusquely.

Angel rose from his seat, placing his finger in one of his unpleasantly dusty tomes. He knew it had taken a lot for Kate to come to Cordelia's apartment, seeking him out. So he didn't want Cordelia and Wesley to give her a hard time. He wanted to make this as easy on her as he could, and then get her out so he could get back to work.

"Right," Kate said. "Anyway, tomorrow's *Times* is going to have a screaming headline about police corruption in the LAPD. I haven't seen the story, and I don't think your name will be in it, but I don't know that for sure."

"Thanks for the warning," Angel said, nevertheless very pleased.

She sighed. "Figured it was the least I could do."

"How'd it break?" he asked her, closing the book. Dust wafted up and Cordelia sneezed. She had recently asked him if an allergy to dust could qualify her for disability pay.

"Peterson agreed to turn state's evidence in return for a plea on a lesser charge. And by lesser, I mean he'll go down for manslaughter instead of first degree murder, but he's not skating on that. He told us all about Manley, Castaneda, and Fischer. Turns out there are more, too, working out of that same division."

It was clear it was hurting her to talk about it, but Angel needed the details and he figured that Kate needed to spill. Her bitterness was eating her up, and he wasn't the only one to have noticed it. She had a bad reputation on the job now, people laughing at her to her face and calling her "Scully."

"Those four are the only ones implicated in the Nokivov murder, but there are other officers down there who have been into all sorts of nastiness. Trumped-up cases against people they want to take off the streets, or against informants who might be able to testify about some of their dirty activities. Planting drugs, guns, and other evidence. At least a couple of other murders. These boys have been busy."

Wesley said gently, "But you think, with Peterson's help, you'll get them all?"

"We've been rounding them up all night," Kate said. Her shame and frustration were palpable. "If there's anybody left to run the division tomorrow we'll be lucky."

"The city is not going to be happy," Cordelia observed.

"Not at all." She lifted her head. Her blond hair brushed her shoulders. "Things are already tense enough with the gang war and the disappearances. Now add police corruption—it's not like the LAPD has the most sterling record as it is—and it's going to be insane."

She crossed her arms over her chest. "Hopefully it'll blow over soon, once we bring all these cops to court and put them away. But it's not going to be pleasant in the meantime."

A knock on Cordelia's door cut off Angel's reply.

"What is this, visiting hour at the zoo?" Cordelia asked as she rose. "No offense, Kate. Actually, I guess Angel would be the one to take offense, since you're just the visitor and he's the exhibit. But then, it's my apartment, so—"

She opened the door. Alina Vishnikoff stood there, holding the machine that Angel had seen in her room at the house. It looked somewhat the worse for wear.

"Alina?" Cordelia said.

"Alina," Angel echoed.

"Okay, you got me," Kate said. "Who's Alina?"

"You might as well come on in," Cordelia told her. "The neighbors hate it when I hold parties in the hall." She stepped aside and allowed Alina to enter.

"Detective Kate Lockley," Angel said by way of introduction. "Meet Alina Vishnikoff."

"Pleasure," Kate said offhandedly, but Angel knew Kate had made the connection: Peterson's bank account. Big payments.

"Her father," Angel filled in.

Kate kept her cool. She was a good cop.

"I'll explain," Cordelia offered proudly. "Alina and her brave little toaster are somehow responsible for all the teen-type disappearances around town. Her friend Mischa introduced us to her, although oddly he has not yet knocked on my door tonight. How Alina got here I have no idea."

"Gunn dropped me off," Alina said.

"Gunn?" Cordelia replied, startled. "And I still haven't met him. Does he really exist? I mean, Phantom Dennis is more visible than he is."

"He said he would come up, but he came up zero and he needed to see Jacquee," Alina said to Angel. "He said you'd know what that means."

Kate peered at the young girl. "You're the one who's been making everyone disappear?"

"Yes . . . well, with the help of this." She held up the Reality Tracer.

"Can you undo it?" Kate asked her.

"Maybe," Alina replied, her lack of conviction evident in her tone of voice, her posture, in everything about her. "Only there's a problem with it, and it hasn't been working right. And tonight, one of those . . ." She shuddered. "I dropped it. So I need to look at it, try to figure out what's going wrong. Only I'm not very good with the technical side of things."

Angel and Cordelia looked at each other. "Willow," they both said.

"Phone," Cordelia added.

As Alina watched, wide-eyed, Phantom Dennis put the receiver in Cordelia's hand and she dialed the number of the de la Natividad residence.

"I can't believe I'm inviting more people over," she sighed.

Chapter 16

Los Angeles

"Everybody . . . everybody just *shhh* for a minute!" Willow complained. "I can't even think with all of you talking."

Everybody fell silent. Willow looked around her. "Everybody" was herself, Cordelia—it was her apartment, after all, even if it looked more like an adjunct meeting of the Scooby Gang—Angel, Wesley, a police detective named Lockley, who seemed very impatient to, like, arrest or save somebody, the Russian girl named Alina something, and presumably Cordelia's pet ghost. They had explained Dennis, and apparently Angel, to Alina before Willow had arrived, and she seemed okay with both concepts.

Cordelia had asked Willow over to work on Alina's defective machine, and she had agreed. But now that she had it open in front of her, on Cordelia's kitchen table, she realized it was like nothing she had ever seen before. Even the component parts looked strange to her, which

Alina explained by telling her that it had been built in the Soviet Union over a matter of decades.

"The first Reality Tracer, my father said, was the size of a Siberian yak," Alina told her. "It took many years to refine it down to such a compact size."

"And still, the technology is completely unrecognizable," Willow said, whistling. "Imagine that."

"I did not expect that you would be able to make it work perfectly," Alina ventured. "But I thought together, perhaps we could repair the damage it suffered when I dropped it. From then, I think it's mostly a matter of me adjusting it and working on my focus as I project through it."

"Through it?" Willow asked, mentally taking notes.

"It requires telepathic control," Alina explained. She looked innocent and frightened and eager to share. Also, proud. "That's why it is so complicated. It is not just a machine, but it's a machine designed to work in concert with a telepath, absorbing and redirecting the psychic frequencies to its own end."

"Wow." Willow was very impressed. She and Alina, with some assistance from Wesley, had removed the stainless steel casing from the device and set it on the tabletop. Inside they discovered a bizarre configuration of wires, transistors, fuses and circuit boards. It looked like something that had been assembled from spare parts by an oddly dexterous chimp. But some wires had come loose and, in one case, a fuse had broken, probably in the fall.

Fuses. Imagine that. You have to go to an antiques store to find 'em, practically. Willow set about reattaching the wires, and Wesley went to look for a matching fuse from Angel's car.

"Whmf egzztly duff id du?" Willow asked.

"I'm sorry?" Alina responded.

Willow removed the screwdriver from her mouth. "What exactly does it do?"

"Oh. It opens doors."

"The doorknob is a perfectly good invention that does the same thing," Willow said, with a sly grin.

"Not that kind of door, silly," Alina giggled. "Doors between realities. Parallel universes."

"The disappearances," Cordelia explained. "This machine has been causing them."

"With my help, I'm afraid," Alina said.

"Huh." Willow was even more impressed.

"My parents forced me to do it," Alina said nervously. "They wanted to ransom all the teenagers for some huge amount of money, which they hope to use to rebuild the Soviet Union."

Okay, Willow thought, *there are delusions involved, as often happens in cases with parallel dimensions and alternate realities.*

"Grandeur much?" Cordelia said.

"It might have worked," Angel pointed out. "There are some pretty rich parents whose kids are missing. Salma and Kayley Moser's parents, for instance, and others."

Wesley stepped up to the expository plate. "They'd pay a lot, and they'd lean on the government to pay more. And then, with the seemingly random nature of the disappearances, any parent who had a teen would want the government to pay up just so their kid wouldn't be next."

"But, restore the Soviet Union?" Willow asked. "Wouldn't that require a lot more than money?"

"Yes, certainly," Alina said. "It would require persuading independent nations to subsume themselves once again to the will of a revitalized party. But the Reality Tracer doesn't just take people away, it can also bring people—or other objects—in from other alternities."

Willow looked at Alina, her head cocked. "Um?"

"Alternities. Alternate realities. We could bring in monsters, or armies of soldiers, or inconceivable weapons." Alina lifted her chin. "The user of this machine would be virtually unstoppable."

"And you're the user?" Willow said carefully.

"I'm the only one so far who can use it, yes. It's more or less tuned to my frequency, and I am the only powerful enough telepath that my parents know of to make it work."

The others looked at each other, and Alina continued, "But that doesn't mean there aren't others out there. That's why, when I ran away, I brought it with me. To make sure it isn't used by anybody else."

"And we're fixing it instead of destroying it because . . .?"

"Because all those kids have been sent to different alternities," Alina said. "They can't be brought back unless we can use the Tracer to open the right doors and find them."

"Huh," Willow said again. She hooked up another couple of wires. Wesley came in with a fuse, and handed it to her.

"Here's one," he said. He looked at Angel. "Your turn signal won't work until you can get to the auto parts store."

"They open at night?" Angel asked dryly.

"Perhaps I'll go myself, in the morning," Wesley ventured.

Angel gave him a half-nod. "Good idea."

Willow took the fuse and inserted it into the spot from which she'd removed the broken one.

"Does this look pretty much right?" she asked Alina.

Alina studied it for a while. "As far as I remember," she said.

Willow was pleased. "So, all we have to do is turn it on and start bringing people back?"

Alina was quiet for a moment. Her cheeks reddened.

"What?" Willow asked.

"Do you remember what I said?" Alina replied.

"You said we could use it to open doors, find them, and bring them back."

"The finding part," Alina said, "is not that simple. They've been randomly distributed, more or less, throughout various alternities. I only know our universe in any detail. So I don't really know where they've been put. Just that they're not here."

"So how does the finding work?" Cordelia asked. "Some kind of homing device?"

"Not exactly," Alina admitted. "Not at all, really. I'm afraid . . . I'm afraid someone will have to go and find them. They'll have to be led to the doorways before I can bring them through. But I'm not sure any human could do it."

A long moment of silence gripped the room.

Finally, Cordelia couldn't stand it. "What kind of someone, then?"

Alina looked around the kitchen, her gaze finally settling on Angel. Willow realized she was looking at Angel, too. So was everybody else.

Angel noticed.

"It's very dangerous," Alina said. "We don't know what we'll find on the other side of the doors. And whoever goes will have to be prepared in certain ways—if I just sent you through and brought you back, you would die immediately."

"What about the people who have already been sent through?" Kate Lockley finally spoke up.

"I don't know, truthfully," Alina said, "if they are still alive."

"You'd better hope they are," Kate responded, all business and harshness.

Alina swallowed. Her voice was small and filled with shame. "They should be, theoretically—until I try to bring them back. That's where the trouble will come, if there is any. We've never had problems sending anything through, but the return is when things go wrong."

"You said that," Angel pointed out.

"There must be some kind of preparations we can make," Willow suggested. "Protective spells, or something."

"You mean witchcraft?" Alina asked.

Willow smiled faintly. "Something like that."

"That's possible," Alina said, pondering. She rubbed her forehead as if she had a very bad headache. "Many of the researchers who worked on the project would only look at it from a strictly scientific point of view. But magick, or witchcraft, certainly would not be something I would dismiss offhand. If you have someone who knows protective spells that would make it safer for a person to travel through the alternities, it can't hurt."

"I think we can come up with something," Willow said, tapping her screwdriver as she got to her feet. "I'll call Doña Pilar and we'll get to work."

"Of course, if you'd like all of them to come back . . ." Alina began. She paused.

"We would," Angel prompted. "What?"

"I don't know that one person could do it all," Alina confessed. "There are many alternities, and many missing teenagers. Conditions may be dangerous where they are. Time, I think, is of the essence."

"It usually is," Cordelia said. She rolled her eyes. "Just once, I'd like to have all the time in the world to save the world."

"That's called human progress, I believe," Wesley said dryly. "Civilization."

"Queen Mother," Cordelia shot at him, and he raised his chin with wounded dignity.

"So we need someone else to go into completely other dimensions and maybe battle who-knows-what to save a bunch of strangers," Willow cut in. She looked around the room. "Where are we going to find a someone else like that?"

As immediately as they had all looked at Angel before, they all said the same word.

"Buffy."

Sunnydale

Another portal had opened, near Weatherly Park, and various creatures had come through into the Sunnydale night. Two innocent joggers had already been assaulted, and word spread quickly through the city that, once again, it was a bad night to be outdoors.

Or indoors.

Or anywhere within the city limits.

The Police Department had dispatched all the officers it could spare, but Sunnydale's finest didn't really know what to make of the creatures of the night, the ghouls and goblins, walking shadows and giant insects, Moon-men and Martians that were being reported, clearly by hysterical townsfolk.

And Buffy was just a tad busy.

Angel had called an hour before. She talked to him for a few minutes, then to Willow for a while. She and Willow had talked twice more in the intervening time, as Tara gathered the necessary items for her spell. Once she had sent Giles to the Magic Shop for a particular powder made from berries that were only found in Argentinian jungles of a certain altitude.

Then Tara announced that she was ready.

Which meant that Buffy was ready.

Or if not ready, at least I'm not as totally unprepared as I was a little while ago.

Some of the details were still a little fuzzy. Such as, where she was going, and what she would do when she got there. It would all be explained to her by Angel, she had been told. Only she wouldn't see Angel until she had passed through a portal to some other reality somewhere.

I can see why they're keeping it vague, she thought. *If I knew what I was really getting into, I'd never agree to it.*

But she also knew that was totally not true. It was important, or Angel wouldn't have called her. No one else could do it. And the end result might be that the portals that allowed all kinds of creepy nastiness into Sunnydale—and sucked teens out of L.A.—could maybe be shut down.

That would be worth just about any inconvenience. And while it wasn't quite item one on the Slayer job description, it wasn't far down the list.

So she prepared in the fashion that Willow had described for her. She took a bath and anointed herself— Riley had wanted to help with this part, but she politely turned him down, and when Xander offered, she declined a tad less politely—with a special oil made from orchid petals. Then she dressed all in cotton. Black jeans and a long-sleeved tee, with some old canvas sneakers she had. Willow had stressed that she could not wear any clothing made from animals, so she even wore a metal belt instead of leather. Fully dressed, she meditated for twenty minutes, fixing the image of a door in her mind, and once she was familiar with its every detail—the color of the paint, the ding on the knob, the rust scaling the hinges—she practiced opening and closing it, listening to its squeal, hearing the firm *ch-thunk* as it latched.

Giles, Riley, her mother, Xander, Anya, Tara and Spike gathered around for this last part. Buffy had to make a magickal circle on a floor—she chose Giles's living room, since it was handy—with the berry-based powder Giles had fetched. She did that, measuring it according to Willow's direction. At two-foot intervals on the edge of the circle she placed candles of pure beeswax, each brand new and twelve inches tall. In a few minutes, when Willow called back, she would light each of the candles by igniting a stick of wood that had never been cut by manmade tools—Xander had broken a dry branch for this part—and touching the burning wood to the wicks. Then she would stand inside the circle, and Willow and Tara and Doña Pilar, working together with someone named Alina, would open a door for her. She'd go through, and everything would be explained on the other side.

If I live that long.

Angel had impressed upon her that this was dangerous. The way he had put it, in fact, was, "I'm going to ask you to do something. I want you to tell me no."

"What is it?" she had asked.

"I'm taking a trip. I'm told it's necessary to get those kids back who have been disappearing. Maybe it'll even stop those monsters from appearing in Sunnydale."

"Salma too?"

"Presumably."

"I'm gathering this trip is not to someplace like say, Paris. Or Disneyland."

"Could be like a little of both," Angel said. "No way of knowing till I get there."

"And you need someone along to keep you company?"

"Apparently I need someone along because one person will never be able to locate all of these kids quickly enough to save their lives."

"And you want me to say no because . . .?"

"Because the chances of even getting there alive are slim. The chances of finding the missing kids and coming back are laughable."

"But you're going."

"Kind of have to."

"I'm going too," was all Buffy had said.

"Figured you would."

She looked at the clock now. Another two minutes and she had to light the candles. She walked the room, starting with Spike. "You be good," she told him.

"Please, that word makes me gassy," he snapped.

"Keep an eye on Xander," she told Anya.

"Are you going to have sex with Angel when you get there?" Anya asked, eyes glowing with anticipation. "Danger can be very arousing, you know."

Buffy felt her cheeks redden a little, and Riley's gaze burning into her. She'd have to reassure him a little before she went.

Xander shook his head. "Woman has a one-track mind," he said. "Fortunately, it's the same track I'm on, so no complaints."

"I didn't think there'd be any," Buffy replied. She hugged him and kept going.

"You be careful, sweetie," her mother insisted.

"I will be," Buffy promised. "No unnecessary risks. And Angel will be watching my back. You know we're a good team." She hugged Joyce Summers hard, and Joyce returned it with a grip that Buffy thought her mother would never release. When she finally did let go, tears rimmed her eyes.

Tara was already halfway to a trance state, staring at the candle from which Buffy would light the stick. Buffy smiled at her but didn't want to interrupt. Anyway, she knew she'd see Tara en route. Tara seemed to notice her anyway. "Blessed be," she whispered softly.

"Thanks," Buffy said.

Giles came next. "I know you'll be careful," he said soberly. "So I won't bother to nag you. Just remember what you've learned, what I've, um, taught you and what you've picked up on your own. You're the best I've known and from what I've read, in the Watchers Council histories, maybe the best there has been."

"I've been in some pretty tight spots before," she said. Her voice caught. *He really cares about me.* "Piece of cake."

"Indeed." He smiled. It was a difficult, brave smile, and she loved him for it.

"Thank you, Giles," Buffy said. She hugged him, too. When she pulled away, he was blinking behind his glasses.

She turned to Riley.

"I wish I could go with you," he said.

"I know. But that Russian girl, Alina, said humans couldn't do it."

"You're human."

"I'm a Slayer," Buffy argued. "That makes me something different. I'll be okay."

"I know you will," Riley said. "I'd just rather be there to make sure."

"Someone's got to stay here and kick monster butt,"

she said. "Until we get the doors closed, they're just going to keep coming through."

"I'll be kicking," Riley assured her. "Count on it."

"I always count on you, Riley Finn." She touched his face. "It's good to know you're countworthy."

He smiled his wide, open smile. She took his hands in hers. "Try not to worry about me," she whispered.

He kept smiling, but she saw the fear there. "I know how tough you are, better than anyone."

"Yeah," she said. She leaned into him, wrapping her arms around his middle and turning her face up. He bent slightly and brought his lips to hers. He tasted like home. She didn't want to break the kiss, but she did. It was time, she knew.

When she turned away from Riley, this time it was she blinking back tears.

Tara had already begun to chant quietly.

Buffy knew what she had to do. She went to the table, picked up the stick, and held it to the candle that burned there. When it had a steady flame at its tip, she took it to the other candles that were arranged around the circle. She began to light them, one by one by one.

Willow and Doña Pilar had worked together enough over the past few days that they knew how to communicate nonverbally—even, as in this case, when they weren't in the same place.

Willow felt a mental tug, and turned—at least, she felt like she was turning—to see Doña Pilar standing beside her. But it wasn't really Doña Pilar, except in the astral plane sense of her. The woman's spirit, for lack of a better name, was semitransparent, and through her Willow could see a red wall. She looked at her own hand, and through that as well. She and Doña Pilar seemed to stand in a small red room, illuminated by a sourceless red glow. After another moment, Tara, or a semi-Tara, joined them there. The three of them joined noncorporeal hands in a circle, and their chanting—which each of them did, barely audibly, in their physical bodies at Cordelia's apartment, Giles's bungalow, and the de la Natividad estate—became louder and more forceful.

In Cordelia's living room, Angel felt a breeze. He looked at the door, then the window. Both were shut tight.
It's happening, then, he thought.
The hairs on his body tingled, as if there were a powerful electric charge nearby. He watched Alina, sitting in front of the Reality Tracer, its electrodes hooked up to various parts of her. She concentrated on it, turning a dial on it in minute increments, but mostly, it seemed, she was funneling her will through it in some way he didn't quite understand.

No one watched Doña Pilar, alone in her tiny kitchen. She gazed into a flickering candle as she sat at the ancient wooden table. The breezes that buffeted her body went unfelt, as her total concentration was far away with Willow and Tara.

In Giles's living room, several people felt the winds, but no one wanted to say anything. Buffy had lit all the candles in the circle and stepped into its exact center. Tara stood before her, chanting, but somehow her chant had taken on a kind of echo, as if other voices had joined her in an unnatural harmony.
Buffy herself felt nothing. She stood in the circle, listening to Tara's chant, which sounded like nonsense syllables. But the sounds drew her back into her meditation, where she saw the door she had imagined before. It was

painted red, fading in spots, scuffed beneath the lock where keys scraped it. People pushing it open with the toes of their shoes had worn the foot of it. Rust pocked the tarnished copper hinges. She knew the door she saw wasn't the real door, that what should be opening before her there in Giles's house was a golden, shimmering portal like she had seen on Santa Ysabel Street. But it stood for that door, and that was what counted.

As she watched, it began to swing open.

Angel's door of riveted steel irised open like a camera shutter. Alina and Willow had assured him that when he stepped through, he'd find Buffy nearby. He was counting on that—she didn't have as much of an idea of what to expect on the other side as he did, and he didn't know squat. He wanted to be able to guide her, at least get her started, on what they had to accomplish over there. Not far from the forefront of his mind was the danger that Alina had warned of—he didn't want Buffy to be caught unaware.

When the door opened, he stepped toward it.

In Sunnydale, Buffy did the same.

Her door had opened all the way, and from the other side a bright yellow light spilled through. It had the warm sunny quality of a summer's day, but a hint of coldness in the center of it tickled her spine. She took a deep breath. Hesitated for only a fraction of a second.

She stepped through the door.

"Godspeed," Giles murmured, as Buffy disappeared.

The circle disappeared. There was a collective sigh.

No one moved, except Giles, who picked up the Slayer's favorite crossbow and a quiver of bolts.

Without another word to anyone, he marched out of the house.

The first monster he saw, he shot and killed.

And the second.

And the third.

I will keep killing them until she comes back, he thought.

Buffy, do come back.

Be well. Be safe.

And come back.

To be continued . . .

Nancy Holder is a writer and a mom. She and Jeff Mariotte have written seven book-length projects together, including two (*Buffy the Vampire Slayer: The Watcher's Guide, Vol. 2,* and the upcoming guide to *Angel*) with Jeff's wife, Maryelizabeth Hart. They are all still speaking to each other.

Jeff Mariotte is a novelist, comic book writer, comic book editor, and occasional bookseller who has forgotten the meaning of the phrase "spare time."

Everyone's got his demons....

ANGEL™

If it takes an eternity, he will make amends.

❖

Original stories based
on the TV show
Created by Joss Whedon
& David Greenwalt

Available from Pocket Pulse
Published by Pocket Books

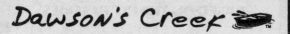
Dawson's Creek ™

**Look for more new,
original Dawson's Creek™ stories
wherever books are sold.**

And don't miss:

Dawson's Creek
The Official Postcard Book

Dawson's Creek
The Official Scrapbook

Available now from Pocket Pulse
Published by Pocket Books

**Visit Pocket Books on the World Wide Web
http://www.SimonSays.com**

**Visit the Sony web site at
*http://www.dawsonscreek.com***

2318-02

. . . A GIRL BORN
WITHOUT THE FEAR GENE

FEARLESS™

A SERIES BY
FRANCINE PASCAL

FROM POCKET PULSE
PUBLISHED BY POCKET BOOKS

3029